JUJITSU FOR CHRIST

Jack Butler was born in Alligator, Mississippi, the son of a Baptist preacher. His work has appeared in *The New Yorker, The Atlantic, New Orleans Review, Poetry,* and numerous anthologies of Southern literature. He has previously published two collections of poetry and one collection of stories and has degrees in English, writing, and mathematics. He lives in Little Rock, Arkansas, where he is a statistical analyst for the state Public Service Commission.

JUJITSU
for
CHRIST

A Novel By

Jack Butler

PENGUIN BOOKS

PENGUIN BOOKS
Viking Penguin Inc., 40 West 23rd Street,
New York, New York 10010, U.S.A.
Penguin Books Ltd, 27 Wrights Lane, London W8 5TZ
(Publishing & Editorial) and Harmondsworth,
Middlesex, England (Distribution & Warehouse)
Penguin Books Australia Ltd, Ringwood,
Victoria, Australia
Penguin Books Canada Limited, 2801 John Street,
Markham, Ontario, Canada L3R 1B4
Penguin Books (N.Z.) Ltd, 182–190 Wairau Road,
Auckland 10, New Zealand

First published in the United States of America
by August House, Inc., 1986
Published in Penguin Books 1988

LIBRARY OF CONGRESS CATALOGING IN PUBLICATION DATA
Butler, Jack, 1944–
Jujitsu for Christ: a novel / by Jack Butler.
p.   cm. — (Contemporary American fiction)
ISBN 0 14 01.0374 0
I. Title.   II. Series.
[PS3552.U826J8   1988]
813'.54—dc19   87-18648
                                                              CIP

Printed in the United States of America by
R. R. Donnelley & Sons Company, Harrisonburg, Virginia
Set in Stempel Garamond

For Johnny, who read this
before it was written.

You got a black voice and a white voice, Nephew said. *A kind voice and a cruel voice.*

Everybody does, I said. *This is a divided country. I want the voices to come together in one whole voice.*

Everybody *don't,* Nephew said. *You don't know yo fellow man. I don't know about no country, but* **you** *sho need making whole. A glad voice and a mourning voice,* he said.

Roger

ONCE, IN A PLACE called Jackson, Mississippi, there lived a young man named Roger Wing. He lived in what had been a laundromat and was now Roger Wing's Studio for Meditation and Self-defense.

The building sat back of an overpass in a tangle of narrow alleyways. Would-be customers had to turn sharply just at the base of the overpass, then maneuver their fat Buicks carefully past dilapidated apartments and barbecue joints with walls of corrugated tin. Either this inconvenience, or the black teenagers staring from the stoops of the apartments in summertime, had driven most of the white business away.

Roger's father had died when Roger was almost eight, and, after a year, Roger's mother had moved them from the countryside, where she found it almost impossible to make a living, into a small town near the capital, Clinton. Grant had stabled his horses there once, in the chapel of the little Southern Baptist college, Mississippi College. Later, there had been a race riot. This was in September of 1875, and it started during the Republican barbecue. Over a thousand Negroes were involved, and there were casualties on both sides. How it got started was never made clear, but all that fall, General J. Z. George, the Democratic campaign chairman, was carrying out a plan of intimidation against blacks. Rifle clubs drilled near black registration centers, with real rifles and live ammunition. The idea was to win the state back from its Reconstruction government, and it worked. The riot lasted five days, but despite a request from Governor Adelbert Ames, Grant refused to send in any troops, stating that the nation was tired of war. In this he was correct. It was a precedent that later generations of Mississippians were to find very useful: no matter how preposterous your position is, just stay in their face until they get tired of you and go away.

Nothing had happened in Clinton since then, although they were still pissed about the horses. Roger and his mother had not lived there six months before she remarried. The man she married had come down from Indiana when his plant relocated. He had three sons by a previous marriage, two of whom were older than Roger. The oldest had been Rookie of the Year for the Dodgers. He was the toast of his new home town, although he had had only one good season since his rookie year, and that one had not been quite as good. The next eldest graduated and went into local real estate, a thriving business, since Clinton was rapidly becoming a suburb of Jackson. His income was going up twenty percent a year, and so was his weight. The youngest of all was determined to become a major-league shortstop.

Roger sometimes thought that his mother had chosen this new husband for the sheer relief of it. His natural father had been bad-tempered, sentimental, cruel and loving, and had died in a pick-up truck. This man, his stepfather, was the floor manager of his plant, he went to church, he took the bass boat out to what would become Barnett Reservoir on Sunday afternoons, he drank a beer now and then, but Roger could not tell which of these activities he preferred, could not tell what the man wanted out of life, or even if he did want anything from it.

Roger's daddy had frightened the wits out of his son, and had kept his wife so angry that she had paid little attention to the boy. In his new family, Roger found himself at once accepted and ignored, like a new rock in a shallow creek. His mother was preoccupied with her new life, which she perceived as a step up the social ladder (carpeting and central air and tv and bermuda grass instead of a screen porch and a window fan and a hound dog and a rusty Chevy on blocks). She did not notice that Roger was becoming increasingly lonely.

In fact, since he had nothing to compare his loneliness to, and had had no instruction in talking about his feelings, Roger was hardly aware of his own isolation. He kept his own counsel without knowing that he did so, talked to his friends at school about small things, and saved the money he made delivering the *Clarion Ledger* and mowing lawns. He worked out in the fenced back yard every day, and as karate became more and more important to him, he began to form an image of his future. It was an image of noble deeds, the deeds of a warrior-saint in the cause of justice, an image of his own studio in Jackson, ten miles away.

Roger Receives His Calling

ROGER HAD A first-degree black belt in shodo-kan karate, and a fourth-degree belt in jujitsu. He was adept at yoga and the Tai Chi as well, though he had had neither formal training nor examination in the two latter disciplines. He had found a common center to all these curious practices and had come gradually to think of them all as one. He was small and roundly built. He was not a good sprinter, or a quick interior lineman, but years of practice had bred in him an economy of motion the eye could not follow.

In the sixth grade he had attended a compulsory assembly program in which a Taiwanese gentleman leapt high in the air and split, with the side of his foot, a brick held high overhead by an assistant. Karate was not a well-known activity then, but Roger accepted the display as being hardly different from any other sort of assembly-time magic show. He had stood on that very stage the year before, in the fifth-grade pageant, a mute spaceman in a cardboard-and-tinfoil helmet holding a leaky orange plastic water-pistol raygun.

In fact, his mind was not on the present show at all, but on the odd taste of water from waterguns and garden hoses, the must of rubber and its kin. It was, to him, a very comforting flavor, and somehow a very old one. Never mind that the long-chain organic polymers are recent and our own creations. The water from a garden hose leads back, all the way back, to the rusty sump of Genesis.

But the next hour in gym class, there had been another demonstration. The nine-, ten-, and eleven-year-olds were lined up along the walls of the gymnasium. Grey mats were unrolled along the floor. The trampoline was shoved into one corner. Dim cathedral light filtered down from the high, dirty, wire-covered windows.

Coach brought out Otis and Tracy and the man who had split the brick, and explained that they were about to see a demonstration of self-defense in a two-on-one situation. The shadow of the window-fan kept sliding around on Coach as he gestured and talked, making a super-hero emblem on his chest one moment and turning him into a hooded executioner the next.

Mr. Lon, the man from Taiwan, was bony and weary-looking. His peculiar clothes had seemed a bright white on the stage earlier but now looked yellowed and dingy.

Coach took a long time with his explanation. He made it funny. He made it clear that he thought the funny-looking Mr. Lon was about to get the holy crap beat out of him.

Otis was blond, large, slow, and powerful. He had been a junior for two years. He was the fullback. Tracy was cruelly thin, with a hooked nose and a hooked grin and brilliant green eyes. He started fights, smoked cigarettes at recess, and talked back to the women teachers.

Coach sent Mr. Lon to one side and Tracy and Otis to the other, and then dropped his arm between them. Otis and Tracy advanced on Mr. Lon, Otis looking good-natured and puzzled, and Tracy bouncing and jabbing. Tracy's right arm flashed out suddenly at Mr. Lon's nose.

Mr. Lon's response was a movement from another world, as if his arm were a length of rope he had pumped into a ripple. Tracy's arm flew helplessly away from the impact. Otis had jumped at Mr. Lon just as Tracy had punched, and, rolling out of the upward block, Mr. Lon sent another tremendous ripple along his body, this one down his back and into his left leg, his heel exploding just under Otis's sternum. Otis sat backwards with a thump, gasping for air.

"You kicked him, you cheat!" Tracy cried, and pulled out his switchblade. Mr. Lon straightened from his kick and seemed to tear at his own chest for a split second, sending the heel of his right fist midway between Tracy's elbow and wrist. The switchblade spun glittering through the air. Tracy sagged to his knees clutching his left arm.

Coach had run over to Otis and was bending over him. He looked up and glared at Mr. Lon. "You lousy Chinaman chink," he said. "I'm calling the cops, you nigger son-of-a-bitch."

"He had a knife."

"Tell it to the cops, you nigger."

By this time Otis had managed to catch his breath. "Trace did have a knife, Coach," he said.

The trouble with Otis was he would never lie, and everybody knew it. He had busted open the windows in the hardware store once and taken all the screwdrivers and hammered them into trees all over town with little signs hanging from them saying, "Cant find a good screw anywhere." And once they had caught him under the bleachers with Chrissy Mellowlake, who was only thirteen at the time. But he wouldn't lie. His father had explained it to him. "Son, the Bible says there ain't but one sin can't be forgiven, and that is blasphemy against the Holy Ghost. And all that is is saying that the workings of the Holy Ghost ain't the workings of the Holy Ghost. But Jesus and the Holy Ghost are the same thing. And Jesus said he was the Truth. So the Truth is the Holy Ghost, and if you say the Truth ain't the Truth, you are blaspheming, and all that is is plain simple lying. A man who lies don't know who he is, and don't know who he can trust, and he ain't only going to Hell, he's already there."

"Get out of here, you little yellow nigger," Coach said. "You better not expect to get paid for this day's work, I guaran-damn-tee you."

"I came a hundred miles. I need the money. He had a knife."

"I tell you what, buddy rough, you just move it on out of here."

"Coach," Otis said, "I'm all right." He heaved himself up and knee-walked over to Tracy, who was curled around his arm, crying. "I think o Trace's arm is broke, though."

Mr. Lon turned and walked away, and when he did, the kids along the wall broke ranks and flooded around Otis and Tracy and Coach. Roger remained against the wall watching Mr. Lon and, when Mr. Lon had vanished through the door at the far end of the gym, ran swiftly, unnoticed, along the wall after him.

He found Mr. Lon and his assistant in the parking lot stowing canvas bags in the back seat of a 1949 Dodge.

"I told you, the little piss-ant had a knife."

"Yeah, and if you were better, it wouldn't have mattered. You could have done it without breaking his arm. You lost your temper, didn't you? No *kime*."

"You know so much about it. You should have been there. I'd like to see you take on a knife."

"Yeah, yeah. You were perfectly justified. But what are we gonna use for gas money?"

The assistant saw Roger and pointed with his eyes. Mr. Lon spun around. The assistant went and got in the car on the driver's side.

"How can you do that with a bone in your arm?" Roger asked Mr. Lon, and the weariness left Mr. Lon's face.

"You mean this?" he said, taking a little step and performing the upward block he had used against Tracy's punch.

Roger nodded.

Mr. Lon dropped to his haunches, his beaming face on a level with Roger's. "Seek a level where opposite states coincide," he said. Then he seemed surprised, or embarassed, as if he wanted to say more, but was not able to. There was a snort from inside the car.

"Son," Mr. Lon said, "do you have any change? Just any little bit of money?"

"I have my lunch money," Roger said. "And a dime for a Coke and a nickel for a Butterfinger at recess."

"Would you consider donating that to the cause of karate? I have often gone hungry for the sake of the sweet science myself."

Roger wasn't sure what science had to do with it, but looking into Mr. Lon's face was like looking into the wisdom of all the East. "Do you need my money?" he asked.

"I wouldn't say need it," Mr. Lon said. "No, I wouldn't say that. A man doesn't *need* anything. But it would make things easier. Thank you. Thank you," he said, as Roger hastily dug in the stiff pockets of his jeans and fumbled the coins into Mr. Lon's hands.

"For inasmuch as ye have taken so much as a cup of cold water or a candy bar out of the mouths of these babes, insofar are ye blessed as a saint of the discipline of karate," Mr. Lon said, laying his left hand on Roger's head.

He got up and went around and got in, all the time looking back at Roger and smiling. Roger heard him say, "Well, we've got enough to get to Buster, anyway. She can pump us some to get home on." Then they cranked the car, backed out, and drove off, Mr. Lon leaning out the window and waving.

When the car turned the corner, Roger felt a panicky vertigo, a sense of tremendous dislocation. He did not know where the other children were now, or how long he had been in the parking lot, or which class he was supposed to be in. The raw February sunlight glinted on the cars and the buildings with a freshness that was almost ferocious. A wind boomed into the lot, which, in the harsh clean light, seemed to be getting bigger and bigger and rising through space.

He turned and ran back to the gym. When he came to the steps, an impulse of flight and freedom launched him over them all, a leap he had never tried before. He landed unevenly, twisting his ankle and banging his face into the cyclone fence on the other side of the walk.

"Fighting," said Mrs. Murray in the dispensary, swabbing the dried blood from underneath his nose with an alcohol-dampened cotton wad. The alcohol made him swoon.

"You ought to be ashamed," she said.

How Abraham Lincoln Gandy Left
Alligator, Mississippi

WHEN HE WENT into the office, Mr. Alfred had his glasses on, doing
the books. The small gas heater, hooked directly to a standing bottle
of butane, had not been lit, and Mr. Alfred was wearing the earpieces
down on his fur-lined cap.

Hip waders hung from a nail in the mantle of the unused fireplace.
A pile of decoys spilled from one corner of the huge room. In
another, a table was stacked with magazines, doll houses, bicycle tires,
cans of oil. Under the table were boxes of papers.

Here and there on the wall were old guns, including an eighty-two-
year-old Colt, not mounted for display, but stuck up on big nails,
ready to grab. Riding harness hung from other nails, yellowing
articles from the *Commercial Appeal* had been tacked up, cartoons
starring Hambone.

"What did you want to see me about, A.L.?" Mr. Alfred asked.

"Mr. Alfred, I'm going to have to be moving to Jackson."

Mr. Alfred looked at him a long time, then looked back at his
books. "Go on, then," he said.

"Don't be that way, Mr. Alfred. I love this place much as you do."

Don't neither.

"You leaving it."

*Not even gone tell me how lucky I am, are you. How good I have it here.
Not like no regular sharecropper nigger. Money in Coahoma bank, call
me Mister at the store. Not even gone bother, are you.*

"My boy is reading, Mr. Alfred. I got hopes for my boy. There ain't
no education for him here. You know that."

"That would be T.J."

"Yessir."

*Want to remind me you know my family, do you. See how you concern
yourself. Ungrateful me.*

13

"He's reading young, isn't he? He wouldn't be over seven. Because Snower Mae had him when it rained all fall. The year the engine fell on Tippee's arm."

"Yessir, he is."

And you taken care of Tippee, didn't you? Just like you would of of me if I'd of stayed. But we both know it's too late. It was too late the minute I said leave. You are just proving yourself to your own self.

"What's he reading from?"

"I have some books."

"You do?"

"Yessir. I gets em here and there. A one'll be thowed out by the road a now and again. All of em ain't fit. I reviews em before I let him see em. And then Mr. Klein have a couple. I reads a little myself. In the evenings."

"You do?"

"Yessir. Just in the evenings. Since you brought in the electric."

"How many books do you have, A.L.?"

"About fifty, sir. I reckon."

"Lord, A.L. I don't know as *we* have *that* many."

"I'm sorry, Mr. Alfred. A lots of them has the covers off. It might be forty."

"I didn't mean that. I was just surprised. You welcome to all the books you want. But you ain't going to like it in Jackson. You're a country nigger. A country nigger and a city nigger ain't the same kind of person. You ain't planning to try and pass, are you?"

"If it wasn't for all the country niggers there never would of been no city niggers. I ain't never wanted to pass for anything but what I am, and what I am ain't a white man. Mr. Alfred, they got a store in Jackson that don't sell nothing but books."

"The Baptist Book Store."

"Yessir, but I reckon they'll let a Methodist buy em."

"It's the only bookstore they have."

"That's one more than anywhere else in Mississippi. Mr. Alfred, I need to talk to you about buying that Studebaker you was trying to get rid of."

"You can make the price on it? I need a good price on it. It ain't but two years old. We'll talk about it."

"More like nearly three, Mr. Alfred. They'll be bringing out the fifty-two's before long."

"Nineteen fifty-one less nineteen forty-nine is two. We'll talk about it. You won't like it there."

"It ain't just the readin."

"What else is it? What are you talking about? Are you talking about Luly? Is it Luly again?"

Gandy stared silently down at the white man. Finally he said, "Just things. Things I can't do nothing about here. Things a child don't need to be exposed to."

"If it is Luly, you ought to say so. Say so and I'll talk to his daddy again. I can't do a thing if you ain't going to say what it is. You got your face set for going, I can see that. Go ahead and go. But you won't like it in Jackson. You put in many a year here, and now you're throwin em all away. You're throwin your boy away, too. Things won't work out any better for him there. If he's finding bad experiences here, he'll find em there too."

Yes, and in Jackson I won't have no white man to protect me. Which is to say, to come between the other white men and me.

"Don't do like that, Mr. Alfred. Don't put a curse on my doings. Don't strike my hope. You got them cottonpickers now. You gone be paying on them, you know you are. You probably figuring on that right now, doing your books. How you gone pay for em. You ain't going to be needin so many hands, and you ain't going to be needin no colored strawboss, and you sho ain't going to want to be paying either one of em."

The white man was looking at his books again. "I'm not cursing you, A.L. You're a free man. You want to go, go."

Maybe he believes that, A.L. Gandy thought. *Maybe he believes he can just let go. Maybe he thinks he don't see me as a proper part of the ground he's give his life to. But if he could let go of any part of this place, he would have been long gone himself, years ago. Because it is killing him. The weather is ruining his sinus, and the worry is thickening his heart.*

"I been here since you was a boy."

You could look up at me. You could say goodbye.

The white man was writing. He did not look up.

Asshole. I been yo pappy and yo brother. I hope someday there's something come along bigger than this place. Something make this place look small in yo eyes, something make it don't count at all. Something you want and can't have.

I hate this place.

He stepped out the door, onto the board sidewalk. Looking around. The Chinese grocery store. Mr. Klein's sundries. Rufus pool hall. The post office. Across the street, the railroad, raised up like a levee, to be above the high water. Curving beyond it in the distance, the bedraggled fields, still spotted with scraps of sodden white.

November clouds. The ducks were up, honking.

No I don't.

Maybe I am free. Maybe things can be just whatever happens next, instead of frozen on the tracks, seeing it coming miles and miles away.

Regardless: I am going to Jackson, Mississippi.

Roger Finds Jesus as his Personal Savior

ROGER HAD BEEN around churches all his life. They were totally familiar to him. It was impossible to be from Mississippi and not be familiar with churches. Mississippi was the holiest damned state in the entire United States of America, which is no doubt why she was reviled and persecuted among the unbelievers. Envied because of her warmth and Southern hospitality, persecuted because of her unwavering stand for Jesus, for states' rights, against sex, against the United Nations, against mongrelization and Adam Clayton Powell: and holy, she was just as holy as hell.

But Roger's father had died just as Roger came into what Southern Baptists call "the age of responsibility." That's the age when you begin to be able to tell sin from salvation, so can go to Hell, and there are documented cases, I mean on record, where wise five-year-olds have understood Jesus well enough to be saved from eternal torment. And because of his father's death when he was so young, and because of his mother's remarriage to a man who was apparently unaffected by the evangelistic imperative (he was, after all, a Presbyterian), Roger had fallen from regular attendance.

As a result, he didn't become a Christian until October of his senior year.

Patsy Wingo knew her weak point was witnessing. Sometimes she wondered if she was even a Christian, since she was so afraid of speaking out for Jesus.

She was a thin, pretty blonde girl with glasses that made her brown eyes seem extraordinarily wide and luminous, like an owl's. As a consequence of a minor harelip, surgically corrected when she was only a few months old, her voice had a soft nasal burr, a pleasing vocal furriness like the sound of a child talking into the spinning blades of a fan.

She was shy, but not because of the harelip. She hardly ever thought of it, because her parents had paid no attention to it. And it wasn't that she was a coward, either. She had trapped a moccasin at the sophomore class picnic, with a forked stick just like it said in the Boy Scout manual, which she had read because the Campfire Girls' manual was so namby-pamby. Then she had horrified everyone by refusing to let the snake be killed, flinging it instead, stick and all, into Lake Mellowlake.

In fact, she was far more popular than she realized. She had made cheerleader on the first ballot, and even the hoods respected her principles.

She was shy because she didn't understand her classmates. They all seemed in possession of some secret attitude or wisdom that she couldn't fathom, some central awareness that gave them poise, gaiety, and certitude.

She had no way of knowing they had their doubts and humiliations, too. But her classmates did have the advantage of knowing who their enemies were—anyone who baffled, threatened, or confused them. Patsy suffered under the Christian injunction to love all men, hating only those who hated the Lord, and then hating not the sinner but the sin.

Patsy thought it was her own lack of conviction that made it hard for her to witness to them, but in fact it was this sense of their alien and superior certainty. She tried to imagine going up to Imolene Train, who had been her best friend until the sixth grade, and who still went through the motions (but Patsy never went to a dance, and Imolene never went to Bible Club): "Imolene, are you a Christian?"

Patsy could never imagine what would come next. The truth was that Patsy and her friends spoke a different language and moved through different habits. They were, as it says in Titus 2:14, a peculiar people, but Patsy did not as yet understand just how peculiar.

Her guilt was particularly acute today. Brother Butler's text Sunday night had been Matthew 10:31–34, and he had borne down hard on being ashamed of Jesus. She had seriously promised God during the invitation that she would witness to at least one person at school Monday, and then she hadn't kept her promise. Now it was Tuesday afternoon, and she had sworn to God during an agonizing two-hour prayer Monday night that she would witness for His Son Tuesday, or would He please hide His Face from her forever.

And the last bell had rung, and everyone was pushing out of the classroom, and Bible Club would meet in fifteen minutes, and everybody there was already witnessing to their own people, so they wouldn't count.

And she still had not witnessed to a single solitary soul.

Roger slowly gathered his books. He didn't like to rush out into the hall and push around, and he didn't have to hurry, since he lived only eight blocks away and didn't have to catch the bus. A voice behind him shouted "Roger!" and he nearly jumped out of his skin. It was Patsy. She said, "Would," and seemed to have to swallow two or three times. Then she said, "you-like-to-go-to-Bible-Club-with-me?"

"Okay," he said.

Patsy was praying silently, a heart-felt, soaring, incoherent paean of gratitude to the Lord for giving her courage, for giving her the person walking next to her to witness to, for just everything. She hardly knew where she was. God asked so little and gave so much. She was happier than she had ever been. Vistas of shining service opened before her. She saw so clearly the wisdom and mystery of submission to His Will. All the great lessons her Savior taught flew through her mind so swiftly she could not tell which was which, and yet she felt her understanding of each infinitely deepened.

If Heaven was like this—

Her life was a trifle, a dry leaf in a flame of eternal joy—

We must give to receive, and at long last she saw why—

This joy was the reason, not some old, iron-grey, inexplicable commandment—

We must have the courage to face our fear of looking ridiculous, only then can we be truly important—

*And yet not **important**, because only the Lord is important, but it isn't selfish of Him to be most important, because He and only He can free our hearts and give us this joy—*

*Didn't the Bible **say**—*

She was higher than a kite. And the whole time, she was chattering away to Roger, giving him a guided tour of the hallways, just as if he were new there, just as if he had not gone to school in this town for half of his life.

Roger had never seen Patsy so talkative. They walked down the familiar tiled corridor lined with lockers, under the grey-white glow of flourescent tubes. He had never been to Bible Club. Never been interested, really. He went to church occasionally with his stepfather. His stepfather's church always made him think of funerals and made him sleepy—the rich wood, the dim light, the air-conditioning, the nice clothes. His mother had been an intense church-goer in the days Before, as he thought of them. Roger had strong memories of bright little wooden churches at the ends of long, long gravel roads, deacons standing around in cleaned and pressed overalls and white shirts. But then she had become a Presbyterian, and then she had quit going.

The last time he had gone to church with her was at a revival service at her old church—their old church—during a visit to her mother. The message had warned against the federal government, the ecumenical movement, and speaking in tongues:

"A lot of peoples thinks they have the Holy Spurt. A *lot* of people. A lot of people *think* they do. Now I am a not a naming any names. It ain't the Jesus way. And I am a not a one to be a talking about a religion I wot not of, such as the Pentecostal. Of which a what I know about the Pentecostal, you could put it in a coffee-spoon. You could, you could maisure it out in a coffee-spoon.

"But friends, I do know this *book.*" A-*wham* on the pulpit with the book, shocking Roger, who wouldn't even put a dictionary on top of the Bible: the Bible had to be on top. "I ain't a being proud to say I know this book. I have studied the word of the Lord all my natural life. And what this book tells me.

"Friends, if the Pentecostal thinks they have the Holy Spurt. Which some calls em Holy Rollers. But I don't, because I have a respect. I call em Pentecostals, because I have a respect. And if they feel like they have the Holy Spurt, well fine. Because it is a blasphemy to be a speaking in tongues without the Holy Spurt.

"I wouldn't say a yea and I wouldn't say a nay on it. I wouldn't be the one could tell you, friends. But do you think the Holy Spurt come down just any time? Do you think He come down for the fun of it? He come down oncet at Pentecost, and He has come down since. But friends, do you think He comes down ever single Sunday that rolls around? Do you think the Holy Spurt has that kind of time on his hands?"

Christ was returning, the revivalist said, and all the false gospel would be found out, all the false speakers in the federal government and the ecumenical movement and the Pentecostal, if there were false speakers in it, which he wasn't saying there were, but if there were, they had better watch out.

The sermon then wandered into a lengthy discussion of the difference in the fleshly body and the resurrection body, and Roger went to sleep.

"That man is so ignorant," his mother said, leaving for home. Roger had thought it a pretty good sermon, as sermons go.

He wondered what Bible Club would be like. Would it be like his stepfather's church, or like the little church Before? Patsy and her friends went to a little mission of the First Baptist Church. The mission was still meeting, in a colder-than-usual October, in reclaimed carnival tents, on sawdust floors, sitting on folded chairs and warming itself by means of two wood-burning stoves. It would continue that way all winter. This hardship at once made church more fun and gave the members a pleasant sense of frontier fortitude, of suffering in the name of the Lord. The church had a few wealthy and elegant members, but most were less well-off and more enthusiastic. The Bible Club was supposed to be all-church, but nearly all its members were from the mission.

Roger had come along to Bible Club not for religion but because he was lonesome. He had come into puberty late, and gradually, perhaps because he tended to keep to himself and he ate less red meat than the average American child. He was just now beginning to get seriously horny, and Patsy, because she sat behind him and was pretty and was a cheerleader, had figured in a few of his fantasies. He didn't know much about her.

Once in geometry Coach had put an equilateral triangle on the board and said it was isosceles (except he pronounced it *isoskeles*, like Popeye). Patsy had pointed out his mistake.

Coach had said you could look at it that way, and had gone on. He had said the two angles at the bottom were equal.

"The one at the top is too!" Patsy cried, then covered her mouth.

"Young lady, I teach the angles. You don't teach me the angles."

"Yessir." Coach turned back to the board. "But the one at the top is too!"

Coach whirled and pointed at the door. "Principal's office! Move it!"

Patsy went white and bolted from the room. She had crept about the corridors in deep embarassment for a month. Her father had had to come talk to the principal and Coach and promise it wouldn't happen again. "That's ok, Sugar," he told Patsy at home. "Stuff like that happens. Just use your brain next time and take care of yourself. You can't stop ignorance."

Patsy made a D in Geometry that term. Coach won 23 games.

And now here they were, and Patsy was explaining for the third time how this wasn't the usual meeting place, but they had to meet here because both pianos were out here, the one from the glee club room as well as the one that was always here, because of the recital, and they went through the double doors, and up behind the curtains, and out onto the stage.

Jimmy McMorris was a spare, moderately tall young man with a flat-top and an attractively broken nose. He was a pretty fair quarter-miler, and his father was pastor of First Baptist.

The nose and his gaunt cheeks would have given him the look of a hawk except for his wide-set blue eyes and his wide, mobile mouth with its full soft lips. It was a face that was well known around the school. It would be better known tomorrow. Just ten minutes ago, the principal had called him in to tell him he was the new SBA president.

Now his tie was loose and pushed to one side, his collar open. A look of weary happiness suffused his face. These few, these faithful, as yet unaware of his election, aroused in him an infinite tenderness. As president of the Bible Club, he had been their shepherd. He was doubly their shepherd now.

"Bring us together again" had been his campaign slogan. He had asked an end to the rivalry of Junior and Senior, Freshman and Sophomore, an armistice in the war of bookworm and jock, teacher and student. He had asked a return to the great common principle of School Spirit.

Years later, during a national election, he was to experience a vague, dissatisfied sense of having known something no one else knew, of not having been heard.

But now the Bible Club waited, and beyond them, beyond the opened curtains, an invisible host also waited, waited in rows of empty seats, his future waited, the future of the world.

He raised his hands to bring them to their feet.

"Patsy, would you lead us in prayer?" he said.

She had *known* he would call on her. How many times had she sat in Bible Club, heart fluttering, and *prayed* he would call on her to pray, *but Thy will be done.*

And as she accepted his recognition, she knew she was saying goodbye to Jimmy, goodbye before their love had even begun, for her fate, Roger, sat here beside her. The ways of the Lord!

"Father, I want to thank you for bringing us all here once again, and Father, just open our hearts today, Lord. We just thank you, Father, for these election campaigns we have just had, and Lord, we just pray Father that the people we choose Lord will just feel Your love in their hearts. Father if there be any of us here today Lord that have anything between our hearts and You, Father I pray we will just give it up right this very minute, because it is just the most wonderful thing in the world Father to walk in Thy love. And pray you Lord be with the sick-and-afflicted and those out on the mission field in Jesus name Amen."

Hey, that girl can *pray,* Jimmy McMorris thought.

They sang "Rock of Ages," and they sang "Bringing in the Sheaves." They took up a collection, and then Jimmy Mac sang a special in his sweet tenor, "In the Garden," Patsy's very favorite song. It pulled at her heart today, because for the last six months, every time she had heard that song, she had thought of herself in the garden with, not Jesus, but Jimmy Mac, walking, then sinking softly in his arms to the leaves. Sinking to the leaves was ok because they were married in her thoughts, he was just coming back from a long trip was why she had been in the garden alone.

> *I come to the garden alone,*
> *while the dew is still on the ro-ses;*
> *and the voice I hear,*
> *falling on my ear,*
> *the Son of God discloses—*
> *and He walks with me,*
> *and He talks with me,*
> *and He tells me I am His own;*

and the joy we share
as we tarry there,
none other...has ever...known.

The empty auditorium was driving Roger crazy. There are only two kinds of people: some of them want the door open, and some want the door closed. Roger wanted it closed, and the auditorium, cavernous on his left, was like the biggest door of all left wide open, like anybody could walk in, like anything could happen next. How could you concentrate?

And to make it worse, he could smell Patsy's skin, and to make it even worse, his workout was going to be at least an hour late today.

He looked at Patsy, but she was intent on the message, the little sermonette that Jimmy Mac was now delivering. From time to time she closed her eyes in earnest prayer, her hands pressed on the Bible in her lap. He watched those hands working, the intensity of her heart pumping in the blue veins of her wrists, and he suddenly felt terribly lonely. Left out.

Maybe that's all Hell is, being left out. For outer darkness and weeping and gnashing of teeth substitute left out. Come to the judgment seat and in the mind of the Heavenly Hosts a flashing process occurs like sweaty hands gripping a baseball bat, and your right hand comes out on top without enough room to grip it whole. You're left out, boy. Didn't get good enough at being good in time enough, now nobody wants you on the team. Morality is real simple, it's just love, courage, work, and wit, that's all there is to it, all real men can do it, you didn't, good riddance, too bad, so long, goodbye.

Le-eft out, Le-eft out,
Dear God sweet baby Jesus don't let me be
Le-eft out, Le-eft out.

Everybody's at the party,
Harry Jim and Becky Arty,
Going on for all eternity,
Posterity modernity,

but I've been Le-eft out, Le-eft out,
Sweet baby God oh Jesus I'm afraid I been
Le-eft out, Le-eft out.

I used to be a nigger,
but my heart has gotten bigger,
I'm a-learning to do right,
I'm a understudy white,

Ti-ime out, Ti-ime out,
stop the game until I figger how to keep from being
Le-eft out, Le-eft out.

Roger found himself drawn to Jimmy's voice. The warmth in that voice worked on him strangely, chemically: his restlessness stilled, dove inward, bloomed in a wild fear. He saw blackberry brambles, all thorn and green. He saw a severed head in the brambles, the brow torn and bloody, the mouth smiling, the eyes looking into his own, as if they were on a level somehow. He knew it had to be the head of John the Baptist, but why the hair of snakes? The mouth wanted to tell him something, wanted to tell him Love, surely, after all this time, that he did really love him, he did he did he did.

A cruel voice said, "Should of happened a long time ago."

Another voice said, "My god, get the boy."

Jimmy Mac's voice said, "For by grace are ye saved through faith, and that not of yourselves: it is the gift of God: not of works, lest any man should boast.

"But now in Christ Jesus ye who were sometimes far off are made nigh by the blood of Christ. For he is our peace, who hath made both one, and hath broken down the middle wall of partition between us ...

"Now therefore ye are no more strangers and foreigners, but fellow citizens with the saints, and of the household of God."

Then Jimmy lifted his hands again, and they rose, and began the invitational: "Lord, I want to be a Christian, inna my heart, inna my heart ..."

A boiling resentment flashed through Roger, leaving him shaken and tingling with chill. It swept up images of his father, his mother furious at him over some small thing in their first house after they had moved here, his most hated customer on the paper route, all of it subsumed into one roaring funnel of anger. And then it was gone, gone for good, Roger felt. Everything he saw stood out in bright and watery detail, the chairs, the curtains, the girl at the piano—oh infinitely good chairs of lustrous metal tubing, oh perfect and pleated fall of drapery, oh magnificent buck teeth, so white, so independent, framed in such black hair, by such reddened pimples!

Then he saw that this perception, this dearness of everything, was not enough. It was the gift of grace, but it would not stay. He was required to answer the gift. An action was required of him.

He felt as though he were moving through one of the *kata*.

"I want to be a Christian," he said into the silence at the close of the little hymn.

Patsy almost fainted. The entire Bible Club was stricken with silent pandemonium. They were like a child who has tied a string to a stick and hooked a five-pounder.

Jimmy recovered almost without a pause. He had Roger come down front, as they would have done in a real church. He took him aside and counseled with him: the pastor is required to be certain the postulant understands the meaning of his act.

Then he had a few words for the others, and then led them all in prayer, and then had them come in a line to the front and shake Roger's hand, one by one, as they sang "Blest Be the Tie that Binds." Actually, that was normally only sung after eating Jesus in the form of stale saltines and diluted Welch's, but it was a good choice this day, a brilliant improvisation: "Blest be ee the tie I that binds. Our hea-arts in Chri-istian love. The feh ell oh shi-ip of ki-indred mi-inds is li-ike to tha-at above."

They left as quickly as they could, nervously, as if they had done something illegal. They would be too late for the Mouseketeers, but it was Thursday night, and tonight Disneyland would be Tomor-rowland, a re-run of the space show.

Jimmy stayed to explain that Roger did not have to be a member of any particular church to be a Christian—the act of salvation had already occurred, and all Christians are members of the one Church, whose head is Christ. However, the essence of Christian service *was* fellowship, after all, and therefore Roger should probably go forward in a church service soon to apply for local membership. Then he gave Roger a hard one-armed hug and walked away.

Patsy was waiting in the hall. She walked him to his house in perfect silence (she too lived not far away from the school, about a half a mile from Roger's house, one subdivision away).

It was cold, and their breathing came in plumes. After a while, they were making their plumes at the same time. The bruised and smokeless sky, the naked glimmering branches, the yellow lights coming on in the houses on the darkening lawns—these were rich and clean and mysterious. Finally she stood at his door, her eyes in the luminous twilight wider than ever. Roger was unable to speak. She put her arms around his waist, rose to tiptoe, and kissed him full on the mouth. Then she turned and ran for the street.

Roger waved. He had never been kissed on the mouth before, except for his grandmother, who tasted of snuff, when he was much younger. He did not work out that night, and Patsy's mother was to notice that her daughter seemed unusually distracted at supper.

Outside, and outside the little town, which, for all the new development, was still surrounded by woods and wilderness, the night darkened in the trees. A small wind came up. It made the pines whisper. And all night long, the water over the spillway answered them, dropping to deeper darkness. *Luther*, the pine trees whispered. *Luther. Luther Jackson.* And all night long, the water answered, *Lawrence, Lawrence, Lawrence. Lawrence Rainey.*

Sword Drill

ROGER AND PATSY fell into a pattern. They more or less assumed they were girlfriend and boyfriend. The only dates they had, though, were to YFC, every Saturday night at six in the Hotel Heidelburg.

YFC was Youth for Christ, a Billy Graham spin-off. The idea was a continuing mission into that hotbed of ferment, the youth of America. The first YFC meeting he went to, Roger was a celebrity because Jimmy McMorris stood up and gave his testimony about Roger being saved. It was proof the Lord was working in a powerful way in the hearts of the youth of America.

After Jimmy gave his testimony, he nudged Roger to do the same. Everyone was waiting. Roger didn't feel the way he had when he was saved, but finally he stood up.

"Jesus has saved me," he said, "and I want to give something back to him. I don't know what I could give, though. I don't have any money and I can't preach. All I'm good at is karate and judo. Could you witness for Jesus with the martial arts? I guess you could, couldn't you? Maybe I'll start like a club, like Jujitsu for Christ. Anybody who wants to be a member who is a member of Bible Club, or Youth for Christ, can join. You can have free lessons at my studio I'm going to have."

Another thing they had at YFC was Sword Drill. The Word of God is the sword of the spirit (Ephesians 6:17). Half a dozen competitors would come up to the front of the room. The moderator would call out, "Attention!," and everyone would stand up straight, shoulders stiff, the Bible in the left hand at the side. Then the moderator would call out, "Draw Swords!," and everyone brought their Bibles forward to the horizontal, left hand supporting, right hand on top, thumb riffling the gold-leaf.

The moderator would call out a passage of scripture by name and number (anything but John 3:16, which everyone knew), pause, and then shout, "Go!"

There was a mad race to thumb through to the passage, and the winner would step forward. When acknowledged, he or she would read the passage.

The first time Roger participated in a sword drill, he won, not because he knew very much scripture, but because he had mind-like-water, and didn't get all jazzed up like the other competitors. None of them knew about mind-like-water. They just thought it was the Lord working in a powerful way. Patsy was infinitely proud.

After YFC, Patsy and Roger and the rest of their group would go to the Daisy Queen, over on the other side of town. It was called the Daisy Queen apparently in imitation of the Dairy Queen shops, but it was the only Daisy Queen that ever existed. It was an adjunct of the dairy business next door, sort of a factory outlet for milk products. It had stools and a counter just like an ice cream bar, but it was way over on the other side of town, and almost the only kids who ever went there were members of the Bible Club/YFC axis.

They would have shakes or malts or sundaes or splits, half-price, and then they would all pile into the station wagon of whatever Christian adult was chaperoning that week, and drive off homeward, singing songs like

I got the good old Biptist Baptist spizzerinktum
down in my heart,
down in my heart,
down in my heart to stay ...

Another verse of that one was

And if the Devil doesn't like it,
he can sit on a tack,
sit on a tack,
sit on a tack to stay.

Roger and Patsy would sing along lustily, or else kiss lustily. They got everything out of kissing you could get out of it without anybody putting a tongue in anybody else's mouth or putting a hand in anybody else's clothing. There were dangerous, exhilarating moments, when someone's tongue-tip would race quickly along someone else's lower lip, and once Patsy bit him, actually chewed on his lip. It scared Roger. He wasn't sure he could control her when she was like that.

The other kids would sing louder when Roger and Patsy were kissing. Roger and Patsy always got the back seat. They were a blessed couple, sanctified by Roger's conversion on the day of their first real meeting, and everyone was proud of them. They were so in love kissing was ok. Everyone glowed and felt romantic, and Roger and Patsy were kissing for all of them. Except of course for the adult driving, who didn't know anyone was kissing, and would have been worried about it, not understanding all the details, and so had to be protected from the knowledge.

And that was it, really. Roger somehow never got around to joining Patsy's church. He was too reserved to give himself whole-heartedly to the little mission church and their enthusiasm. Most of his friends were on the football team, and they went to First Baptist, or the Methodist church, or the Presbyterian church. Roger felt he was a Baptist, because he had been converted by Baptists, but he was not interested in going to First Baptist.

Patsy would come over to his house after school sometimes. Roger's mother called her "that odd little Christian girl," which Roger thought was pretty uppity. On the other hand, he never outright told his mother that Patsy was his girlfriend and they were going to be married. He just sort of left it to be gathered and she never gathered it. Probably not gathering it was her message to Roger not to get involved with this girl too deeply, and Roger not telling her outright was his message of acquiescence. But figuring out all those messages would have been way over Roger's head back then. That's the trouble with innocents. They aren't innocent of doing, just of knowing what they're doing.

Anyway, this one Sunday afternoon, Patsy came over and Roger's family was gone. She came in the door calling out, "I missed you at church." Nobody answered. "Well, shoot," she said. She wandered the hallway, its varnished wood floors with the big heater grating, the buff-colored wallboard and plaster walls, the hollow-core doors opening off of it. "Well, shee-oot," she said.

She heard a grunting sound from maybe the bathroom. No. Then again. The bathroom window. She stepped into the tub and lifted up on tiptoe to look out. Roger was out in his back yard practicing. "Well howdy-doody," she said to herself.

It was thrilling to watch him this way, him not knowing. He was in the white jacket of his ghi, and she guessed his jockey underpants, because his legs were bare but something white covered his bottom. They had a high privacy fence all around the back yard, so no one could see.

Her sweetie was coiling into the cat stance, then, faster than she could blink, stepping and striking a padded limber board that had been planted in the ground like a fencepost. Roger would step and strike, step and strike, bat-at-at bat-at-at, high-middle-low, left-right-left. He did it over and over. Then he changed to a mirror of that stance, and began striking right-left-right. It was early spring, and very warm, and sweat was running freely along his smooth thighs.

She felt her knees go weak, and she came down off tiptoe. As quickly as she could, since her legs were not cooperating so well, she ran along the hall, into the kitchen, and out the back door.

"Hi, sweetie," she said as he turned around. Then she went over to him and sank to her knees and hugged his legs. It *was* his undies. His sweat smelled good, like the smell the sun would have if you could smell it.

"It will—it will—" he said, in a strangled voice, but it already *was*, expanding and pushing, warmer and wiser than any snake. It sought and found the vent of his briefs, bloomed on the naked air.

"Oh, your *thing*," she said. "Your pretty thing." She knew about things, because her mother and father had made sure to leave informational books on the kitchen table, and had made sure to tell her so. She had absorbed the theory, and had checked the illustrations against her own anatomy, but she had never seen a real live thing before. She had not realized they were so pretty: as pink as the inside of a sea-shell, and the tip was so *cute* and *soft*.

She rubbed it along her cheek, and Roger gasped. "I'm sorry," he gargled, his pelvis twitching, thrusting along her cheek, between her cheek and hand.

"Oh sweetie, it's all right. It's all right. I ought to show *you* a pretty-pretty, your thing is so sweet. Here," she said, pulling her white sweater over her head, and then undoing her bra to show him her small pink nipples. "It's heavy petting, but it's all right. We won't do it but once," she said happily.

Roger did not know about things, her things or his thing. He had one, and he knew what it did, but he didn't know exactly why, or how it did it to her. She knew he didn't, because he had told her so. They had agreed to have a talk so she could tell him what she had learned from the informational books. They were going to have it somewhere where they could be alone, but where it would be safe in case they accidentally got excited, like a park, where they couldn't do anything because people would see them. They had been waiting for it to get warm enough to go to a park, and now it had, but now this had happened first.

She spread her sweater on the grass and pulled him down over her bare breasts. They were small, but she pushed them together to rub his thing between them. "Oog, oog, oog," he said, and came on her throat.

"Ooo!" she said, reaching up to play in it with her fingers. "What is it?"

He had collapsed over her, and now burrowed down to her shoulder with his face. "I think it condenses," he said in a muffled voice. "I don't know, but I think the pressure condenses it. It isn't—I hope you don't mind, it isn't nasty any more, it changes."

"That isn't what it is. I remember now. This is completely different stuff. This comes from a completely different place, it just comes out the same way."

"How?" he said, so she told him. She told him about the vas deferens, and urethras, and how blood pressure made it stiff. She told him why his nipples had gotten swollen and sore a year and a half ago. Once she started, she remembered all of it, and she told him all of it. Roger thought it sounded improbable at best, and totally goofball wacko at worst, but he had never known Patsy to make things up.

He could have gotten the information, in a more garbled fashion, and in a ruder terminology, from the other football players. He could have had it years ago, but he had misunderstood a remark by Dibby McDonald to be about his mother, and he had cleaned Dibby McDonald's clock. That had been in the ninth grade, when they had the slightly illegal peewee football team, all eighth- and ninth-graders who made it under the 121-pound limit. They went 8 and 0, and the average score was 47 to 1. Only one touchdown was scored on them all year, and a safety. Next year the state legislature changed the rules to provide for an age limit instead of a weight limit. That was the same year that Clennon King, a professor at Alcorn, went to Whitfield for thinking he could go to Ole Miss, and General Edwin A. Walker thought over recent events and came to a few decisions.

Anyway, after he cleaned Dibby McDonald's clock, nobody would say anything sexual around him any more, so he never learned. They liked him ok, but nobody could figure out how he had cleaned Dibby McDonald's clock, and they weren't taking any chances, especially Dibby McDonald.

Patsy had worked her way through ovulation cycles and was onto relative penis size, and was telling him that his was maybe a little bigger than average, no giant, you understand, but a nice big thing, especially for a sort of short round boy, when he said, "It's getting hard again."

She rolled him over and grabbed it in one hand to see. "Mm," she said, and began nibbling the tip of it.

"Oh Jesus," he squealed.

"Don't take the mm Lord's mm name in mm vain," she warned.

"Are you sure this is *all right?*" he said as she slid her mouth over the end of his thing.

She raised her head to say, "This isn't doing it. We probably aren't supposed to be doing this because it could lead to doing it, but we love each other, and we won't do it. I'm pretty sure this is ok. It's probably heavy petting, but it's ok."

In fact, as far as Patsy knew, she was inventing what she was doing. The books she had read were comprehensive on the details of the plumbing but didn't have much to offer on habits. And it was so radical and so strange that it had never even occurred to her parents or any of the other good Christians responsible for her to forbid it.

"Sweetie," she said, "don't you move, because I am going to take my undies off, and you are going to do this to me while I do it to you. Don't you dare dare turn around, because that would be too much temptation and we might do it."

And as she settled over him, her little pink asshole he couldn't help seeing heading directly for the tip of his nose and her furry little divide directly for his mouth, he took the Lord's name in vain one more time, amazed and gentle:

"Jesus Mmf," he said.

Mr. Blake Understands Heaven

THE MAN WHO HAD had the washateria before Roger was named Blake. He was an independent contractor. He was competent and honest and hard-working, and did pretty well for himself as a contractor. After a while, though, he found himself getting into real estate as a sideline. He knew a lot of people in the real estate agencies and loan companies, and he usually knew when a good piece of property was on the market and usually had no trouble getting loans on good terms. He would buy a lot or a house and a lot and build or remodel himself and then sell the property a little below market but a good bit above what he got for contracting the work.

A lake was put in outside the city, and as it happened he had 3.7 acres on the shoreline, which he divided into eleven lots. He built a lakeshore house on each lot. Sailboats and party barges and motorboats were seen on the lake, and subdivisions clustered around it, and people sprang up from nowhere to fill the churches and houses and golf courses and Seven-Elevens, well-dressed upwardly mobile young people with ignorant savage children. From the time he sold his houses on the lake, Mr. Blake was really more in real estate than he was in construction.

He never thought of running for the state congress or for alderman, or sought to become a deacon. When his son graduated from high school, he went off to Starkville and not to Oxford. Mr. Blake was a member of an odd modern class: well-off, suburban by habitat, but country to the bone. He was wide-thumbed and big-knuckled and calloused and leather-faced. His eyes were clear and powerful in their lenses. You felt his descendants would bear the same marks generation after generation undiminished, though every man jack of them be born and brought up under the picturesque trees, the wide trim lawns, the false Colonial fronts of Sylvan Meadows henceforward forever.

The washateria had been one of his mistakes. He was philosophical about it, having salvaged most of the machines for another washateria that did quite well indeed. A man made mistakes, mortised both ends of a mortise-and-tenon, for example, or blew up a saw plugging it into a 220 he should have known was a 220 and not a 110.

One day he had showed up at the washateria, simply because he was out that way, and he liked to check on his property. If no one was around, he might pat a house he had built like another man patting a dog and saying, "Good dog." He parked a block away and walked up. There were bodies moving around inside. He stopped, obscured for the people inside by a large sheet of plywood bolted to the plate glass where someone had cracked it. Voices floated out the door, voices that looped and swooped and sang and moaned disgracefully on every ordinary syllable.

"Niggers," he said to himself.

He heard a lifted, plaintive, unintelligible question. It was immediately punctured by a staccato, diving remark that brought a musical boil of laughter.

He stepped in, and things got quiet. The silence didn't surprise him or make him uncomfortable. In fact, it was too familiar to notice.

Light angled through the dirty glass, cutting a shaft through steam, catching baskets of heaped linen, little dime boxes of detergent, blue plastic half-gallons of bleach empty and cut open for scoops.

The women murmured in little groups. One old stubble-faced toothless man nodded to him, a chewed-up felt hat in one hand, a sweat-stained hand-rolled cigarette stuck to his lower lip.

"Moanin, Mist Blake," he said. "Sho is a fine moanin." There was a pause. "Sho is." A longer pause. "If it don't rain, though, I don't know what the farmer gone do."

Blake was checking the washers and dryers. "Morning, Jerry," he answered. "Between the weather and the guvvamint, the farmer don't stand a chance, that's for sure." There was no obvious damage. There were no messages scratched into the ceramic or scrawled on with crayon saying "Cheat" or "Cocksucker tuck my quater." Two machines had coathanger wire twisted through the tongues of their slots, but he had done that himself.

"Ain't it the truth," said Jerry. "Ain't it the truth."

Something was bothering Mr. Blake, and he couldn't figure out what it was. Why were the women flicking covert glances his way? And why were there so many more of them here today than usual?

He said, "I got some corn out there by the line been dried up since April. But the time my hay gets ready, that's when it'll up and rain and won't quit for a month."

"Ain't it the truth," said Jerry. "Ain't it the truth."

Mr. Blake figured it out. Only one dryer was turning, and it had no clothes in it. Several washers were going, but only the one dryer. When his eyes had gone to it, the women had ceased even to whisper. The dryer spun crazily on. It had been spinning since he walked in, he realized.

He pulled open the door, and still it kept spinning.

"Yessa, Mist Blake," Jerry said, "sho is. I's gone tell you sho is broke. Need to fix it, yes you do." Blake felt the blood in his face. He was going to have to fix it. He hadn't brought his tools, and he was going to have to go out and get them and come back, and no telling how much free drying the women were going to get off him while he was gone.

But then, at the door, wheeling around to tell them not to use the broken dryer while he was gone, a command he knew was totally useless, he had the only religious experience of his life.

The dryer would be running anyway, whether the women dried their clothes or not. He would be losing that energy anyway. If they were to use it, he would not be losing one whit more, and they would be gaining. And their clothes would be dirty again tomorrow, next week. They would have to come to him with their quarters again, and might be gotten to come gratefully.

He felt he understood for the first time where all the extra loaves and fishes had come from. He felt a generosity that almost squeezed his heart through the front of his chest.

"You ladies might as well use the dryer till I get back," he said, and stomped on down the block to his truck.

That night, over fried chicken, he spoke to his wife about the experience. "Was a dryer at the washateria got stuck today," he said. "Wouldn't quit running."

"I imagine them niggers got their clothes dry off of you, then, Mr. Blake."

"They did," he said. "That they did." He struggled mightily to phrase his vision. "It seemed like they might as well," he said.

"You're a good man, Mr. Blake. If it wa'n't for you, I don't suppose a one of their men would have a clean shirt to wear to the Welfare line this week."

Mr. Blake found himself irritated at the way she described the colored folks. They had to be nobler to be worthy of his impulse.

"We got any more that lemon icebox pie," he said.

After Sunday School that Sunday, and before the preaching services, Mr. Blake told the story to Brother Goodman. "It seem to me like, in Heaven, wouldn't a blessed thing be wasted. Even a accident, they would use it," he concluded.

"Good, good," Brother Goodman said, smiling in an absent-minded way and clapping Mr. Blake on the arm. "How's Mrs. Blake this morning? Good to see you."

That was his last attempt to communicate his moment of illumination. But fifteen years later, at the onset of the last of a series of strokes, when he could not remember his son's name, or call Mrs. Blake's face into his mind, that one deed stayed with him, as clear as yesterday. Of all the gifts he had given, of all the sacrifices he'd thought he'd made, that memory remained, his last conscious approximation to the possibility of a saved and regenerate immortal soul springing brightly, humbly, infallibly within him.

When he sold the place to Roger, he was aware that he was dealing with an innocent, and wanted to warn him of something he didn't think the boy knew, that the neighborhood was a black neighborhood, and also to let him know a moment of grace had once occurred there. "They're good people," he said. "A lot of colored, though."

Marcus

ROGER WAS LAYING linoleum tile when he met Marcus.

Mr. Blake had removed all the washers and dryers before he sold the place, and where each washing machine had stood was a square of tar-blackened concrete with two pipes protruding from a corner.

Roger had made storage closets and bookshelves of the dryer recesses, except for two. He had removed the partition between these two, and placed his Japanese sleeping mat in the resulting space. This, with a small reading lamp and a curtain over the opening, comprised his sofa and bedroom. He cooked on a Coleman stove and washed his dishes in the lavatory of the mirrorless washroom—one plate, one spoon, one fork, one sharp knife, a ceramic-coated tin cup, a one-quart cooking pot, a skillet.

Now he was filling the vacant squares with linoleum, cutting the linoleum with that wooden-handled tool whose blade, in profile, resembles the beak of a parrot.

He had had a problem with the pipes. At first he had thought to saw them off flush with the floor and had bought a hacksaw and some blades. He spent several sweaty hours sawing on first one pipe and then the other, getting nowhere. He sawed with the blade bent, and as soon as it got into the metal at all, it bound, got hot, and snapped. He tried to saw without the saw, with only a blade held in his fingers, to get closer to the floor, but his hands cramped and got sweaty, and the blade slipped and cut his finger.

Depressed, and stymied, and by such a small thing, he prayed. Then he meditated. When he was calm, he went out and bought more pipe, a pipe wrench, WD–40, and a whole batch of ninety-degree elbows. He also bought curtain rings and bamboo curtains.

With these, he connected the projecting pipes into an upright frame, and from the frame he suspended his bamboo curtains, effectively dividing the studio into two areas, one for work, and one for private life.

He had painted the interior of the place a gleaming white, and now he was finishing up by laying the linoleum precisely around the pipes.

He sat back on his haunches for a breather, and there was Marcus, swinging on the doorjamb, peeping at him through the glass front, then swinging around and looking at him plain, a skinny shirtless kid in grimy knee-length skin-tight shorts that might once have been blue jeans. His head was large and beautiful as an angel's over the knobby body outgrowing itself, and his complexion golden and clear as wild honey. He was waggling his eyebrows at Roger and grinning like the devil. His eyes were a startling hazel-green, and Roger did not realize he was a Negro till he spoke.

"What you doing yo pajamas on," he said. "Why ain't you in school?"

"It ain't pajamas, it's a ghi," Roger said. "It's comfortable. I'm through with school. Why ain't *you* in it?"

"I'm thoo, too."

"You ain't done it. You ain't eem let out for the summer yet."

"I don't have to go I don't want to. What you doin?"

Marcus had come over and squatted down like Roger, only he let his arms trail on the floor like a monkey, and put his face between his knees and filled his cheeks with air and slapped them with his knees to make a wet, farting sound.

"Laying linoleum."

"I seen that. What you up to, what I mean."

"This is going to be my studio. I'm going to teach karate and jujitsu and yoga."

Marcus was up instantly. "Karate?" he shouted. "I know karate!"

He sprinted over to the window-ledge of the studio's glass front, jumped up, whirled, and struck an imaginary pursuer like a man throwing a hatchet. Then he leaned way back for balance and kicked his opponent in the chin. By this time, however, another enemy had caught him around the neck from behind and dragged him off the ledge. Marcus bumped his butt backwards and flipped the new attacker over his head, then fell on the man's nose with his knees.

"You don't *know* karate, you *practice* it," Roger said. He had met this response before, if usually in a somewhat more muted form. It irritated him. Karate was not a quick fix of machine-like invulnerability, but a discipline, a stringency, an attention, a purification, a life.

Marcus jumped up and ran toward Roger, but was slammed backward by someone who leapt on him and began strangling him. Gasping desperately, he began flopping his body up and down like a fish until he built up sufficient wave-action to topple the strangler. He jumped on top of the villain and pummeled him, crying, "Bammity bambam bam bam bammity bam bam bam!" With each blow, his elbow flew past his ear.

"You hit anybody like that and you'll break every bone in your hand," Roger said. He rose and went over as Marcus stood up panting. "Let me show you a basic stance," he said, reaching to move an arm and a leg to place Marcus into the cat stance.

He almost jumped with he touched the boy, whose skin was dry and hot and electric. "You've got to remember your center of gravity, keep it low and not overbalance it," he said. "You've got to learn to feel it as a living spot moving around in you, and keep it always here"—Roger indicated a spot below his navel—"or a feather could knock you over."

Marcus suffered the strange, insistent touch for just a moment, but when Roger hesitated, he was off.

"Leeray say he gone beat me up, but I say you ain't gone do no such thing Leeray, I give you a chop upside yo head make yo eyeballs roll like a slot machine." A vicious scuffle ensued, Marcus belaboring the kidneys of someone much taller who had him in a crushing bear-hug. Suddenly he was flung to the ground. He jumped up and went for his opponent, but was held at arm's length, flailing away. He stopped and grinned at Roger. "I bite a plug out his tit. He say, 'Git that crazy thing away fum me.' He say, 'I don't want no more a him. I don't have to fight no crazy people.' It taste just like salty metal.

"Leeray in the sixth grade," he added.

"Look out!" Marcus hit the deck and rolled over machine-gunning a jet coming in over Roger's left shoulder. Roger went back to work amid the whine of ricochets, the whump and fall-out of grenades, the screams of incoming mortar.

He was trying to decide whether to use a piece he had cut an extra slice out of, or go out for more linoleum. He hated sloppy work, but he was tired. He didn't notice how quiet it had gotten.

Marcus slammed into his back and bowled him over. He nearly flipped and kicked before he realized what had happened. The blade of the cutter was biting through his ghi into his chest. Marcus was sprawled beside him shaking with silent laughter. He grew still and his luminous eyes looked up across six inches of floor into Roger's eyes.

"We friends, ain't we?" he said.

Roger could smell the pungent honey-and-vinegar of the boy's sweat. There didn't seem to but one answer.

"Yes," he said.

First Supper

MARCUS RAN ALL the way back to his house, and all the way up to the third floor, and burst through the kitchen doorway. His fat mother, bending over to put the cornbread in the oven, didn't look up.

"Momma, I bring my friend for supper?"

Her gown was hiked up to where her stockings ended in a roll. She sighed mightily and closed the oven door.

"Momma." She straightened up and went to the sink to wash the batter bowl, the yellow evening light slanting through the window on her, the old light, the sad light. Marcus hated it.

"Momma."

"Don't make me no nevermind."

Marcus was out the door, down the stairs, down the street. He ran into the laundromat. Roger wasn't there. On a little card table was a camp-stove, and on the camp-stove a pot of rice was boiling. It wasn't what Marcus had expected. He had expected Roger to be still toiling away with the linoleum knife, but the cement and the linoleum pieces and the tool had been put away, and the floor was clean. It was as if Roger had never existed, and some stranger had come in and begun boiling rice and then left. Marcus was frightened, and angry. "You can't take him away now," he said. "He ain't change nothin yet."

"What?" said Roger, coming in the back door.

"You gone eat with us," Marcus said. "My momma say so."

Roger was surprised, and with him, surprise always led to silence.

"You can just thow this rice out," Marcus said. "You won't be needin it. Where yo gravy?"

Roger pointed to a bottle on the table beside the stove. "I use soy sauce," he said, apologetically. "It's a lot like gravy."

"Look like a wine-bottle to me. You better hurry and git dressed."

"I don't want to change. I like wearing my ghi."

"You ain't eatin with my momma dress like no Chinaman," Marcus said.

So Roger found himself, twenty minutes later, in coat and slacks and shirt, at the front door of Marcus's apartment building. A young girl was in the foyer when they went in. She wore her hair in a way that he had never seen anyone wear hair before: it was a great bushy globe nearly two feet in diameter, like a trimmed hedge, like a large strange hat from outer space. She fixed a look of such malevolence on Roger that he turned to see who was behind him.

Marcus took the steps two at a time, and Roger hurried after. The girl was still staring at him as they rounded the landing.

"That girl—her hair..."

"She ain't arn it," Marcus said. "She mad at white people."

Marcus opened the door and pulled Roger into the kitchen. At a linoleum-topped table in the corner sat a large gaunt man in a grey undershirt, his hair grey on his chest and in a fringe around his head. His coloring and eyes were exactly the same as Marcus's, and Roger realized he must be looking at Marcus's father. A huge black woman was halfway to the table with a steaming bowl of mashed potatoes. She stopped dead, and her hands started to fly to her mouth. Then she grabbed for the bowl three times, lurching forward, fumbling it into the air like a wingback after a bad lateral. Roger jumped to help, and she slammed into him. He went down sitting and the bowl landed upside-down on his head.

For a second he was too stunned to move, and then he jumped to his feet shouting *"Damn!"* and raking potatoes out of his burning scalp, flinging them by handfuls back into the bowl.

The man at the table held a stick of cornbread halfway to his open mouth.

"Hello," said Roger shakily.

Mr. A.L. Gandy pushed his chair back, stood up, and strode to the refrigerator. He pulled out a jug that had once held a cheap orange drink and now held cold water. He circled Roger's chest firmly with one arm and poured the cold water over Roger's head with his free hand.

"Always seem to help to me," he said. "Put cold in, bring hot out."

Mrs. Gandy lay sniffling on the floor, her robe up over an enormous expanse of white cotton panties. Now she began to howl. *Pull yo goddamn dress down, crybaby,* Mr. Gandy thought.

Mrs. Gandy clambered to her feet and ran sobbing to a back room, shaking the floor as she went. A door slammed. "You hate meeee," she wailed, muffled by distance and the closed door.

"Be with you in a minute," Mr. Gandy said to the closed door, in a tone so gentle his wife could not possibly have heard it.

"Here now," he said, taking Roger's potato-splattered coat off and leading him to one of the chairs. "You come on in that door and bring me the butter," he said sternly, studying Roger's face.

Marcus came two steps back into the kitchen. "It ain't butter, it's marjrin," he said.

"You bring me that yellow stuff in the refrigerator that you know blessed well what I mean. And a wet dish-tile."

Roger was in shock. The old man's voice went on and on, erasing time. Roger was a baby. His shirt was off. A wet cloth was gently cleaning him. And now something greasy. He saw the man's fingers on his hairless chest, working it in. Now on his scalp. It hurt. It soothed. Roger could smell the man. The smell of a nigger, some bitter voice said in his mind. It was the smell of a man who had done hard physical work all day, sharp and strange and demanding. The fractions of labor. It was pleasant. It was not the smell of a white man. The woman was crying, far away in his mind.

"You be all right now," the man said, and patted Roger absently on the head, a father's gesture. He went away. Roger could hear his patient voice alternating with the anguished voice of the woman.

Marcus came to the table and began helping his plate.

"My daddy fix you," he said. "You need to be more careful." He proceeded to put away an astonishing quantity of food, including some of the mashed potatoes from Roger's hair. By the time Mr. and Mrs. Gandy emerged from the back room, Marcus had finished three helpings, located a pecan pie and severed a quarter of it to take with him, and vanished once more.

"This is Snower Mae Gandy, my bride," said A.L. Gandy. "The prettiest little woman in Christendom." Roger thought Christendom was a pretty strange word for a Negro to be using. It was in his own passive vocabulary but certainly not in his active one. Snower Mae inclined her head to Roger, laughing happily, and said, "Liar." She was, in contrast to her husband, extremely dark.

"Where's Marcus?" Mr. Gandy asked when they sat down to eat. "Eaten and gone, I see. Well, he can't play kick-the-can all night. He'll have to take his spanking some time, he knows that. I guess he just don't want it just yet."

They had greens cooked with fatback and cornbread and green onions and black-eyed peas with relish and buttermilk and mashed potatoes with left-over chicken gravy. "I'm sorry about yo head," Mrs. Gandy said to Roger, raking the top layer of potatoes into a separate bowl. "We can just take the used potatoes off the top, and I believe the rest will be ok."

"I think Marcus ate most of them," Roger said.

"Well, yo head was clean anyhow, I seen that," Mrs. Gandy said. "A little Wildroot won't hurt nobody."

"Where's Eleanor Roosevelt?" Mr. Gandy asked, later in the meal.

"Over to Missy's," Mrs. Gandy said.

And then later he said, "T.J.?"

"Over to Valley Street with Leon. He said."

"You know I don't want him hanging around with Leon."

"He said. You was there. He just goin to the grocery to hang around. Maybe help Mr. Smith a little."

"You and me hope. I like to see Leon help anybody but Leon."

They sat back after the meal, to have room for huge wedges of pecan pie and big glasses of sweet milk.

"You want to take coffee in the study?" Mr. Gandy said when they were through. They went into a tiny room that Roger had assumed was a pantry off the kitchen, Mr. Gandy carrying a chair from the kitchen table. He waved Roger to a big worn-out armchair under a floorlamp. He took the kitchen chair himself.

The walls were covered with books. They came in all colors and sizes and conditions, nearly all paperback. There was one shelf of hard-cover editions. "I believe in education," Mr. Gandy said. "I never went through but third grade, but I educated myself." Roger had never given education a second thought. It was just something that happened to you, mostly after you got into high school. Mr. Gandy spoke to him as if he were an associate professor somewhere.

"This here's my library. I have just about every kind of book there is. I don't have em all of all of the kinds, but I have as many as I can. Yo library is probably better, but this is as best as I can do, and I am happy with it."

Roger had never imagined so many books in anyone's house. It was more books than he would ever read.

"My oldest, he read when he was five. Thomas Jefferson Gandy. Go on and look around you want to."

Roger found that the books were in alphabetical order by author, or by subject matter, apparently depending on which Mr. Gandy thought was more important. A book called *Invisible Man* nudged up against a treatise on Einstein and four-dimensional space. Roger flipped through the *Invisible Man* book looking for an action part, where he went invisible, but he couldn't find it.

"Thomas Jefferson reads a book almost every night," Mr. Gandy said. "He can read a book in one setting. Here he is now."

Roger turned to see a large young extremely angry black man standing in the doorway glaring at him.

"What is this *honkie* doing in my house?" he demanded.

Current Events

THE LARGE YOUNG black man who called Roger a honkie was T.J., of course. Leon and T.J. had not in fact been at the Valley Street grocery. They had *gone* there, to collect a couple of Cokes, a bag of malted milk balls, a jug of orange juice, three Zeroes, and three Baby Ruths. "We a need em later," Leon said. "You'll see."

But then they had left the grocery, and gone to Leon's aunt's house. She was out with her man, and no one was home.

Leon was Leon Cool. When you asked him what his name was, that was what he would say. He had been born Leonidas Didier in New Orleans. He and his mother had moved to Jackson when he was five, because she had family there. Then she had married a fellow who moved them out to Los Angeles, and that was where he had lived until last year. She had become afraid for him there. He seemed angry half of the time, and mercurially cheerful the rest. He was always broke, and depended on her for spending money, but now and again would turn up with a roll of twenties. He ate when he remembered to, stayed out all night, and slept on the street for days on end. "At least he keeps himself clean," she told her friends. She saw hope in that.

He did keep himself clean. He was the one who invented starched and pressed blue jeans. When his favorite pair became ragged along one cuff, he rolled that leg up to midcalf in a wide band, then pressed that. His high-tops gleamed white. He looked like a professional soldier in one of those oddball uniforms, a zouave or something.

Finally his mother sent him back to Jackson to stay with her sister, safe from the L.A. streets. He went because otherwise she would have given him no money at all, and because he and the sister had fucked each other for a while when she had come to L.A. for a month-long visit. He had been thirteen, and the sister twenty-five.

When he got to Jackson, he found out there were to be no repeats. She expected him to clean his room, go to school, treat her man with respect, and behave.

He went to school, but only to have somewhere to hang out. "This ain't no *school*, man," he said. "You think this is tough? Podunkarama, man. Low blow for Pogo, white joe got *all* the dough. You want a tough school, go to L.A. They all tough there."

Leon was tall, as tall as T.J., but gaunt where T.J. was fat and pretty. T.J. was the first-string quarterback, at six-four and 203 pounds, though he was only a junior. He had a B average and was vice-president of the junior class at Lanier. Leon's height put him on a par with T.J. in T.J.'s mind, since Leon's fierce eyes could look directly into his own.

Now, in his aunt's kitchen, Leon took out four skinny hand-rolled cigarettes and said, "Now. Now, my man. Now we gone get you bad. You bad but you not bad enough. Do like Leon does." Leon lit one of the joints with a kitchen match. He drew a deep breath from it and held it. He gave the joint to T.J. T.J. took a pull on it.

A seed popped, and T.J. dropped the joint. "Hey, look out," Leon said, and scooped the lit joint from the table-top. He got it settled in the pinch of his thumb and finger and drew another long drag. This time he did not pass the joint to T.J., but held it, burning end up so it would burn more slowly. Finally he exhaled, took another drag, and passed it to T.J. T.J. took a pull, and this time did not drop it. "Hey," said Leon, reminding him to pass it. They smoked it all that way.

Between drags, Leon carried on a halting monologue in a grinding, half-withheld voice. "You like me, you a natural-born leader. But you too good. Yo daddy selling good and you buying it. Like a big dumb meat-cow, just being good till they whop you between the eyes. Big and smiley and pretty as a Hollywood movie star. Got to get bad. Bad is bad because they can't control it, see. When you been good too long, ain't nothin left but bad. Bad is just good that got smart.

"Look at Leon. People don't understand me, you know. I'm a leader. I can motivate people, you know? Motivated you, didn't I? I can be one of those executives. Sure I can. I got the brain for it. Be sittin in current events witch you makin that B talkin bout Nixon make a fool a himself. Yeah. Didn't think I's listening, honh? Think ole Leon's stoned. Leader don't miss nothin. But what I care two white men have a play-like argument? You think there's any difference in them two white men? Naw. What one of em do the other one do. Time for the nigger to quit waiting on the white man. Set down at the counter and say, Serve me now, baby. You know the State Sovereignty Commission is paying the mothafucka Citizen Cuntholes five thousand dollars a month? You know who I heard that from? You got to meet the man. You got to meet the man what am. You ever been out to Tougaloo? Current events, shit. Don't eem know what's happenin at Tougaloo.

"You ever wonder why the girls say, *Hey, T.J.*, in that singy teasy way when you come along, like they making fun of you, but you can't figure out what they makin fun of? It's because you ain't solid bad, my man. Good mean thinkin about what other people think. Bad mean I take care of *myself*, honey, I a sho take care of you. Oh yay they vote for you, just like they vote for any white man, but they a be laughin the whole time."

Leon regarded the defunct stub solemnly, then ate it. He said, "You can pay me the dollar and a quarter now. Naw, I don't have no change. Tell you what. I'm pretty sure we gone smoke all four of em, ain't you?"

T.J. did not have any idea whether or not they were going to smoke all four. He didn't know what it was like to be stoned, but he couldn't tell any difference.

"Pretty good stuff, ain't it?" Leon said.

T.J. realized that although the dope wasn't doing anything to him, this kitchen was a fine place to be. It was fine to be taking his destiny into his own hands. Here they sat, two strong men, turning the world over in their minds. Changing it. By just looking at it different. This was a pivot-point, a focus for tremendous beginnings. He could feel the future humming in the air.

And it was appropriate that such changes should begin in such an humble place: this little kitchen. He was amazed at the thought of all the living that had been done in kitchens, all the talking, just like this. All the meals that had gathered themselves on this very table, to be taken up into invisible lives, to be changed into love and work and ideas. He thought of cornbread and turnip greens turning into the theory of relativity, into music, into freedom. He realized that time itself was a made thing, that the very moment they sat breathing and beating in had been made out of the stuff of prior lives. He could feel the lives, like clear layers of water, like a clear river with levels of light he could float through. He floated in time, level after level, down to the bottom, the riverbed bottom of the table. The table-top was a wavy-patterned formica, like the sand of a river bottom. The light threw his shadow over the sand. He hung in the current flicking his fins.

There were many many lives in the sand, like crawdads drifting over the river floor, then jetting backward a little. He saw his daddy walking the fields to court his momma. His momma pretty and skinny like in her picture. He saw Mr. Alfred, calling his daddy to come back and work. Mr. Alfred beetling across the fields in the shiny new Studebaker. He was high in the current over the fields, the lives.

He was in the river but also in the sky. He saw his sister born. He saw his family driving into Jackson for the first time in the old Studebaker, Marcus a tiny howling baby in his mother's arms. He did not see himself. He was the shade that kept them cool, the shade of a big cloud in the sky that they rested in and never looked up and saw him. Momma, Momma, it's me, he wanted to call out, but clouds can't talk. I'm big now. I a take care of you. Look up, Momma. See me.

"Pretty good stuff," Leon said, and T.J. shot up out of the sunlit river into dark starry space. Hell yes it was good stuff. Of course it was good stuff. Everything was good stuff. Their heads were planets in flooding space, throwing long swiveling shadows in the smoke, lightbulb a far sun.

"Just give me the whole five now, and we'll call it all square. We a just go ahead and smoke the other three. The five."

Three. Five. The five. Oh yeah. Pocket. Hand. Tell hand go pocket.

T.J. brought out *the five*.. Leon was laughing. T.J. could see why. It was funny. Money was funny. It had Abraham Lincoln's picture on it. What if it was his daddy's picture? That would be even funnier. There was his old grey-headed daddy, partly bald, in the oval in the middle of the bill. The green embroidery around the edges was the green of cotton fields, stretching into the distance all around him.

"What are you laughing at?" Leon said.

"You know."

Money was so funny. Money wasn't real. Here he was waving it in the air, funny little piece of paper with drawing all over it. He half expected a bunch of white people to come crashing in the door and grab it. They were so funny. Thought it was real. It wasn't real like the river bottom was real. Just a scrap in the current.

"The white man thank it's real," T.J. explained. "That's his trouble. That's the trouble God give the white man, he thank a dollar is real. The trouble God give the nigger is to live with the white man. That's where a white man live, on a dollar bill. He cut his yahd to look like a dollar bill. If the white man could go to the bottom of the river, he would be a good man. When the river sleep, and have a dream about the sun. We need to show the white man the door to the river."

"You got potential," Leon said, and snatched the five from T.J.'s hand. "But you need to learn the value of a dollar."

"I'm bad," T.J. said. He stood up. "I'm *bad*," he roared. "I'm *bad* and I'm *hungry*. Got to *feed* a bad man, Leon. Why you want to make a man *bad*, and then *stahve* him, Leon? Naw, I don't want none of yo candy junk. I want some *food*. Gimme that." He grabbed the new joint Leon had just lit, and drew a huge breath from it. He held the breath, then blew it out: "Wah-*hoom!*" He drew another huge breath from it, then handed it back to Leon.

"I'm *hongry*. I can pick this refrigerator up. You believe me, Leon? I can. I have before. I want to hit somebody. I love to bounce off of people. Can't wait till two-a-day start. What they got in here. That *ahnj* crap. I ain't drankin that ahnj crap. Ain't no nigger. Nigger be drankin that ahnj crap. Cheese. *Cheese*, Leon!"

T.J. got out a big cylindrical chunk of cheddar cheese wrapped in black wax. He set it round side down on the table. He rambled in a drawer and found a butcher knife. He whirled around with the butcher knife raised high in his hands. Leon jumped up, turning over his chair. T.J. brought the knife down on the cheese, yelling *Whonk!* A chunk of cheese rolled to one side. T.J. flipped the knife sideways without looking. It lodged, reverberating, in the wall.

"Shit," Leon said.

T.J. peeled the black wax off the cut chunk of cheese. He sat down and began to eat it. He picked up the remaining chunk, a truncated black cylinder with one orange face.

"Look, Leon," he said, "a spotlight. A cheeselight." He saw the cheeselight coming out in a beam. He turned the beam on Leon. "You caught in the cheeselight, Leon. The sirens going off. Waow waow waow waow waow waow waow."

Leon had backed up against the wall. He looked left at the window, right at the door. Two people came in the door.

"Waow waow waow waow …"

"What you doing here, you shitty little dickey-bird?" the man said to Leon. He was half a foot shorter than Leon.

"Raboo, this is my house," the woman said.

T.J. kept making his siren. This hardly seemed the time to stop. Leon scooped the joints off the table and put them in his pocket. "You so dumb," he said. "You don't live here."

"Leon, you ain't talking to Raboo like that," the woman said.

"He make me so mad, Aingie. Start right in, don't even give me no chance."

"Smoking that shit in here," Raboo said.

"Waow waow waow," T.J. said.

"Raboo, you don't know they was smoking shit in here—"

"The hell. Don't tell me I can't smell shit. And I can see it too, if it

47

do stand up and walk on two legs."

"Waow waow waow waow ..."

"I ain't coming back till you shut a this piece a peter-meat, Aingie," Leon said, and disappeared out the door. T.J. followed him. He heard Aingie wailing behind them:

"Done stuck a *knife* in my wall!"

Outside in the dark, Leon said, "We a have to smoke the rest of em later. You could whip that son of a bitch, but it wouldn't be smart to get arrested right now. We got too much to do. Bar yo daddy's car."

"What?"

"I say we a smoke em later. Can you find yo way home? I got some business to do."

"Sure I can find my way home," T.J. said, looking around. "I'm *from* here. I ain't from California." He looked back to grin at Leon, but Leon was nowhere to be seen.

"You from California," T.J. said.

He looked around again. Just follow the railroad. That would take him home just like it brought him here. But which way?

The world had switched around while he was under the river. Good was bad and bad was good. Right was the same as left and North the same as South, and a nigger was free. So how could a person get back home? What did the signs mean now?

He picked a direction and went. He went jog-jumping from tie to tie. The longer he went, the more familiar it became, and the safer he felt. But he was losing the strange clear truth that had been so easy a little while ago.

Never mind. He was tired, really tired. He would get the truth back later. Now he needed his home, his bed, his family, his dark warm colored family, safe and friendly and drawn in close. Forget the weird cold world of the white man.

He was working up a sweat. That's what he would tell his daddy, that after he left the grocery he went out running the ties for a work-out. His daddy didn't like him to run the ties, he thought it was dangerous. His confessing to that would keep his daddy from thinking of anything else T.J. might have done.

Then he came to the overpass and there was his street. His home. He went up the stairs and in, and there was his daddy, sitting talking to a white man.

Supply Preach

LATER THAT SUMMER, Roger began to get seriously lonely. Nobody came by to see him. He routinely ate supper with the Gandys, but during the day he had time on his hands. He had begun the studio with no real conception of how to go about building up a clientele, and he was living off his savings. He lived cheaply, since his only expenses were payments on the ex-laundromat and food. His laundry he took home. It irritated him that he had not thought to have Mr. Blake leave a washer and dryer in the building and add them to the price.

His mother was glad to have him bringing the laundry home. Roger's plans had not been real to her until the month before graduation, when he had begun negotiating the purchase of the laundromat. Suddenly she realized that he would not be going to college or getting a regular job like the other kids. He would be out there in the dangerous world where things ran on money and nothing protected you from anything.

She insisted that he stay with them at night and take the bus to his studio in the mornings. At first he did, his stepfather having no objections. But it was easier to stay out at the studio. His mother was sad when he was away, but when he was home she didn't know how to be close. So she got very busy, planned too many picnics, took him on shopping trips with her. After a few weeks of this, he was staying at the studio all the time, only spending a night or two at home on the weekends. The thing that made him the most lonely was not seeing Patsy. At home, she had come over in the evenings after school, and of course they had seen each other at school every day.

Then there had been Bible Club and YFC and sometimes church. Now, the only time he saw her was when they came by on Saturday night to pick him up for YFC.

When Jimmy McMorris had graduated, his father had given him the old family station wagon as a present. Actually, it was only three years old. It was when Ford changed the grill from the straight-line shark-mouth to a rounded ram-jet style with a bar across it. Now Fords looked like fat spaceships, not boxes with fins.

So Jimmy Mac now drove the group to YFC. He was attending Mississippi College, so he was still available to go. Several of the group's members had moved away to go to college or join the Army or get a job. Two now lived in Jackson. One had married. Attendance was a lot less regular. YFC worked a lot better for the youth of America when they were still in high school.

But Jimmy and Patsy and Roger were regulars. Every Saturday at twenty minutes to six, the big low-riding blue and white wagon pulled up in front of Roger's studio, and he got in, and off they went. Patsy would be in the front seat, and she would get out and get in the back with Roger. They didn't kiss anymore, though. It didn't seem right to kiss without an adult there to not see it. And very often, Roger did not even go to the Daisy Queen with them. There was a back road near the Daisy Queen that led home to Clinton, and it was easier for them to drop Roger off at his studio, which was nearer downtown, and then go on to the Daisy Queen and then home by the back road than it was to double back into town and drop Roger off after going to the Daisy Queen. As Jimmy pointed out, he had church the next day and needed his sleep so really couldn't afford to take the extra time.

Those were the loneliest nights of all. It would already be too late to eat with the Gandys, or even to visit: they too had church and went to bed early on Saturday nights to be fresh for Sunday mornings. Roger would mope around for hours, vaguely guilty because he knew he *wasn't* going to church the next day.

Roger often invited the others to come visit him during the day, but only Jimmy had a car of his own. And in the same way that Roger did not know how to build up a clientele, he did not know how to make other people want to visit him. So they said they would love to and then discovered that they were always a little too busy to feel like making the trip. Besides, what could they do when they got there? Those colored people out on the steps staring at them made them nervous.

They could go have some barbecue at Mosey Froghead's little tin barbecue shack. In fact, it had the best barbecue in Jackson, and probably in the state, and maybe in the entire world. But it wasn't the cleanest place in the world, and it was dark, and so were its customers, and so were the things they said, at least when the white kids were there. Also, you could get beer there, which made it a den of evil.

Roger knew it wasn't a den of evil. He would go over sometimes and have a beer with Mosey. Mosey didn't mind Roger because Roger didn't talk too much, and Mosey knew Roger was crazy, although Roger didn't know it.

"Is Froghead your real name?" Roger asked him one time.

"No. Mosey my real name. Call me Froghead because the way my head put on. Put on at a angle you know. Don't look like no froghead, though, they wrong about that. Ought to be Mosey Fish-head."

Mosey was right. He had a large round head with wide and bulging eyes, and it was joined to his shoulders without the intervention of a neck. It joined them at the angle most people's heads have when they are looking at the top shelf of a bookcase, so that Mosey resembled nothing so much as a gigantic bass floating to the surface of a lake to snap a mayfly. It was a scurrilous lie to say that he looked like a frog.

Roger worked out mornings and afternoons. He meditated in between, fixed lunch, napped. Mr. Gandy didn't mind if he wanted to go over and read some of his books during the day, but Mr. and Mrs. Gandy both worked, and Roger was uncomfortable in the house alone, or when only Eleanor or T.J. or Marcus was there. Eleanor, who was twelve, tended to sit in a chair across from him and stare. Besides, Mr. Gandy did not have many books on the martial arts.

One Wednesday afternoon in late August, Roger had finished a workout and was trying to decide whether to go read a book or visit Mosey or just take another nap, when the blue and white Ford pulled up. Roger's heart jumped, and he ran out to meet Patsy and Jimmy, still in his ghi.

But Jimmy Mac had come alone. He was offering Roger a chance to supply preach.

Roger took him over to Mosey's and they had Cokes and barbecued pork sandwiches and potato chips and warm cole slaw. Mosey wouldn't make them any french fries, so they had three sandwiches each. The pork was in thick slices and was moist and rich with fat. You could taste the nutty flavor under the cutting flavor of the sauce. The sauce wasn't very sweet, just a little, and it wasn't super-hot. Back then barbecue sauce didn't usually emphasize jalapeños the way it began to do later, when the Mexicans and Cajuns got out of hand. Mosey made it with gallon jugs of ketchup and blackstrap mixed half and half with honey and sweet pickle juice he had left over from pickles, and the Cokes that people hadn't finished that they hadn't put their cigarettes out in, and whatever seasonings he had on hand that hadn't caked up or gotten weevils. This batch he had also dissolved a couple of licorice whips in. He used a batch a day, two on Saturdays, and cooked each batch on extremely low heat for three days, letting it set up a little overnight, so that he always had at least three big pots simmering.

"Well, where is it?" Roger asked.

"Well, you take Eighty east to Brandon, and then you take a right on Eighteen to Raleigh, but you don't go to Bay Springs. If you get to Bay Springs, you went too far. You take a left on I don't remember the number, but it's the first gravel road after the Leaf River bridge. After five miles, you come to a fork and you stay on the left one until you cross Choctaw Creek, then you see a sign, Bethany Baptist. You can't miss it. It's a white church on a hill. But can you get a car?"

"I might be able to borrow somebody's." Mosey, behind the counter, knew he was thinking of Mr. Gandy's bullet-nosed 1949 black Studebaker, and shook his head at the foolishness of it all.

"You know, it would be really good experience for you, it really would. With your commitment to Jesus and all. You're just about the first person I thought of."

"But you think I can? I never praught, or."

"Praught?"

"Preached?"

"You just talk. Do like you did when you witnessed at YFC, when you gave the devotional. Only do some demonstration. Don't talk so much. You were real good, I don't mean that, but do a demonstration."

"But can you do jujitsu in a sermon?" The truth is that Roger was far more expert at shodo-kan than at any style of jujitsu, but in the last year he had decided that jujitsu was closer to the heart of things than karate was. This feeling was based on what he perceived as the more meditative, less aggressive nature of jujitsu. It was more Christian. Perhaps even more important was the fact that he liked the sound of the word *jujitsu* better than he liked the sound of *karate*, although he was not deeply aware of this preference. In any case, he had definitely decided his club was the Jujitsu for Christ Club and not the Karate for Christ Club.

"Sure you can. You can do anything in a sermon, just so long as you do it to the glory of God. You need a joke to start out with, and then you need a scripture to read to them, that has your subject in it. And then you get to the serious side of your subject, whatever it is we're doing wrong, like not loving one another or giving God enough praise, and here's where maybe you give a demonstration, to like wake em up if they are beginning to wander off, especially if you aren't a real good speaker, and tie it all in with the scripture, like your club, you know, and what it's for and all. And break a couple of boards. Personally, I don't like to give demonstrations because I don't have anything to demonstrate, but I'm a pretty good speaker, so it's like my sermon is its own demonstration. And I always have a lot of fresh jokes. It's just my personal homiletics, but it works for me."

Bethany Baptist was in the red clay hills and pine woods east of Newton, Mississippi, where the junior college for preachers was. There were only 34 members, Jimmy explained, so they couldn't pay a regular pastor. They made do mostly with a succession of young student pastors from the preacher college, retired missionaries back from China or New Guinea or Africa, and lay preachers whose love of the Lord had enabled them to give up drinking or sell a large number of automobiles. They had liked Jimmy so much they offered him 35 dollars to come every other Sunday.

"So if you can get a car, the round trip will be about five dollars for gas, and you can give me ten, and that will leave you with twenty dollars, and some good experience with gospel work. You could start doing a lot of this."

Roger found himself for some reason thinking of swatting flies.

"You could go around and witness for the Lord and help pay for your studio. I have a feeling this is really the Lord's will, the way it all works out so neat. This could be a really important Sunday for this person I have to counsel with. They're a Christian, but they're thinking about dedicating their life to Full-Time Christian Service. They really need to talk about God's Word, because they are confused right now about what to do. It's a critical time for them, and I just couldn't tell this person no."

The person was in fact Patsy, but Jimmy did not feel this fact was central to the situation. Besides which, it might confuse Roger, knowing how crazy he was about Patsy. They could talk it out later, when Patsy had figured out her commitment to Jesus.

"Maybe I better skip YFC," Roger said.

That seemed like a good idea to Jimmy. "You want to be rested up for the supply preaching job."

Roger was glad to get out of going to YFC. Every white person in Mississippi was secretly happy to be able to miss church or prayer meeting or Sunday school or the Tuesday night meeting of the Women's Missionary Union or Royal Ambassadors or Girls' Auxiliary or Bible Club or anything. None of them knew it, but they welcomed headaches and arthritis and sick stomachs and bleeding sinuses and palpitations and falls from ladders and automobile accidents and pinkeye and I don't know what-all, because all they had to do was stay home and be taken care of. One of the things that subconsciously worried them about Heaven was that the new body was going to be incorruptible, and they would have to attend all the services.

Sin was a drag, and hearing about it a hundred times a week was even worse. There was joy in doing The Will of the Lord, but it was such a *theoretical* joy. The rest of the time you went around feeling sinful because you didn't feel enough joy so you must not be *really* doing TWOTL. TWOTL. As in The Will of the Lord, you know. So there was Sin again. What they needed was a TWOTL that wasn't so dadblamed hard to do, a TWOTL that made you feel good when you did it.

But of course something like that would have been too much like sex.

"The plugs needs cleaning," Mr. Gandy said when Roger asked to borrow the Studebaker. "It ain't firing right."

"I don't know how to do that," Roger said.

"Honey, what *do* you know how to do?"

"I don't know."

"Well you needs to know *something*, son. All right," he sighed. "I reckon you can bar it. But the plugs does need cleaning."

A huge rainstorm came through Saturday night, and that Sunday dawned improbably cool and fresh. Roger launched himself, in an alien vehicle, toward his first real sermon. He crossed the muddy Pearl, swollen to many times its normal size, and headed east.

Mr. Gandy had been embarrassed to let him in the car, although he was usually proud of it. It smelled of the lives of its users. The front seat cushion was torn, and there was a wide, dark stain on the back cushion. At first Roger felt as if he were violating a privacy. But the morning sang under his tires on the empty highway, and these intimate disrepairs became familiar, even friendly.

At forty miles an hour, six or seven miles past Brandon, the engine quit.

Roger pumped the clutch instead of the brake and sailed frozenly on in the sudden silence. The car jerked and the motor cut back in when he released the clutch. It happened twice more, and so when he crossed a bridge he was too distracted to notice whether it had been the Leaf River bridge. He took the first gravel road to his left in case. Then there was a fork, but it was a three-way fork. He took the left-most. The car went out again, and this time rolled to a stop when he let the clutch back in. He turned the key off and back on and jiggled the choke and it cranked. He went on. Sunday school started at 9:45.

At 9:30, he was panicky.

At 9:45, he stopped and rested his forehead on the wheel and prayed. "Please, God," he whispered.

He found a service station that was also a house. The station was closed. The owner came to the door in a flannel shirt, stubbled, smelling of onions and whiskey.

"Lord, sonny, you bout half a county over. Go back the way you come till you hit the second right, then you taken it and go about two mile and taken a left, and then follow yo friend's directions. Hell, you ain't bothering me. You gone be late though."

The car quit again five minutes after Roger took a left and this time would not crank. He lifted the hood and peered under it helplessly. He jiggled wires. He got his fingers black and smudged his white shirt, which was sweat-soaked now and clung to his back. He got back in and ground the key. Got out, looked, jiggled, got in, prayed, cranked, no good. Got back out, prayed, jiggled, prayed, got in, cranked, gave a short desperate cry that he had intended to be a prayer, cranked. It started.

At 12:45, Bethany Baptist Church broke shining into view on its hills. White, rust, green: church, clay, pine. If the church was not locked, he could sleep on a cool pew, wait for the night service.

But there was a big pink Cadillac in the driveway. It was Deacon Mecum, smoking Old Golds.

"I reckon you want to come with me. We usually feed em. That's all right, it watten no bother. Several of em gets lost. We had an extra song and Brother Vanderburg gave his witness from his gall-bladder operation. Brenda didn't have her stuff for a chalk-talk or she would've. I wanted to check out the toolshed back of the church anyways, somebody's been getting in it. So after I did that I just waited a little. I had a good smoke. Brenda don't like me to smoke around her, and I'm old-fashion, I don't believe it's proper to smoke on the grounds between services. You just come on in my car. No, it was just devilment probably, whoever got in the toolshed, won't nobody bother your car."

In the Cadillac he said, "Dinner will be a little cold, but that's ok. You'll like Brenda. She likes to talk to the young men from the colleges. She has artistic ideas. You can tell by her name, practically. Everybody thought I was a regular scannel, marrying a girl with a modern name." He chucked with satisfaction. "Yep. Thought I was a regular scannel." Roger was emotionally exhausted and found it easier to let Deacon Mecum do the talking. He did not have the strength to explain that he wasn't really a college student. He *was* in a way, he guessed, since his friends were. It felt good to think of it that way.

Roger washed up in the bathroom with cold water from a pitcher in a basin and a fresh sun-dried towel, and they ate at a table on the shaded back screen porch. They had cold fried chicken, warmed-up canned butterbeans from the year before (the last jar, Mrs. Mecum said), pan cornbread, squash cooked with sugar and then browned in a pan with onions and bacon grease, green beans, and iced tea, with fresh peach ice cream cranked for dessert.

After dinner, the deacon took his nap.

Mrs. Mecum was a brisk, short, pear-shaped woman with neat grey hair, a very clear complexion, and blue eyes lively behind steel-rimmed glasses. She showed Roger the garden. It was hot in the sandy furrows, the tomatoes rioted green and red and made the air close and hot with their breath, the corn sprang tall and scratchy, but back in the yard she drew him a glass of cold water from the pump, and they sat on a bench in the shade of oak, mimosa, pine, pecan, and one black tupelo from God knows where, and he felt cool and alert: not at all stuffed and stupefied, as he might have expected.

It may have been the breakdown of the car and his despair on being late for his first real sermon: the exhilaration of falling without a net and finding oneself safe after all, borne up on the wings of angels, the temptation Satan nearly got Jesus with, there high over Jerusalem.

"We think it so fine of you young men to devote your lives to the Lord and come up here and help out. Some of the young men are just as *scared*. And some go a little far out. I can't agree with just *anything*. My Jesus means too much to me. But they're just discovering their own thoughts, and I know they mean well." Roger understood that she was giving him some discreet guidance on the limits of his message for the evening.

"I don't like too much hellfire and brimstone," she went on. "We need to be afraid of it, all right, but most of us here was Christians before they were even born. A lot of em preach hellfire and brimstone because it's the easiest way to make a sermon, I think. But I like a teaching sermon. What do you preach on usually?"

The light and shade carved the water where he held it to his eyes. "Self-defense and Jesus, mostly," he said.

"Self-defense and Jesus? But Jesus is our shield."

"But unto them that hath it shall be given, too, and from them that hath not it shall be taken away. And that goes for defending yourself, too. It's kind of like martial arts. It's kind of like this Chinese and Japanese fighting."

"You mean that ju-ju?"

"No, that's that magic. I mean judo and stuff. Jujitsu and karate and bare-handed defense and all." He was trying the terminology out on her, seeing if she knew any of it, attempting to gauge at what level of simplicity to reduce it to.

"Fighting and Jesus! Well, I come as a Sword. There was this boxer at Meridian once, he was colored, but he was famous up North, the deacon would know who. Of course, he couldn't have been in the church building, but it was a tent revival and they had him come in for a testimony for the colored, it was a big white-and-colored revival and the colored sat all across in the back, and he said he prayed before fights. After the services, I went up and asked him what would happen if he turned the other cheek while he was boxing, and he said, 'The other man would knock me out.' I said, 'Well?' He said, 'The Lord don't want me to be knocked out.' I said, 'How do you know?' he said, 'The Lord wants me to take care of my chilren, and if I am knocked out, I can't take care of my chilren.' But it didn't sit right with me, I don't care what he said."

"But you don't understand," Roger said. He was feeling the old frustration again, the inability to make others see what was perfectly clear to him. "You don't understand. It ain't to kill people with your bare hands. They think it is, but it ain't. *Karate* means 'empty hands.' It's supposed to be, if you have two equal people, the aggressor, the mean one, is supposed to lose. Because he's not clear. He's mad, and he wants things. He don't have the peace that passeth understanding. See, in jujitsu, a man comes at you, and you don't fight, you just grab him how he's coming and help him along with it a little more until he is doing too much of it and he begins to see the error of his ways. It's just like when Jesus said heaping coals of fire on his head. You don't hate back, you just use love, and they keep coming, and, and, and you flip them, and—"

Roger waved his hand impatiently to stimulate the stopped flow of his explanation. "And you can make Christians out of them," he said.

"Tell me some more," Brenda Mecum said.

Roger and Brenda put their heads together and came up with a grand plan for the evening service: a combined sermon/demonstration/chalk-talk. Roger had not brought his ghi, so Mrs. Mecum stitched up the front of a pair of the deacon's old pajamas, then tailored the legs just below the knee. It was easy enough to tailor the sleeves of an old white shirt, and take out the collar and make a belt to wrap round and round. This get-up had something like the correct appearance, but was much flimsier, and they agreed he should wear some long underwear for decency's sake.

They got to the church early and set up. Roger sat on a small bench up on the rostrum, and Mrs. Mecum stood by her easel below. On the easel was a large pad of artist's sketching paper. On a child's high chair beside her was an open box of big blocky colored chalks.

Roger was wearing a choir robe over his impromptu ghi.

People began to filter in, staring curiously at Roger and Mrs. Mecum. They didn't filter long, with a total membership of only 34, as it said on the little slotted board up front, and that was really only the Sunday School membership, as they didn't bother with Training Union on Sunday evenings but just went straight into the worship service. And really the "34" needed to be changed, since two of these had recently died. There were only two young people, twin teen-aged brothers, sullen with having to be there instead of out tomcatting around.

"Y'all ready?" Mr. Mecum said, standing up and facing the congregation, and proceeded to lead them in a couple of hymns, *a capella*, since the pianist was among the recently deceased.

After a prayer, Mr. Mecum departed from ceremony. "Brenda and the young preacher have worked up a real special service for us tonight," he said. "And since there isn't any announcements, I'm just going to turn the services over to y'all without no further ado."

Brenda nodded at Roger, and he stood and came to the edge of the podium. "I'm not really a preacher," he said. He looked at Brenda, who nodded again.

"I'm a soldier of the cross," he said, and flung off the choir robe, to stand frozen in the ghi.

The twins woke up and sat forward. The church rustled with

surprise. Roger held the pose in silence. Brenda began to sketch. She sketched a heavy Roman soldier in a tunic and sandals, a soldier who bore an ominous resemblance to Bluto in the Popeye cartoons.

"What is a soldier of the cross?" Roger asked, stirring from his pose. "Does he carry a heavy shield?" He indicated a shield on one arm. "Does he wear a heavy helmet? What about a spear? What about a heavy breastplate?" Brenda was sketching in these details as Roger mentioned them. He added greaves, a visor to the helmet, a mace, a sword.

"No!" he cried, resoundingly. "Because if he does ..."

Brenda flipped the page, and there, already drawn, was the Roman soldier, pinned and helpless under a jumbled pile of armor and armament.

"No," Roger said again. "A soldier of the cross should put aside every weight, and the sin which doth so easily beset us. Because our whole armor is the armor of the spirit. We carry our armor inside of us, not outside of us.

"Like me," he continued, indicating his costume. "I may not look like much, and I bet you think this outfit is silly. But I know something." Brenda flipped the page with the fallen soldier and began to sketch again, another large hairy man much like Bluto, but this one angry and charging toward the onlooker out of the page. He charged with his arms raised high at a peculiar angle, and with his head oddly lowered. His legs were dwindled from what must have been foreshortening, and a small round shield swung at his groin.

"Just like a person can know Jesus, I know karate," Roger said, and went into a flurry of strikes.

"We must fear not, for Jesus is with us," he said, breathing hard. "Our enemies may be great and terrible"—he indicated the drawing— "but since I know karate and jujitsu, I don't have to carry any worldly armor to protect myself. If a bad guy comes at me, I can just flip him. And if you know the love of Jesus"—here Brenda grasped the sketchpad—"you can do the same thing. You can change the enemy"— Brenda turned the sketch-pad upside-down—"into a friend."

And lo and behold, the upside-down drawing was of a friendly smiling man, hands in the air, dancing. The shield was a head, the head was a satchel, the curious legs were arms and the curious arms were legs.

The church was delighted, but Roger and Brenda were not through with them.

"And just in case you don't believe me, or believe Jesus, because he is really the one that is saying all of this: Brother Mecum?" This last was the deacon's cue. He rose from his seat carrying the brick he had brought from home. He mounted the rostrum and stood there waiting.

Roger was feeling great. He was beginning to think he could maybe do a lot of this, that maybe even the Lord would call him as a preacher.

"Sometimes, out in the world, it's like you run into a brick wall," he said. "Sin and injustice and I don't know, and all you have is just you and your heart and Jesus. And you feel like that brick wall just won't give. I know I do sometimes."

"Deacon," Brenda Mecum whispered from her post below, and the deacon raised the brick high in his huge gnarled hand.

"But look what the love of Jesus can do to that old brick wall," Roger said. He stepped back three quick steps like a dancer, then took two quick sprinting steps forward and sailed high into a turn, his right foot flashing out.

Then he was down, and the deacon's hands had come apart and down, half a brick in each. He stared from each to each, blinking the brick powder from his eyes and snorting.

"Well, I be swan," he said.

The church broke into applause, and Brenda Mecum called out, "Amen! Services over!" and everyone came up and swarmed around them. The two boys insisted that Roger autograph a half of the brick for each of them and then would not leave without some personalized instruction.

He was on an adrenalin high, which he attributed to the Lord. He wanted it to never end. He kept Brenda and Deacon Mecum late on the front stoop of the church, talking and talking. The stars were beginning to come out. The late summer evening was full of glory and wild dying blues.

Somehow, in the middle of a sentence that he had thought was interested agreement on their part, they said goodbye, got in the pink Cadillac, and drove away. Roger had 35 dollars cash in his right hand, and he was the only one left at the church.

He got in the old black Studebaker. It started. It took him five miles and stopped. Nothing he did would get it started. He felt alone and abandoned, and he could not figure out how he had lost the happiness he had felt back at the church.

He had dozed off in the back seat when a long black limousine pulled up beside him. An old man in a heavy black coat (in spite of the heat) got out and peered in the window with a flashlight. Roger rolled the window down.

"Car don't belong here," the old man said. "What's wrong?"

"It won't start," Roger said, and began telling him the long history of the Studebaker's breakdown.

"Suffer fools gladly," the old man muttered. "Never did make no sense to me. Got the suffer part right, though." He turned away and went and got behind the wheel of his limousine. He sat there a moment and then blew the horn, short, repeated blasts, until Roger got out and went over to him.

"You coming or not? I ain't got all night," the old man said. Roger got in on the other side.

At first they drove back the way Roger had come and then went for miles through wilder and wilder countryside. At one point the old man piloted the limousine along a lane that was little more than a path through a forest.

They arrived finally at a large ramshackle house, already lit up, although there was no one in it when they went in. There were guns everywhere, lugers, revolvers, automatics, carbines. The guns and their parts littered table-tops and cabinet-tops and couches. On the walls were pictures of naked women, some calendars and some glossy pages torn from magazines and some thumbtacked 8-by-11s of mouse-haired women with slumped shoulders and shy smiles sitting bare on the edges of anonymous beds. Roger blushed.

The old man went directly to a wall telephone that could have come from a gangster movie and began making calls. He kept at it for an hour and a half. When Roger found that the old man was ignoring him, he began to study the naked women. He felt as though only five or ten minutes had passed when the old man took his shoulder and said, "Wise Man's gonna help you." Then the old man left the room.

Roger studied the guns. Then he allowed himself to look at the pictures some more. He wanted to masturbate, but he didn't know when the old man would be back. He went to sleep on the couch.

Another horn woke him up. Someone was out front. When the old man did not appear, he went to the door. "Come on," a black voice called from the pick-up. "You, come on here."

Roger went out. "I'm Wise Man," the man in the pick-up said. "Fix yo car. Git in." Roger got.

"Do you know the way?" Roger asked.

"Do I know the way," Wise Man said scornfully. Roger wondered why he was called Wise Man. He invented a story in which Wise Man was one of a set of triplets, each of them called Wise Man. But Wise Man did not seem to want talk any more than the old man had.

When they got to Roger's car, Wise Man took out the plugs, which were covered with carbon, and filed them clean with sandpaper. He removed the distributor cap and cleaned the points. Then he cranked the car. Roger was ready to go, but Wise Man wouldn't let him. He adjusted the timing by ear. Then he adjusted the fuel mixture on the carburetor. Shaking his head, he changed out two of the plugs for new ones he had brought with him, and changed one of the wires. When he was through, the car purred.

"Need new rings," Wise Man said to Roger. "Oil blowin by, messin up yo plugs. But I can't fix it here. How much money you got?"

"Thirty-five dollars," Roger said.

"That ain't enough. Give it to me. I'll be takin yo back seat too."

"What?" Roger said.

But Wise Man was already dismantling the back seat of the Studebaker. When he had it loose, he dragged it, grunting, out the door and heaved it in the back of the pick-up.

He came back over to Roger. "Dawson's runners blowed a hole in my old one," he said. He smiled. "But Old Man Lattimore fix him. He bit Dawson boy finger off. Done it himself, didn't send nobody. Told the boy, 'Son, this will hurt you, but if he pays attention it will keep you and yo daddy alive. You tell him I said that, those words exactly.'

"Mr. Lattimore the only good white man I ever known," Wise Man said. "Rest of em werfless fools." Teeth white in the night, making it plain he included Roger too. "Whole state full of werfless white folks. Like yo cah. Wouldn't be running at all wadn't a few smart niggers around.

"Whole state of Missippi ain't eem there. Ain't no such of a place. Cross over the Alabama line in the middle of the night, road don't change, woods don't change, dirt don't change, night don't change. Ain't no such of a thing, Missippi. It's all just in yo imagination."

Wise Man went and got in his pick-up. "I got a whole lot of opinions," he said, leaning out of the window of the truck. "I never seen a white man had mo than two opinions, and he a try to make em do for everything. I got a whole different opinion for everything I run into. Why they call me Wise Man," he said, and leaned back in, started the truck and drove off.

It was nearly dawn. By the time Roger got back to Jackson, Mr. Gandy had caught the bus to work, so at least Roger didn't have to face him right away. Mrs. Gandy had had to stay home, but she had nothing to say beyond hello.

Roger went over to Mosey Froghead's. "Tell him a bear eat it," Mosey said, when Roger told him about the seat. "A bear eat the seat a my truck one time. Because of the persimmons blowed up in it. Twelve gallons of persimmon beer. Good thing I wadn't in it, or I might not be here now. Them bears love them simmons. The flavor stayed in the holstry, you know. Come out a the woods and eat it up. Eat the springs and everything. Wadn't all the way a bear. Mo of a labrador dog, really. Damn lab dog will eat a brick wall. He will eat a whole damn tree. How come I don't live in the woods no more, damn lab dogs eat up all the trees. Lab dogs and Paul Bunyam. Couldn't make no living hauling timber with Bunyam around. Hell, he eat up the *bear*."

When Mr. Gandy saw Roger next, he didn't ask about the seat. "Car sho does run well," he said, and waited.

"A bear," Roger said, and blushed furiously.

"What?" Mr. Gandy said.

The Finest Thing That God in His Wisdom

THE WAY ROGER finally began making some money on his studio was this: Raymond Otto was a member of the Hinds County Country Club, and he had been mightily impressed with Roger at the YFC meetings. The country club liked to have theme lunches once a week, and there were usually speakers at these luncheons. Probably their favorite such luncheon to date had been the one in which the governor-elect himself had dressed up as Colonel MIM. MIM was Money In Mississippi. Another favorite had been when the cartoonist who did Hinnie for the *Jackson Daily News* had come out and given a talk and sketched some impromptu cartoons. Hinnie was a jackass who appeared in a single panel on the front page and gave a humorous opinion on current events, after the manner of the old colored man in the *Memphis Commercial Appeal*, Hambone.

Raymond Otto was not only the head of the local chapter of the YFC, but also a homosexual. In fact, years later, he was arrested for something the papers would not describe in the men's room under the bus station. He was immediately freed on bond, and then the charges were dropped. His homosexuality was no surprise to the other members of the country club, and they thought it had been in rather bad taste for the police department to arrest him. He liked young men, but so did most heterosexual women. And they *were* men: Raymond Otto did not molest boys. His character was excellent.

He had been impressed with Roger's health and innocence, as well as his devotion to Jesus. When he suggested to Roger that he capitalize on his success at Bethany by giving a luncheon talk at the country club, Roger agreed.

Soon after he picked Roger up to take him to the luncheon, he was quite certain that Roger was heterosexual, but that was all right. One had to find these things out. Lucy was a good cook, and the lunch would be excellent. And he still enjoyed Roger's company.

Roger was at just that stage of naiveté not to be concerned with the fact that he was appearing before the elite of Hinds County in a skimpy canvas suit, and his talk was a great success. He was getting comfortable with talking about his subject, Jesus and self-defense. In fact, he was beginning to credit himself with a great original idea. The connections between the two realms were so many and so dynamic that he could not understand why no one had ever seen them before. He ended by telling them about his club, Jujitsu for Christ.

The club sounded like a wonderful idea to June McMullen. June was 26. She had gotten her B.A. with a major in art at Vanderbilt and then come back home to live. She was still not married, although she was very pretty. True, she was a freckle-faced girl with a pug nose, but she was very trim, she had wonderful brown hair and wonderful big warm brown eyes, a laugh like Mozart pouring whiskey out of a gallon jug, and a body odor like freshly-ground coffee. Anyway, if you were white and lived in Mississippi and didn't want to marry a freckle-faced pug-nosed girl, you were in trouble. The only white girls who weren't freckle-faced and pug-nosed were the ones who won Miss America 17 years in a row, from 1956 through 1972. And they had all been raised on cream. They soaked their feet in a bucket of honey every night of their life, and they were never allowed to get fucked by anything but a quarterback.

The trouble was, June was too restless for Jackson, Mississippi. She had come back there to live because it was home, but college had put ideas in her head. When you had a degree in art, you felt like you ought to do something. You could go to New York and get a job with an ad agency in the art department and become alcoholic and live in Queens and commit suicide when your oldest child by your second marriage was nine, a lot of people did that. But they were mostly people from less fortunate families. They were the ones who made Mawmaw's eyes so hollow at Christmastime.

What she did instead was get into a lot of different activities. She started the first arts council Mississippi ever had. Jackson, Mississippi, is a world-renowned cultural center now, you can tell because they had some ballet on public television, but in the old days it didn't use to be that way. June was single-handedly responsible for the state-wide realization that there was much art that had nothing to do with dogs or ducks, and even less to do with black velvet. Which is something that states like Arkansas would still do well to learn.

She was a leader in the Colonel MIM movement too, for a while, until she realized it had more to do with banks and less to do with patriotism.

One of her greatest achievements was that no one called her Juney.

June thought the club was a great idea, and she was also piqued, as Raymond Otto had been, by the glimpses of pectoral definition that Roger's ghi afforded the luncheon. She talked two of her best friends, Katie and Linda, into joining the club and signing up for lessons at Roger's studio. When he found out about it, Katie's fiancée, who was also named Roger, Roger Tutwiler, insisted on taking the lessons too. He wouldn't forbid it if Katie wanted to do something foolish and adventurous, but he would make sure he was there to take care of her if anything went wrong.

June tried to talk to Roger about the details after the luncheon, but Raymond Otto was in a hurry to go. Lunch with a heterosexual male was ok, but once lunch was over, there was really no more reason to hang around and talk. Since neither Roger nor the Gandys had a telephone, June gave him her number and made him cross his heart to call her the very next day.

Roger took his promises seriously, whether or not he had crossed his heart, and he found a pay phone and called her the next day. June was amazed to find that he had no charter and no by-laws. He hadn't really realized that you had to have charters and by-laws and officers and meetings to go from idea to reality. You do, though. At least, you do if you are a primate. Maybe if people were descended from intelligent lizards, then maybe not. Then there might be another way to go from idea to reality. But people, as it says in Genesis, are really just monkeys with expanded memory, and that is the only way they know. Artists are the only people who don't do it that way. They go straight from idea to reality without committees or parliamentary procedure or constitutions. Which is why their realities are not generally approved of. They are one-man realities. Or one-woman realities. And which is why other people are afraid of artists. They think they are descended from intelligent lizards.

June explained charters and bylaws to Roger. She was a good little monkey in spite of the fact that she still hadn't gotten married. She organized the first meeting of the Jujitsu for Christ Club. She got Roger elected president. Raymond Otto was the vice-president, although he first had to make sure that he did not have to take karate or attend meetings to belong to the club. She was secretary-treasurer, and Mosey Froghead was sergeant-at-arms.

Katie's Roger, Roger Tutwiler, insisted on making Mosey the sergeant-at-arms when he found out who Mosey was. "You never heard of Mosey's barbecue?" he asked, astonished. "My God—it's probably the best in the South. It's like Doe's Eat Place, but for barbecue." Roger Tutwiler's idea was to get a discount on the barbecue. But Mosey was nobody's fool. Pork sandwiches were 35 cents, and they were going to stay 35 cents if the white folks made him President of the U.S.A. French fries were extra. Which he told them, but told them to go ahead and elect him if they wanted to. He meant President.

But that was later. Right now, on the phone, June asked Roger how much he charged for lessons, which was another thing Roger hadn't thought of. He figured his expenses at two hundred a month. He divided by two lessons a week for four weeks a month for four people and said, "Seven dollars," pleased at his audacity and figuring to spend the excess on pleasure.

"Per person per hour?" June said. "That isn't *nearly* enough. You're a professional. You have to charge like a professional or people won't respect you." She suggested fifteen dollars per person per hour for two two-hour sessions per week. That frightened Roger. They settled on nine ninety-five, June insisting on the fraction if he was going to charge less than ten dollars an hour, so people would think he was using psychology instead of just not respecting himself enough. As it turned out, one more person signed up, William Percy Alexander Sledge, of Sunflower County, Linda's intended, a second-string fullback for the Rebels and a friend of Roger Tutwiler's (it was through Percy that Roger Tutwiler had gotten his season tickets, and through Roger's father that Percy had gotten his car, a cream-colored convertible with maroon leather interior).

The sessions started the very next week (June didn't like waiting). Roger was a good teacher. For one thing, he knew what he was doing. He didn't just know the techniques, he understood the soul of the techniques.

Not that he could talk very well about it. He knew what he did and why he did it, but words were too slow. But his understanding showed through in everything he did.

Technique was not a set of instructions: it was not a bag of tricks, or a quick way around effort. Technique was simply belief. Not that loud advocacy that went by the name of belief in the world, but belief that worked, belief that was who you were. It was a thousand thousand bodily decisions. It was a commitment made in the nerves to do it *this* way: to twirl in the air and trigger this this and this move, trusting the air to sustain you, trusting your body's memory to serve you more quickly than will.

It was a decision that bypassed decision, and therefore egoism as well. One went from move to move, and the moves were playing themselves out without interference, without doubt or hesitation. It was acceptance of the Path instead of quarreling about the map.

It made for a fearsome speed and economy, and those whose eyes were watching for all the messy display of the usual wasted energy could hardly see what was happening. They were expecting the spark and static of faulty connections, in fact had come to think of such fritz and fission as the sign, not of a bad connection, but of connection itself. For such witnesses, the results of good technique were the results of magic or accident, and without probability, and when they praised those results, they praised the gods of chance and not the gods of order.

Another thing that made Roger a good teacher was his patience. He needed it. Katie and Linda were full of giggles. For them, this was just another lark, some more of June's prestijubilation.

June was entirely serious, however, and so was Roger Tutwiler, though he had come along simply to keep an eye on Katie. That was his place, since she was such an empty-headed goose. That was one of the things her parents liked about him, that he promised to take such good care of their little goosie. He hadn't expected to like this Eastern foolishness, but he did like it. Soon, in fact within two months, he and June had yellow belts in shodo-kan.

June and Roger Tutwiler began their lessons by bringing their master a bottle of sake. Roger had never been a master before, and it felt good. After the workouts, they would sit around and sip a little sake warm, until they all had the giggles like Katie and Linda. These were magical times for Roger, being a master and watching the sweat cool on June's brow. After the first few lessons, she quit wearing a bra under her ghi because it interfered with her movements. At least, that's what she told Roger when she asked his advice about it. He turned red and said he could see her point. Then he turned redder, but she didn't seem to notice. Now he could see her nipples when she leaned forward laughing to pour the sake. It had become a part of the ritual for him. They began each session with mutual bows, then a bow to the east in unison, then a short prayer to Jesus to bless this the fruits of their bodies to his service Amen, then stretches, then the *kata*, then some sparring. Then a warm-down, more stretches. Then sake warmed up on Roger's Coleman stove, and then June's nipples.

It was good to be able to see nipples twice a week, and Roger needed it, what with the way Patsy had dropped out of his life. You got used to nipples. They always made you feel good, like looking at ripples in a clear creek, but warmer. That's why titties have gotten so big, is too many people don't get to see nipples in their formative years. No nipples, our subconsciousness says, well ok. I'll go for cleavage then. You won't give me the dots I want to see, I'll set up a feedback into the social structure and select for big titties.

As soon as the human race invents antigravity, we'll grow titties as big as mountains. As big as planets. This little bitty woman will be stuck on them somewhere, way at the back, neglected, a curiosity item. Nobody will notice her. They will all be too busy building civilizations on her titties. Big double planets floating in space.

The first time the Jujitsu for Christ Club met, Mosey and Percy Sledge nearly had a misunderstanding. Percy was also known as Little Wide Load. He was five foot ten and weighed 230 pounds. He could clean and jerk 487 pounds, and he could press 372. He had a scholarship, but he wasn't on the first team, and the scholarship was about to be taken away from him. The reason was that he liked to hit too much. He was a fullback, but what he really liked to do was run into people. Give him the ball on an 82 flex right, and he would head straight for the biggest man on the other side. He had the longest unofficial run in Ole Miss history, 147 yards, when he had picked up a fumbled snap in the end-zone just before it went out of bounds and proceeded to run over every tackler on the Tennessee team except one, and he was chasing that one up into the stands when he slipped and fell.

He was a mean motherfucker, although he wasn't anywhere near as mean as Buck Randall. They called him Little Wide Load in deference to his brother, Wide Load, who was a big man.

Roger had led them through a sequence of stretching exercises and a few basic blocks. They had all been impatient to learn some strikes, but Roger would have none of it. They weren't ready.

"You have to learn defense first," he said. "Defense is the heart of the martial arts. Not because of self-protection—that would just be fearfulness, and fearfulness isn't a clear mind. But because successful defense requires understanding of your opponent. When your soul is his soul, when you *know* what he is going to do next, then you are safe. You can defend yourself without thinking, without fearfulness. You are like Shadrach, Meshach, and Abednigo, walking in the fiery furnace. But the funny thing is, you have to learn the *forms* of the blocks before you can learn to read your opponent's soul. It's like a child with his alphabet-blocks before he can learn to read. You can't begin to imagine what they are for, and you want to do the wrong things with em, like the kid wants to chew em or stack em up or throw em. He don't see em as letters. But someday he sees how letters can make a word and words can make a sentence and with sentences you can tell what people are thinking. It probably seems real artificial right now, but don't be impatient. If you can't wait, you can't act. Percy, cotton-pickin, you know better than that. There ain't no point picking your foot up at all if you ain't gonna get it all the way up. You just screwing up your balance and makin it easier to knock you over and one a these ladies is gonna hook a heel in there and clean them jewels right offa you. *Up, boy, up.*"

It never occurred to Roger to talk to Little Wide Load any other way. He was the coach, after all. He knew the stuff and Little Wide Load didn't. Which was ok with Little Wide Load. If it hadn't been, he would have bit Roger's head off and swallowed it. But he thought it was all neat: weird exercises he wasn't good at, that hurt, and he had to suffer to learn. He loved it.

This was after the workout. Roger Tutwiler had sprung the surprise of the first bottle of sake.

"Whut's 'at?" Mosey Froghead had asked. He had come in to watch the others work out, though he did not join in himself. "Looks ridiculous," he had said. After a while he said, "Ain't nowhere to sit." After a while longer, he had sat on the floor.

Now he grabbed the bottle from Roger and took a long pull on it. "Taste like fish-water smell," he said. Little Wide Load took it from Mosey and drank from it. He didn't wipe off the mouth of it first. "Here now," Mosey said. He looked insulted. He grabbed it back and took a pull on it. He did wipe off the mouth.

Then it occurred to Mosey to be polite. He offered the bottle back to Roger Tutwiler. "You want some of this?" he said. He was pleased with himself. He was being a gentleman. He wasn't even sitting in a chair, and he was still acting with civility.

"Actually," June said, "you damn savages are just about to ruin the whole thing." She rose from her cross-legged position without using her hands, in one fluid motion, and took the bottle. Mosey had never been called a savage by a white woman before, at least not in a humorous tone of voice, and he was charmed. He decided June was the finest white woman he had ever seen.

"Roger, where are the little cups?" June asked. Roger Wing was thinking, *Cups? What cups? I don't have any cups,* when Roger Tutwiler got up and went out to the car to get the pot and the little cups. "And the pot," June called after him. "You're supposed to warm it, and serve it in little cups," she said to the others. "The fumes go right to your brain."

Roger Tutwiler came back with the pot and the little cups, and June got Roger Wing to pump and light the Coleman, and soon she was humming and heating the sake in a saucepan. Little was watching her ass. She was still wearing a bra, this being only the first session, but the ghi she had ordered had not arrived yet, and she had worn her dancing tights from last year when she was studying ballet. In fact, she had ordered ghis for everyone, there not being any stores that sold them anywhere around, and none of them had arrived. They were dressed in a motley of outfits, Little huge in grey sweats, Roger Tutwiler cool and trim in his tennis whites, Linda in twill workshirt and cut-offs,

70

and Katie in t-shirt and overalls. Roger wore the only ghi. He, too, was watching June's ass, though he was trying not to. He was doubly disturbed, because of wanting to watch her ass and yet be faithful to Patsy, and because drinking wine was a sin, and he was about to drink wine. Then he remembered that the Bible warned against looking on the wine when it was red, for it was a mocker, and sake wasn't red, so he felt better.

"The finest thing that God in his wisdom put on this earth, the nearest thing to an angelic being that treads this terrible ball, is a well-bred Southern white woman, or her blue-eyed little baby girl," Little said, misquoting Judge Brady. He pulled Linda close, but kept eyeing June's ass.

"Amen," said Mosey Froghead.

"Aw come on," said Roger Tutwiler.

"The man is a literary genius. A genius," said Little. "And do you know he never before wrote a book?"

"Amen," said Mosey.

"The finest thing," said Little Wide Load.

"Don't be a dumb-ass, Percy," Roger Tutwiler said. "The man is a servile idiot, and he writes like one. It's money that pulls his strings, whether he knows it or not." Roger Tutwiler could call Little a dumb-ass because Little knew that Roger would one day own Lamar Life or Deposit Guaranty or both or something like either or both of them, and the only way Little would ever be a VP of anything was if somebody like Roger gave him a job. Little was 230 in the body and Roger ran about 160, but Little knew damn well he was only 115 or so in the real world and would never gain a Troy ounce, whereas Roger was 195 and still to get his growth. He wasn't *dumb*. He also knew, as servants have always known, to what extent he could kick against the pricks and get away with it.

He misquoted the judge again, word for word the same as the first time.

"Amen," said Mosey.

"The hell," said Roger Tutwiler. "The whole thing is nothing but economics. It always has been. Did you know Mississippi spent one-third of her annual budget for artificial limbs in the first year after the war? The *war* was economics. All this segregation shit—ladies, I'm sorry—"

"I like the blue-eye baby girl," said Mosey.

"Say what?" said Little Wide Load.

"—all this *philosophy* of segregation, this Carleton Putnam and daddy-Brady bullfeathers, is just after-the-fact glorification of economic necessity. Ever since L.Q.C. Lamar and his cronies decided to back Rutherford B. Hayes on condition he stay out of Mississippi's affairs—"

"Roger, you're playing the hard-nosed junior banker from Harvard again," June said.

"But that don't mean I don't like the white woman too," Mosey said. "A white woman have a low ass, for one thing. She have a low ass and a high mind."

"Say what?" said Little Wide Load. "What are you saying?"

"Princeton," Roger Tutwiler said. "Seriously, ever since World War I, when the Negroes began to see the rest of the world and get some real education, and ever since the flood of 1915 and the drought of 1916 combined with the end of cheap immigrant labor in the North—"

"But I like a blue-eye baby girl the best. A blue-eye baby girl is the sweetest thing God put on the earth. A blue-eye baby girl grow up to be a big fine white woman don't have no big old high ass," Mosey said.

"You in trouble now," Little Wide Load said.

"You shut up," Mosey said. "Shut up yo own mouth and say from that book some more."

"All ready," June said, coming back to the group with a flowered teapot in one hand and a stack of sake cups in the other. "There's not any tray, so." She sat cross-legged by Roger Wing, again not using her hands, and not spilling the tea or dropping a cup. She began passing the cups around.

"The sacrilegious young nigger from Chicago or New York will perform an obscene act or make a smart remark and assault some white girl," Little Wide Load said, glaring at Mosey.

"He will, too," Mosey said. "You gone have to kill that nigger. He don't have no respect for the blue-eye baby girl."

"The hell," said Roger Tutwiler. "Hating the Negro is just as much a crock of uh uh crock as the glory of the Southern woman. Hate was just the only currency they had to spend after the war. It was a way to control the government and then the economy. The planters *created* the redneck. They bought the colored votes, squeezed out the red-dirt farmers in the east, and then when the Vardamans and the Bilboes started up, they had to play who-hates-the-nigger-the-most to keep—"

"Here," June said, leaning across the circle and handing him a cup to shut him up. Then she gave Roger Wing a cup and poured for him. "Now you're supposed to pour it for me," she said. "You never pour your own sake."

"Uh," said Roger, struck by the flush in her cheeks, the fine beads of sweat on her upper lip. "Ah...sure."

"Now everyone have some," June said. "You boys hush. Hush now. Katie, you help. Linda. You girls don't just sit there like a goose. Here."

"It's a wonderful book," Little Wide Load said. There were tears in his eyes. "I'm only sorry I took so long to get around to it. Call myself a son of Old Mississippi and take what? Five, six years to get around to the literature."

"I love that book," said Mosey Froghead, accepting a tiny cup of sake and tossing it back. "I'll kill any nigger that say I don't."

"You're gonna have to grow up someday, Percy," Roger Tutwiler said, shrugging and holding out his cup to be filled. He held it a moment to feel the warmth, then toasted Katie and drank.

"Sweet Roger," Katie said.

"Huh?" said Roger Wing, who had been dreaming of June. Then he blushed.

"Sweet Roger," June explained, with a gesture toward the loving couple but smiling at him with some degree of ambiguity.

Roger felt warm. He felt the blush warm him all over. He loved this group of people, he thought. They were his family, his family away from home, his spiritual kin, his true kind.

He was wrong. He had a family, all right, but he didn't know who they were. It was right in front of him the whole time, and he never figured it out until it was too damn late.

Captain Mississippi and Bluejay

WHEN ROGER WAS thirteen and in the eighth grade, he was in the last school pageant he ever took part in. This one was a parade of famous comic-book heroes. Roger admired Batman far more than he did the other super-heroes, because Batman was human. The way Roger looked at it, Superman had it made in the shade. He never had to raise a sweat. He didn't have to *do* anything to be super. In fact, they had to invent troubles with kryptonite to add any suspense at all to his stories. Batman, on the other hand, had to work out every day, which Roger could sympathize with. Anyway, he liked Batman's build better. He was muscular, but he had more of an acrobat's build. He wasn't beefy like Superman.

Roger liked Batman so much he was sure he would get the part. He had his mother sew him a Batman mask. He was very particular about the ears, which had to lie flat against the skull and stick up just barely higher than the crown of the head—but the crown should curve down to follow the skull itself—no straight line from ear to ear. His mother had the horrifying notion that the ears should stick straight out, and be about five times larger than they were in the funnybooks, because that was the way bats' ears really were.

As it turned out, he didn't get Batman. Bruce Weinert got it, because, as he pointed out, he was taller, browner, more handsome, and had much whiter teeth. Roger got to be Robin, whose mask was just an eyepiece on a rubber band. You could buy one like it in the five and ten, and he did, resentfully.

Roger had kept the Batman cowl, however. This afternoon, he sat in his studio, naked except for the cowl, looking at himself in the back of his four-quart boiler. (It would have been vanity, and not discipline, to have bought himself a mirror. Fortunately, he was so disciplined that he kept the pot as shiny as the day he had bought it.)

He was depressed. He had been living in the laundromat for nearly six months now, and he had time on his hands. Attendance at his karate classes had been extremely irregular ever since late summer. When the new had worn off, the late-summer heat had proved discouraging to his students, though it hadn't bothered Roger himself, who trained outside summer and winter and considered it a part of his discipline not to notice the weather. Then when fall had come, attendance had not picked back up. Sometimes only June was there, and sometimes she left word that she couldn't make it either. Now it was December, a warm December, true, and although Roger did not have air-conditioning he did have a space heater that kept the small studio warm enough. But the long days were over with, that summer-freedom feeling was gone, Roger Tutwiler was thinking about his job, Katie was planning for a June wedding, Little Wide Load was with the team, and June was finding her attention drawn to downtown renovation.

It wasn't as wonderful as he had thought it would be to have four hours a day to work out in. He didn't attain higher levels of insight. Instead he got bored and tired. And he still had a good twelve hours a day to kill, except when somebody showed up and he gave a class. Then it was only ten.

He was face to face with the true meaning of work, hadibut. As in, had he but realized. Work was invented to take care of drudgery, hadibut. It wasn't that work *was* drudgery, like everybody thought. No, life was the drudgery: there was a certain irreducible majority of time that was going to be sheer hellish drudgery, doowaddy. As in do what he would. God himself hadn't been able to weed it out, doowaddy. Heaven was just earth without the kapok. Heaven was Eternal, but only for a few hours. Then it was over, God's day off was over, and here was the shitpile of creation again, earth again, time to start over, Day One: Work.

Work was invented to channel drudgery, to put all the shit in the same place and keep it away from the fun stuff. To give us something tangible to blame the boredom on. That's why the people you work with are idiots and shitheads, so you can go home and live with nice people. Though a lot of people don't understand the principle and so live with idiots and shitheads at home, too.

People who don't work run the risk of having disorder run rampant and flood over its levees and stink up their whole lives. That was Roger's situation exactly.

Or maybe not exactly. Maybe there was one other element, one thing more that work took care of that Roger was missing. You could take a more positive view of work. You could say that work is what connects us to the rest of the world. Because work is the way we marry the world, pretty much. For better or worse, work is most of how we enter the earth aside from our families. And a novelist who doesn't have work, whose time is his own to spend as he wishes —why he or she may find his or her writing getting more and more ingrown, less and less connected to how most people spend most of their time.

All summer Roger had had Marcus around to beguile and distract him, but now Marcus, in spite of all his assertions of independence, had had to return to school. Mr. and Mrs. Gandy both worked, so that left Mosey Froghead, locally speaking. Roger could take only so much of Mosey's conversation at a time, and, for that matter, Mosey wasn't interested in having Roger around if he wasn't going to drink any beer, and Roger wasn't going to drink more than one a day, not any more. Any beer at all was against his religion of course, but he had come to his religion late, and his stepfather had always kept a few dark bottles in the refrigerator and made them seem innocent enough.

It was just that after a couple of beers, Roger was in over his head. He couldn't tell how much he had had, or when he needed to quit. This may partly have been because his body was so finely tuned, and to so single a purpose. It requires long training to drink really hard, and the training runs counter to the requirements of most of the other endurance sports.

The last time Roger had gotten really drunk had been back in early August, when everyone went home early wilted from the heat, no sake, no nipples. Roger had gone back to Mosey's just to have something to do. There were three or four black men in the place already, and later there would be many more, with wives and girlfriends and children sometimes, although Mosey's place was so small it looked full with five. They looked around at Roger when he came in, and said a word or two to each other, but Roger was with Mosey, and anyway he was crazy, as they could plainly see. No harm in a crazy white man. One more crazy white man for the nigger to take care of, that was all. *Live that way it a make you crazy. Nevvah thank no real thought. Talkin that jibba-jabba. Can't tell what is a what and what ain't. Wurrin about they grass.*

That night Roger had had many beers. He had not danced on the tabletop, there being no tables, but he had tried to demonstrate jujitsu on Mr. Gerald Sheffield, age 75, who was in fact the same Gerald Sheffield who had once discussed crops and clothes dryers with Mr. Blake. Stooped and grey-headed, he had said to Roger, "What you want? What you want now?" He had been surprisingly wiry, spread-legged and stiff, like a scared pony, when Roger had tried to show him the hold, though Roger assured him he wouldn't really throw him.

"You sho won't," Mr. Sheffield said. "I a cut you."

"No, no, see, if you come at me with a knife, then—"

Roger felt a gentle stroke across his throat, Mr. Sheffield's finger. "Won't be comin at you with no knife," Mr. Sheffield said, stamping angrily back to his stool to get his hat. "Be done gone with *my* knife," he said. "Shut up, fool." This to the half-dozen who were laughing at the show. "Mess with *me*," he muttered, stamping out the door.

The next thing Roger remembered was lying on the counter, although he did not have the impression he was on a counter. He felt that his head was slanted down and he was on a sort of moving conveyor belt, like an airport baggage line or a funeral-home casket conveyor, except that this one was bound through the dimensions from one world to the next, and bent over him were the faces of the handlers, all for some reason black, commenting and drinking beer.

"Dronk."

"Dronkern Cooter Brown."

"One dronk white man."

"I known old Cooter Brown," came a voice Roger recognized as Mosey's.

"Po some water on im."

"You a drown im, fool. That ain't never woke nobody up lessin them damn moom pitchers."

"Bed not puke in my beer."

"Ole Cooter wadden no drunk. Not like people say he was. Oh, he have a beer or two. But he have a bad wife, that's all. Rag him all the time. All the time. Man need a drink, he have to live with that. She the one staht the whole story. Goin around telling dronk on her own man."

The conveyor belt stopped. Something was about to happen. Roger lost the ability to see.

"Bad-mouthin po ole Cooter," Mosey said in the blackness.

The next day, Roger had sworn never again to drink more than one beer a night, unless he got really thirsty, and then only two. And the upshot of that was that he spent less and less time in Mosey's.

He had not seen Patsy since the fall. She had missed YFC three straight weeks, and then Roger had given up and missed a night that happened to be the night she went, and then he went and she didn't, and then Jimmy Mac couldn't drive any more because he had too many other commitments. It wasn't Jimmy Mac's Ford, it was the Lord's, and He let Jimmy Mac use it. But with the privilege came responsibility. Some things you really cared about had to go, and one of them was YFC.

Then Roger had stayed in Clinton a week, but Patsy was in school all day, and he felt weird hanging around the school. And the last half of the week she was in Enid, Oklahoma, on a band trip. The last evening he was in town, Roger walked over and mooned around under the streetlight by her house, feeling lost and lonely and deliciously blue. Somebody saw him however, and called the police, and a patrol car pulled up beside him. There were police everywhere in

Mississippi then. It was necessary because there were so many outside agitators. The outside agitators had even infiltrated the family, seeking to destroy the Mississippi way of life. Some of our own children had grown up to become outside agitators. You couldn't be too careful. Somebody under a streetlight where usually nobody was under a streetlight—better check it out.

Roger had to explain that he lived in the area, but it didn't feel like they believed him, even when they drove him to his house and his mother identified him. She acted embarrassed, and he spent the evening feeling criminal and shabby, instead of forlorn and desolate as he had planned. Duke Bevo, the deputy who had rousted him, later became sheriff and was indicted for a kickback scheme involving a local burglary ring, but he never felt as criminal and shabby as Roger did that night.

The next day Roger had gone back to his studio. He hadn't seen Patsy since, though he had talked to her twice over the phone. When he took a dime over to the pay phone at the grocery and called her, if she was there, she seemed nervous, but glad to hear his voice. But all she wanted to talk about was maybe going to Mississippi College next year when she graduated. She was feeling called to full-time Christian service. She was pretty sure God wanted her to be a minister's wife.

"I may be going to be a minister," Roger would say. "My supply preaching at Bethany Baptist went real well."

"I know, I know," she would say. "Jimmy told me Deacon Mecum told him it was real different. Well, sweetie, the Lord's will be done."

And then somehow, there was never a lot to say. They would hang on the line a while, awkwardly, and after a while say, "I love you," and "Goodbye."

What was worse, they had never done it, and Roger needed to do it *bad*. That was his greatest fantasy now: that ultimate pink portal, that he had seen so many times, whose every whorl and detail existed in huge and tender magnification somewhere in the right lobe of his brain—that place, that thing, invaded by his huge penis.

So now he sat, naked except for his Batman mask, regarding himself in his pot-bottom and masturbating to visions of Patsy.

"What you pullin on yo pecker for?" Marcus said.

Roger clapped the pot down over the aforesaid pecker, then yelled with pain. "What are you doing here?" he said, groaning and hunched over.

"We have a half a day for the teachers." Marcus regarded Roger's mask. "You have a secret identity?"

"Yeah," Roger said perversely. He got up to get dressed, keeping the pot in front of him.

"I see yo boody," Marcus said. "Hee hee hee, I see yo boody. Who you ia? You ain't Batman. Bruce Wayne ia Batman."

"I *know* that," Roger said, thinking angrily of Bruce Weinert and the eighth grade pageant. He pulled on a black turtleneck and lapped the edges of the cowl over it, then donned his ghi. He lashed the ghi round with his ceremonial black belt. He presented himself to Marcus. "I'm Captain Mississippi," he said.

"Say what? I ain't seen him."

"He's new. He's like Captain America, but for Mississippi. Black and white, see, like magnolia blossoms in moonlight shadows."

"When he coming out?" Marcus asked suspiciously. "He ain't got no cape."

"I don't know. He's new. I just got his orders. He ain't supposed to have a cape."

"So it a be like he know karate and everything, and he a save Mississippi?"

"That's right."

"He have a partner?"

"He's new."

"He a need a partner. A little guy to help him out. Robin can help him."

"Robin's with Batman."

"Yeah." Marcus thought it over. "He need a new partner."

Now Roger thought it over. "What color stuff you got?"

"I ain't got no stuff."

"You got stuff, you just don't know it's stuff. You got an old pillowcase?"

"I can git one."

"Well go git one then."

Marcus ran back home, and into the bedroom he shared with Eleanor Roosevelt. He pulled open the tiny closet door and began pawing through the linen pile. Eleanor Roosevelt sat on the bed leafing through a movie magazine. "What you think you doin?" she said.

Marcus's reply was muffled.

"What?" she said. "Come out of there."

Marcus emerged with a blue pillowcase and a matching sheet.

"Roger say to get yo old sheet and pillowcase."

"What for? It ain't old. What you want it for?"

"Roger say to." Marcus decided to change the subject. "He wa pullin on his thang."

"What did it look like?"

"He clap a pot over it."

"What did it look like before he did?"

"What you thank it look like? It wa big."

"What color wa it? Wa it white?"

Marcus thought a while. "Purple," he said finally. "I ain't got no mo time to stan here yakkin witch you. I got to go."

When he went, Eleanor Roosevelt stared into space for a while. Then she got a box of crayons from under the bed, took a stubby paperless burnt sienna from the pack, and colored in Carol Baker's face in her magazine. When she was through, she held the page up to the light from the window, the old light, the sad light. Carol Baker's face glowed. "You don't know nothin, Marcella Louise Timmons," she said to the face. "You don't eem know what a white man look like. You and yo ole colored boyfriend." She stabbed the picture with the sharpened point of the pencil she had brought home from school at noon. She stabbed it again and again, till it was riddled and torn, and then she flung the magazine on the bed. She hoisted her skirt and pulled her panties to her thighs and sat on the shredded picture. She sat on it several times, bouncing. She pulled her panties back up. "Stupid," she said to Marcella Louise Timmons. Then she went to the refrigerator for something to eat.

Roger, meantime, was cutting a section out of the sewn side of the blue pillowcase. He pulled it over Marcus's head so that his face showed through the cut-out. The top corner of the pillowcase stood up like a crest over Marcus's head, leaning to the left. It wasn't what Roger had had in mind. Marcus grabbed the pot to take a look for himself.

"Look ridiculous," he said. "Stick up like a bluejay."'"

"Hey, no," said Roger, suddenly inspired. "Hey, that's who you are, see?"

"Who?"

"*Bluejay.* Like *Robin,* see? You get it?"

"Who he ia? I ain't seen him. When do he come out?"

"He ain't come out yet, he's new. He's new, like Captain Mississippi. *You're* him. *You* are."

Marcus studied himself in the pot-bottom. "Ain't got no mask," he said. "They a know who I am. They a kill my family."

Roger held up a finger. "You wait," he said, smiling. He went to one of the storage cubicles he had made and pulled out the box of mementoes. He pawed through it and came out with the mask he had worn as Robin in the pageant years ago. True, he had taken it out in the back yard that night after the pageant and pissed on it, but it had been washed several times since then. For some reason he had not thrown it away. You never know when you might need a good mask.

Marcus tried it on and smiled. Blue crest and black mask: he really did have the look of a bluejay. He pulled the sheet over his shoulders and knotted the corners. It trailed on the floor behind him. "We need to go out on patrol," he said to Roger.

Roger looked around the divider curtains, out the glass front. It was dusk. "Your momma and daddy'll be getting home any minute now," he said. "You go eat supper and come back, and we'll go out on patrol. Tell em you're going to spend the night with me." Roger wanted to finish what he had been doing when Marcus broke in.

After that, and while Marcus was gone, he cut the sheet down to size and stitched a rough hem in it and in the pillowcase/cowl. He thought about barring the sides of the cape with white and grey like a real jaybird, but he didn't have anything to do it with unless he stitched some cut-up white sheets to it, but he was tired now, and didn't have any extra white sheets anyway. He had been excited in a giddy way for a while, but now he was tired and irritable. This was silly. He didn't even want to mess with it, and he certainly didn't want to mess with Marcus anymore.

Then when Marcus came over, about 7:30, he said, "My daddy say ok but I have to go to bed early. Tomorrow a school day. He say you a be needin to get mo sleep than you been doin, too."

Suddenly Roger was very angry. Ever since he had come back without the back seat, Mr. Gandy had been very magisterial with him, though he had never mentioned the seat. He treated Roger like one of his sons, only slightly older than Marcus, and definitely younger than T.J., just as if Roger were not a grown man out on his own, making his own way, a property-owner. And anyway, he had not been staying up late. He had been sleeping with the light on because he was lonesome.

Suddenly it was all too much: not seeing Patsy, Mr. Gandy bossing him around, people not showing up for lessons, and having to keep

Marcus from thinking about what he had seen Roger doing—it was just all too much.

"When you're going out on patrol, you can't be worrying about what time it is," he said coldly.

"That's true," Marcus said.

With that, they dressed for action, Captain Mississippi wearing his high-top sneakers in spite of Bluejay's opinion that they looked ridiculous. Bluejay himself had on engineer boots.

"Well I have to have *something*," Captain Mississippi said. "They ain't sent me his boots yet."

It proved to be hard to know what to do once they were outside. What was their mission?

"We bed check on the grocery," Bluejay said. "Make sure they ain't robbin it."

"We can't let nobody see us," Captain Mississippi said. He was a little nervous. "We on a secret mission."

So that defined the game: sneak down to the grocery store and back without being seen. Which wasn't hard to do, in spite of the clear skies and half moon. There weren't many streetlights in that part of town, and there were a lot of shadows.

Six streets over, in one of the shadows, Captain Mississippi stepped on a body, and the body sat up and yelled.

"Law," said the body, when Captain Mississippi and Bluejay had quit skipping away. "Law, you gimme a scare."

"Who you ia?" said Bluejay, although Roger was beginning to be pretty sure he knew. It was Elrod the drunk. He had pissed on himself and fallen asleep, as usual, but this time he had done it a long way from his home, which was the basement of a burned-out church nearly a mile away. This church had burned naturally, the last one to do so in Mississippi for the next several years.

"Who *you* is?" countered the body, and pointed a wavering finger at Captain Mississippi. "Where you get them horns? You ain't the devil, air you? Devil come along to git me with a little nigger kukla klan?"

"Hush up," said Bluejay. "You talkin to Captain Mississippi. He a save Mississippi."

"Bless you, Captain Mississippi."

"And Bluejay."

Elrod began to cry. "Nobody take care of po ole Elrod. Po ole Elrod miss his momma's han. Nobody been good to po ole Elrod since his momma cool his face. I know I ain't lived right, Jesus, but every han turn hard. Every han turn hard on me. Bless you, Captain Mississippi, if you'd just soove my face. Just a bad dream po ole Elrod havin."

"We got binness to take care of," said Bluejay. "We ain't studying you, you ole drunk."

But Captain Mississippi had already stepped forward and bent over, compelled by a dreamlike necessity. He was deep in *déjà vu*. He had seen this before. The moon, the shadows, the crying voice, the ghostly costumes. It had happened, must happen, was happening twice at the same time.

Elrod laid his cheek along Captain Mississippi's palm. He sighed. "Soove my fever brow," he said, and fell asleep.

"We need to get back to headquarters," Captain Mississippi whispered urgently to Bluejay.

"You have to finish a mission," Bluejay said. "When you start a mission, you have to finish a mission."

There was no arguing that, and Captain Mississippi knew it. They set off for the grocery again, but Bluejay scampered back to the sleeping Elrod. "You bed not do no crime," he threatened. "Captain Mississippi a be watchin you. Bed not pee yo pants no more."

"Come *on*," Captain Mississippi hissed from the next shadow, and Bluejay had to go.

At the store, in the shadows, Bluejay wanted Captain Mississippi to take his mask off and go in and get him a candy bar, but Captain Mississippi wouldn't do it. They would know his secret identity from the rest of his costume. And anyway, he didn't have any money with him. But Bluejay could loan him the money and then Captain Mississippi could pay him back when they got back. But Captain Mississippi still wouldn't do it. "Well, I'm tired, then," Bluejay said.

So they headed back, Bluejay lagging behind and complaining. Captain Mississippi kept having to wait for him to catch up. After a few blocks, he quit even complaining. His mask bothered him, and he took it off and plodded down the middle of the street, his head down.

When Captain Mississippi rounded the corner where they had seen Elrod, he put the brakes on and faded back into the shadows. Somebody was talking to Elrod.

"You ain't nothin," the man was saying. "You ain't nothin at all. Step in you, I a wipe off my shoe." He sang it and laughed crazily. "Step in you, wipe off my shoe."

"I ain't nothin," Elrod agreed eagerly. "You a lot mo better than I am."

"Think you so smart, witch yo regular job and everything," the man said, leaning over Elrod. "I a do anything I want with you." Roger saw the gleam of a knife. The man slid the thin blade into Elrod's throat.

It didn't compute. Roger didn't have a trained response. Marcus came around the corner and Roger grabbed him and buried his face against Roger's chest. He didn't know if he should go stop the man, or if he should call the police, or what the moral thing was to do. He only knew that Marcus mustn't see it, mustn't ever ever see it, and so he grabbed him and muffled his face and head and held him tight while the man pulled his knife loose and slashed the slumped-over body a little and grew bored and walked away whistling.

And he carried Marcus back to his studio another way, and undressed him, and put his pajamas on, and lay awake all night staring and holding Marcus fiercely, so that he wouldn't see it, not even in his dreams, so that he wouldn't ever ever have to see it. Though there was no way he could keep Marcus from seeing it someday sooner or later in some way shape form or fashion. No way at all, doowaddy.

He lay awake all night, giving himself silent hell for screwing things up and holding Marcus. Bless you, Captain Mississippi. You punished the guilty and protected the innocent.

Bless you, Captain Mississippi.

Ring in the New

THE NEXT DAY the police came. There were only two of them, and a patrol car. There were no crowds gathered around to watch. In those days it wasn't considered healthy to be around the police. The police had killed more niggers than the rest of the white people in Mississippi combined. These two were ok, though. These two were moderates.

"Hell, just leave em alone and they'll kill each other off," the fat one was saying as Roger walked up.

"Just leave em alone and let em do it," said the one who had just gotten out of the Marines.

"Shit I hate to mess with this," the fat one said.

"Least he had a bath," said the Marine.

During the night the weather had changed. It had clouded up and rained. It was cold now, bitingly cold. Elrod lay half in the street, twisted face down, his ragged clothes sodden and beaten down flat. He looked like a dead squirrel, slight and wet and matted. He looked as though he were there to stay, as though he would never be carried away for burial, but, like the squirrel, would simply decay and slump and disappear into the street.

"Probly the first one he ever taken," the fat one said. "Here come a little white boy. What you doin here, little white boy? You know anything about this?" The fat policeman didn't want to mess with Elrod. He would rather mess with Roger.

"You kill this here nigger, little white boy? You responsible for this great loss to society?"

"Speak up or we ain't gone know where to send the medal," the Marine said.

"No," Roger said.

"Well who the hell did, then? Tell me that, little white boy. Come on, Booger, let's take im in and beat the truth out of him." The fat policeman grinned to show that he was kidding.

"This ain't gettin anything done. Come on, let's get the show on the road. I'm tired of standing around. Call the boys and then let's go knock on some doors."

"We got to question this little white boy, don't we? He's in the vicinity, ain't he?"

"Question im, then, and then let's get the show on the road."

Roger was sick and angry. He felt shabby and criminal, just as he had when they had caught him standing under the streetlight near Patsy's house. Only this time it was scarier, because something really bad had happened. Something had gone wrong, and he was involved, although he hadn't done it. He was beginning to turn up on the wrong side of the law, but how? It wasn't fair. He was a nice guy.

He thought of the crazy man in the Batman mask in the moonlight. Here in the grey bitter cold, the sharpness of that vision was like a hallucination, like a memory from a dream. But it wasn't a dream, it was infinitely real. It was all connected: wanting to do it with Patsy, masturbating, going out in the Batman mask, the murder. It was all the same thing, and he was in it and would never get out of it.

He was learning that there is no such thing as right or wrong in the presence of an evil event. When something evil happens, it isn't polar: you can't stand on the justified side of it and be safe. It's a vortex, a great big sucking whirlpool, and all the sides of it are the same. No matter where you are, it wants to drag you in. That's how it lives, by feeding on what it can pull in, like a black hole sucking up light and getting stronger and stronger. Roger could feel it, ankle-high, pulling.

He was learning that morality is nothing more nor less than trying to keep bad things from happening, because once they happen, there's no such thing as innocence. You can only be innocent of a bad thing that doesn't happen. After it happens, you may be lucky enough to stay far away, so that the pull of guilt is only a very small pull for you. But afterward, that's all there is, degree of pull.

So morality is not a matter of trying to be on the right side. All it is is trying to keep as many bad things as possible from happening to as many people as possible. But that means you have to study the way bad things happen. You have to understand what people want and how they try to get it. You have to know how things work. You have to understand the mechanics of ignorance, you can't be ignorant yourself. Ignorance and need, those are the two main things you have to study.

And of course all along you have to study your own behavior, because you can't do much about other people's, right? Your only handle on keeping bad things from happening is what your own behavior might encourage or discourage. So you have to study your own behavior, but then you have to study how other people will react to your behavior. Sometimes you find out things like the fact that being too obsessed with keeping bad things from happening can make bad things happen, or like Leon Cool says, you have to be bad to be good, though when he said it he was putting a good idea to bad use. It gets complicated, but what choice is there?

But Roger didn't have any of that worked out just yet. He was reeling, wavering like a reed in the current, giddily realizing the whirlpool.

They questioned him and let him go. He hadn't heard anything or seen anything. He had slept all night. He saw their eyes change when they discovered he lived in the neighborhood, and it was as if the gears of the whirlpool had been cranked up another notch.

Marcus had had to return to school for the rest of this last week before Christmas, so he missed the police. The body was gone when he came home, and so for him Elrod disappeared into a neighborhood story, not one that was terribly important to him, and he did not even really realize that the death, which he soon forgot, and the patrol of Captain Mississippi and Bluejay, which he never forgot, in fact remained grateful for all his life, the one fantasy he ever fully acted out—he did not even really realize that they must have happened on one and the same night.

Later that day Roger's mother called and asked him to come home for the holidays. As well as she could, she was clinging to the same routine as the mothers whose kids were off in college. The college kids were about to have a month off for Christmas, so it was time for Roger to spend a month at home.

Sanctuary. Roger went.

As usual, the emotional temperature there was only a couple of degrees above that of liquid helium, but this time Roger found it a tremendous relief. The central air purred, his bare footfalls were soundless on the buff wall-to-wall carpeting. His younger stepbrother was out of school but was gone with his friends most of the time. His stepfather worked, and his mother was either cultivating the yard or cultivating her friends. Roger slept late and ate heavily, cold ham sandwiches and peanut-butter-and-grape-jelly sandwiches with big glasses of milk. He watched *As the World Turns* and *Days of Our Lives*. There was a way in which their stories were very realistic, and yet there was no reality to them. He couldn't figure out what was missing, no matter how hard he tried. But they went well with the decor. They depressed him, like too much aspirin, but it was a comfortable numb depression, better than thinking about, well, you know, things. And stuff. He brushed his teeth after every sandwich. He showered four or five times a day. He did not masturbate. He did not even call Patsy.

Torpor, zero, neutral, muted. He shrank as far as he could toward nothingness. Then he ran into his own soul, irreducible boundary. You can't get smaller without destroying it. You can drill little holes in it and pour in acid and cockroaches and pestilence, which is insanity, or you can strap dynamite to it and blow the fucker up, which is suicide. Otherwise, you have to live.

The shape the boundary took this time was being pissed off at his stepfather.

"All I'm saying is a Catholic I'm just not sure where his highest allegiance is is all. Is he going to report to the American people or is he in his heart of hearts gonna report to the Pope is all."

"That's duh—"

"Because they have been like brainwashed, I know you don't like the term, but what else would you call it? I mean from birth they get it drilled into them that the Catholic Church is the most important thing there is and all I'm saying is separation of church and state—"

"Yokel yokel yokel. God, I'm getting tired of these cornball bigoted damn yokels. Sissy, your boy is a sweet kid, but he's fulla crap, am I right? Just because these Mississippi cornballs ain't used to Catholics—"

"Maybe if you didn't come down so hard it would be easier to have a reasonable discussion," Roger's mother said sternly. She was accustomed to dealing with belligerent men, actually still far more accustomed to that than to its obverse, even after all these years of relative calm. "And let's do please try not to curse so close to Christmas."

"Well ok. But he's not trying to be reason—Well, ok."

"No, seriously, all I'm saying, and I don't mean to argue or anything, I'm saying it's a serious worry I have is all. Whether like he can be true to his convictions that he has to have if he really believes in his religion and also still keep church and state separate—"

"I don't see how it's any different than here. You have to be a Baptist to be anything here, and not just a Baptist, you have to be like your little girlfriend—"

"She's not my girlfriend…"

"And be a chicken-fried Baptist. I don't think you understand about how Catholicism works. The Catholics know you're going to fuh scruh goof up, and they allow for it. It's no big deal, you don't think about God all the time, you know, you sin, you say a billion Hail Marys, you start all over."

"Well see and that worries me, too, because to me that isn't, I'm not talking against anybody's religion but that isn't like very high principles in a President—"

"So you want him to have real high principles but not ever use them, right?"

"No, I'm just saying, all I'm saying is should he even *be* President, considering everything. I mean if those are the choices."

"Well it sounds to me like something I read in one of Bum Festrich's columns. It's too late to be worrying about who's President, anyhow. He's the man now, what the hey. Unless somebody shoots him before next month, he's the man. The man's a millionaire, smart, good-looking. Hey, what do you want?"

"Is it Christmas, or what?" the youngest son said. "Are we gonna eat, or what?"

"You need to be worrying about this Barnett character now, if you want to worry. You characters are unbelievable. Coleman was smart, but he wasn't death on niggers. He wasn't death enough. He didn't believe Mississippi could whip the U.S. of A. single-handedly, and for that you clowns toss him out and bring in El Chumpo de Chumpo. You got a death wish, or what? Or you just enjoy looking stupid to the rest of the world?"

"I don't think you understand pride. I don't think—"

"Hey, Sissy, for crying out loud, I'm hungry already. We gonna eat or what?"

"Tell me about pride. Well maybe Barnett'll have the sense to keep the unions out. That's where we made our mistake, with the unions. You clowns sit around worrying about some jigaboo marrying a nice little white girl—"

"It's the children I worry about," Roger's mother said.

"—but if you really want to keep the junglebunnies down, don't let the unions in. You think you got problems now, with them making a buck twenty-five, try eight, nine dollars an hour and see what you got, my friend."

And Roger thought, unwillingly, of Marcus. Of Mr. A.L. Gandy, of Elrod the drunk. For the first time, when he heard *nigger*, *jigaboo*, *junglebunny*, he saw in his mind not some abstract menacing black man, but people he knew. Marcus in his arms asleep, safe from the whirlpool. And he began to rehabilitate his soul.

"Hey," he said. "I think, there's some pretty good. I mean a nuh a colored man has a right to make just as much as a white man, I mean—"

"Half white, half colored," his mother said. "Where will they live? They won't belong anywhere. They're the ones I really feel for."

"Am I a bigot or what?" his stepfather said. "I was in the army with them, I had them at the plant for years. Let a spade stand up on his hind legs and talk to me like a man, I'll treat him like a man, right? Fair is fair. But they're different than we are. Go ahead, let the unions in, you'll see."

"Hey, are we gonna talk politics all day? Do I need to like go out for a hamburger or something?"

"You think you know it all," Roger said, trembling with what he thought was anger. It was really fear, because he was in unknown territory, morally speaking. Defending the blacks—there were no precedents, no trails, so far as he knew.

His mother had gotten up and gone into the kitchen. Now she came back bearing a tremendous brown turkey on a platter. Juice started in Roger's mouth. Nervous energy was making him truly hungry for the first time in days. He had not been hungry eating the sandwiches. All they had been was stuffing.

"All *right,*" the youngest son said.

"No, I just think I've been in the world longer than you have, and I know a little bit more about what's what," his stepfather said, rising to carve the turkey. "Hey hey, what a beautiful bird," he said. "Way to go, Sissy."

"It's Jesus's birthday," Roger's mother said, beaming.

"That too," his stepfather said, cutting.

After the blessing, Roger found a heaped plate in front of him. He prodded a greyish-white pile with his fork. "What is this?" he asked.

"Oh, that's dressing," his mother said.

"It doesn't look like turkey and dressing," he said.

"That's the way stuffing always looks," his stepfather said. The youngest son's cheeks were already full, and he was digging in for more.

"That's a classic New England recipe," his mother said, "bread and oyster stuffing."

"It isn't cornbread?"

"No, it's a classic New England recipe," his mother said.

Large tears fell from Roger's eyes, dropping on his plate. "Is there any giblet gravy?" he asked.

"Roger?" his mother said.

"Giblet gravy?" his stepfather said. "You don't put giblet gravy on good stuffing."

"That's it," Roger said, pushing away and standing up. "He's taken everything. He took you away from me, and he took us out of our little apartment I liked so much, and he's always putting me down, and now he's even taken away my turkey and dressing. That's it."

"Roger, baby," his mother said.

"Let him go, Sissy," his stepfather said. "I'll talk to him later."

He did talk to Roger later. "Son," he said. "I love your mother. But I didn't know you thought I was taking her away from you. It never seemed to me like you guys were too close to each other anyways.

Personally, I think there's some stuff going on in your life that's worrying you, I don't know what it is and it's your business if you want to talk about it or not, but frankly I don't think it has anything to do with me or your mother. I remember some of the shit I went through when I was your age, and it was pretty confusing. So later if you decide, and I won't say this but once, you need some help or somebody to talk to, you can talk to me if you want to." He clapped Roger on the shoulder, and Roger nodded ok. "Good," he said. "Let's go watch the game."

But Roger went back to his studio the next morning anyway, getting his mother to drive him in. Over at the Gandys', Snower Mae looked out her window and said, "We need to have that boy over for New Year's Eve Day dinner. He's awful lonesome."

Mr. Gandy, who had been hoping to go in his study and listen to Doug Elmore and the Rebels take on LSU after dinner, said, "You can't tell that from here."

"Yay I can. Anyway, would he be here instead of with his family if he wadn't?"

"He's lonesome, all right," Mr. Gandy said. He meant it the way John Hurt meant it when he sang, "So lonesome here I can't see my baby's face," or as in "po lonesome boy."

The upshot was that Roger had New Year's Eve Day dinner with the Gandys. It was a subdued dinner, because Mr. Gandy was feeling sullen about having Roger over, and T.J. was depressed about going back to school soon—he had been getting an education knocking around with Leon, he had been feeling dangerous and alive for the first time he could remember since childhood, and now it was back to good grades and deportment. Eleanor Roosevelt ate slowly, her eyes hardly leaving Roger's face, saying nothing. Mrs. Gandy chatted away, trying to liven things up.

"I declare I don't know what happen to that blue sheet of yours," she said to the silent Eleanor Roosevelt once. "I cannot find it anywhere, nor yo pillowcase go with it either one."

Roger turned bright red, and bent to his black-eyed peas. His embarassment was not lost on Mr. Gandy, who said, "I spec a bear eat it."

"When we gone eat the peach cobbler?" Marcus asked, oblivious to the question of the blue sheet, which he no longer connected to his Bluejay outfit, stored over at Roger's for safe-keeping.

After dinner, which Roger had enjoyed hugely in spite of his depression—at least it had not been a classic New England recipe—Roger begged off from listening to the game with Mr. Gandy.

"Well you welcome to," Mr. Gandy said, hoping like hell Roger would say no.

Roger was still nervous about the sheets. "I preciate it, but there's some work I got to do, you know how it is and all."

So he went home and waited out the new year alone. Alone, that is, until ten o'clock at night on January the 31st. A little cream-colored brand-new Volkswagen pulled up in front of the laundromat, Patsy's pre-graduation present.

"Roger," she said, "my heart is heavy with this. I just couldn't let the new year come in without just clearing everything up, and starting out fresh."

Roger's heart wasn't heavy. It was banging around like a terrified kangaroo.

"It isn't that I don't love you, sweetie, because our love has been really special to me, it really has. No, hush now, you let me finish. But I feel God calling me really strong to be a preacher's wife, and—hush, no, *hush* now, no, I don't think you will be a preacher. You don't really know what you are, sweetie, and I don't know when you're going to find out. You're just a real sweet man, but I just don't think you're feeling his call the way I am. With everything that is going on in our state, I just think that God's people are going to really have to answer the call. I know the Congress meant well when they passed that act, but I don't think they understand how much we love Mississippi. The black people and the white people are just going to have to pull together until the Congress understands, and God's people have just got to be ready."

It was no surprise to Roger, though he pretended it was. And he was not terribly hurt, though he pretended he was. What he was was terribly angry.

"I was so glad to see you," he said. "I was so happy when you walked in the door, and now this. I just don't know what to say. I've been wanting to touch you so bad, and now." He buried his face in his hands.

Touch was their word for sex. Patsy looked down at his pants, where indeed there was a hard-on, an impressive hard-on, and a spreading wet spot. A wave of tenderness swept over her.

"Sweetie, it isn't the new year yet," she said, laying her hand on his cock. "But this will have to be goodbye."

She unzipped him slowly, felt for the vent in his briefs, and pulled him free. "I love to see it spring free in the air like that," she said. She licked him from his root to his tip, like a dog, while he struggled free of his jeans. She paused to let him get his underwear off. "Look, it's dripping the clear stuff," she said, and licked away the drop. "So pretty." She plunged him deep in her mouth, to let him pump while she took off her blouse. Her breasts had grown a size since the last time he had seen them, and he was shocked at how big and full they were. She quit sucking him, to rub the clear stuff over her rigid nipples. Then she hurried out of her skirt and panties, and he smelled her, strong and rank as bitterweed. Her slender body was limber, but with the limberness of steel or hickory. She sat on his belly there on the floor and leaned her new big titties over his face, but when he tried to pull her hips down toward his cock, she whispered *no no no* fiercely into his neck and he could not move her. And she would not go to the bed with him, because she was convinced that if she ever once lay down beside him in a bed that would be all she wrote. They could roll on the floor any way they liked, but a bed would make it impossible not to do it. He felt the heat of her pussy a small round hot spot like a blister on his stomach and she reached around behind her back to pump him with her hand and then she came on his belly almost squeezing him in half with her thighs and then she settled into him like water pooling in the low spots. He pleaded but still she said no, now not talking but only moving her head no against his shoulder, and he began to cry, the anger and grief after all welling up, the helplessness, and his impossibly swollen cock, so rigid it hurt, still circled by her fingers, feathery and relaxed.

"Hush, sweetie," she said. "I know, baby, I know." She rolled off of him and slid her mouth again over his cock, as he lay sobbing. And then she worked him, bobbing her head up and down, her short blonde hair tickling his thighs, the peanutty smell of his balls rising to her nostrils. He quit sobbing after a while, but he did not come and he did not come. He felt as though his cock was about to split its skin, but he could not come. Maybe it knew this was the last time, and didn't want it to end. Finally she said, "Sweetie, it's almost the new year. Do you think you'll be through soon?" Still he could not come. And then she stopped, and said, "Roger, I have to go now."

"No," he said, gasping it out. "The clock's fast, the clock's fast. We haven't heard the First Baptist bells. Clock's five minutes fast."

"Really, sweetie?"

"Honest," he said, though Mr. Gandy had timed the bells by the radio once when Roger was there, and they had discovered that the bells of First Baptist were six and a half minutes late.

So Patsy slid him into her mouth one last time, and he wrapped his hands in her hair and pulled, and she, feeling his need, amazingly did not gag but relaxed and let him slide all the way in and down her throat, all of it in, all the way in at last. And he, dreaming himself buried in pussy to the hilt, came to the bells of First Baptist.

Afterwards she was hoarse and could not talk (in fact her throat was sore for days, and her father got worried and made her go to the doctor, who said nothing except that it wasn't strep throat, looking at her with old grey eyes, and then tried to make a date with her after the examination). She dressed and left. When she looked back for the last time, she saw Roger lying, eyes closed, still naked, still hard, in the middle of the floor.

Later this day, and a hundred miles away in Greenville, two white men on a motorcycle pulled up beside a couple of black men, no doubt to wish them, in their own high-spirited fashion, a happy new year.

Which would be a good place to end this chapter, a move I have made before, but I've been doing some thinking. I've been thinking about it, and I figured some things out, and I want to answer Sissy's question. The one about where the children will live. The ones she feels sorry for. I figured it out.

The future, Sissy. We all pick up and move to the future, gel, because there ain't no room in the past. Too many whirlpools. Turns out this is a science-fiction story, a time-travel story. Tune in yo future-vision, gel, set it say 25 years ahead. Look at yo tv then. You a see where all a the pretty little coffee and chocolate children went.

Went to the future. And that ain't all. We still movin. Niggers on Mars, gel, niggers on Mars.

The Man in the Green Room

THE MAN IN THE green room took off his glasses and rubbed his eyes.

The woman looked at him. She was irritated. She was worried about him, too, but even that was irritating. Having to be worried all the time, watching him wear himself out day after day, never getting away from it. She was tired of seeing him tired all the time. It was like taking care of a sick person. You loved them but they exhausted you and *you* got sick of *them* after a while. Only this sickness was worse, because it promised health for others, so no one wanted you to get well.

"Those two boys are here to see you," she said.

"Who else have I got?"

"You got Mrs. Maples and her husband, and then the Baptist preachers."

"And then?"

"And then supper."

"Who have I got after supper?"

"You aren't planning to work after supper, are you? I didn't think you were planning to do that."

"You know what has to be done as well as I do."

"Well, then, I suppose you know who you have after supper. I don't. I didn't think you were planning to go back to work after supper, so I don't have any idea who you have. But I expect you'll be able to figure it out. It must be somebody. It must be somebody important."

"Don't be that way. It doesn't make it any easier for you to be that way."

"I'll bring the boys in now," she said.

When she had shown the two young men into the green room, she said, "I'm leaving now. I have a ride home with Mother. It's time to fix supper." She closed the door, and they heard her leaving.

"Hello," the man in the green room said. He put his glasses back on. "What can I do for you fellows?"

"How are you, sir," Leon said.

T.J. nodded hello, too nervous to speak.

"Well, we just wanted to help," Leon said.

"Yessir," T.J. was able to say.

"What are your names? She told me, but that was this morning."

"T.J., sir. T.J. Gandy."

"Leon."

"Leon who?"

"Uh, Didier."

"DDA?"

"Yessir."

"That's a strange name."

"Well, it's sort of French I guess. Momma from New Orleans. I notice yo street call Lynch Street. Pretty funny, I guess. You pick that out yourself? I have a quick mind, I notice things like that."

"I see. What kind of help did you have in mind, Leon Didier?"

Leon reviewed the points he wanted to make. Be bold, he reminded himself. You a bold man, and you need to let it show. He a preciate that, he a bold man hisself.

"Just about anything," T.J. said.

"What I'm best at, I'm like a leader of men," Leon said. "I know you are too. I been admiring you for a long time." That's good, Leon thought. Lean on that. Everybody likes flattery. "Most people, you know, just sit on their butt. Don't move, don't do nothing, don't get fired up, don't change nothing. If it was up to them, nothing would ever happen. But every now and then come along a man like you, set fire to their butt, stir em all up. That's what I can do too. It's like a rare talent I have. I ain't saying I'm as good as you. I know I have to start off on the ground floor. But the black man need to quit taking shit from the white man. Ain't gone get nowhere being nice to the white man. That's what he want. Black man don't have no self-respect."

The man felt the tug of Leon's anger, his own latent anger stirring with it. But anger got you nowhere, anger by itself. Anger had to be applied, judiciously applied. Pull with love, push with anger. Like an engine. That was what was so exhausting, having to monitor and apply your anger. Having to keep it in perfect balance and drive yourself on. Just giving way to it, that would be release. Relief. That would be the end of it. That was the way it had been for centuries now, the sermon of perfectly passive love, Carver and the Atlanta Compromise, glorify common labor, and Tuskegee, all the white donors happy to support so safe a school, and Taft echoing him fifteen years later, fit to be a race of farmers, but adding "first, last, and always." What it always came down to when you gave them what they wanted, they whittled it down to even less. And then the other side of it, the rage, smothered under the love sermon for so long, breaking uncontrollably loose, and that gave them the proof they wanted, a race of savages. The whipsaw. They worked it so well, year after year, age after age, it was hard to believe they didn't have it all written down somewhere in a single volume every white politician had to read and pass a test on, *The Old Whipsaw: How to Control the*

Nigger.

This kid was dangerous, he realized. He had something, a knack to touch the nerve. Look how easy he got to *you*, he thought. A little transparent flattery, a flash of impudent anger. All very obvious, but here you are ready to kill.

"Have you finished school yet?" he asked them.

"These schools here, they ain't nothing. You want a tough school, you need to go to L.A."

"This is my senior year," T.J. said.

"I disagree with you. Our schools are severely handicapped by the way the politicians strip us of proper funding, and many of our teachers lack adequate training. But I think the education that our schools provide is our strongest weapon. Do you know that something like eighty percent of the students in our schools are taking an American History course, compared to only a third of the white students in the state? Numbers like that make a difference. You can't fight history if you don't know history. And graduating shows me something else. It shows me finishing what you start. Shows me follow-through. Anybody can mouth off against the white man. That's what Joe Blow on the street does, mouth off. If you listen to him, you hear how he isn't going to take any more of this, but he doesn't have a plan, and next day there he is again, taking it."

He could tell he had gotten to the kid who seemed to be the spokesman. Leon. Leon Didier. The other kid was out of his depth, but he seemed earnest. He might amount to something someday.

"It don't take education to know you been robbed," Leon said.

"But it does take education to prove it in a white court," the man said. "Are you more interested in hollering about being robbed or in getting justice done about it? I got a man right now who is going to lay it all on the line for his right to get a good education. This is a grown man"—he came down hard on the adjective—"who's graduated from high school, been in the Air Force, and goes to college. He goes at Jackson State, but he wants to go to Ole Miss. What do you think is going to happen? Do you know who Clyde Kennard is?" The man's voice broke momentarily on the name, and, angrily, he controlled it. "Do you know who he is?"

"He tried to go to Southern," Leon said.

"Tried to go to Southern," the man agreed. "Arrested for drunken driving. They planted whiskey on him. Then arrested him for stealing chicken feed. Seven years in prison. This is a man who was a paratrooper, who was already a student in the University of Chicago. Betrayed by the registrar that led him on. Now what do you think they will do to this new man."

"I don't know," Leon said, irritated at being lectured. "They a probly kill him."

"I think maybe they'll try it. I think maybe they have already killed Clyde Kennard, though they don't know it. And these are qualified men, full-grown men, with experience and accomplishment behind them."

"That's what I'm tellin you," Leon said. "We been stepped on too long. Time to get mad."

"We've *been* mad," the man said. "We've been mad for a long time. I have been nearly crazy mad since they shot George Lee in 1955. Do you know who he was?"

"I wadn't eem livin here then. I was in L.A. You think it's bad here—"

"George Lee was a preacher. What he did wrong was register to vote. He was a preacher, and he had a little grocery store. They shot out a tire on his car, and pulled up alongside and shot him in the face. He got out of the car and tried to run, with most of his face gone. The coroner said he had an accident when his tire blew out. He said the buckshot in George Lee's face was fillings that got knocked loose in the accident. There were witnesses who identified the killers, but they faded out of the picture."

"You might as well quit tryin to scare me," Leon said.

The man got up and pulled open a file drawer. He went through the folders until he found what he wanted. It was a yellowed newspaper clipping, a column from the June, 1955, *Clarion Ledger.* "I'm not trying to scare you," he said. "Read that and we'll talk." He handed the column to Leon. Leon ran his eyes down it, twisted his mouth in disgust, and thrust it at T.J.

"I asked you to read it," the man said.

"I'm a speed-reader," Leon said.

"Sure you are."

"'Thugs and terrorists paralyze the business life,'" Leon said. "'White people are beaten, raped and robbed in Harlem.'"

"All right," the man said.

T.J. was absorbed in the column. The column was about the murder of George Lee. Here is what it said:

The FBI is still investigating that murder of a Negro preacher at Belzoni, to which the nation's press has given considerable publicity. We can't help but wonder why the FBI never seems to investigate violence and breach of civil rights in labor troubles.

Some poor workman trying to support his loved ones can be beaten to death by labor goons up East, merely for refusing to join a union against his will. Thugs and terrorists can paralyze the business life of an entire area, indulging in violence and vandalism to their hearts' content, yet nobody ever demands federal intervention.

In Harlem and other Metropolitan Negro centers, whites are beaten, robbed, raped, and murdered by vicious hoodlums almost with impunity. Taxi drivers actually refuse to take white people into Harlem after dark. You can enter Central Park after nightfall at your own risk. Brutal crimes occur there every night, yet the Department of Justice seems unconcerned with such a shocking situation.

But just let a couple of Southerners whip a colored person, or let a Negro get himself killed under unusual circumstances, and every pressure group in the nation promptly howls for FBI action, plus rigid laws that would destroy our basic liberties. Whoever said "Justice is blind," certainly knew the score.

T.J. looked up. "How can he do that?" he said. "I don't understand. It doesn't make any sense."

"There's no point in saving all his columns, but I held on to that one. That one is a classic. That particular column is a window on the soul of white Mississippi. They think *they're* persecuted. You notice that white people get raped and murdered, but a Negro gets himself killed? You notice that he openly refers to it as a murder, though the coroner said it was just an accident? But then the murder gets reduced to a death in 'unusual circumstances,' and then the whole thing gets classed with such minor and entirely normal activities as whipping a 'colored person'? Reality is what you make it. It changes according to the point you want to make."

"If we ain't supposed to get mad because it won't do us no good, and if you ain't trying to scare us, how come you making us read old shit-mouth there?" Leon asked. "What *do* you think you up to?"

"I work by details, Mr. Didier. You have an anger in you that wants to flash away like fire in straw. Like trying to run a steam engine on straw. It won't run long. We don't have but one weapon in this fight that will work. Do you know what that weapon is? The law, Mr. Didier. These people are legally wrong. Forget morality. They are *legally* wrong. But the law works by details. In some ways, what they did to George Lee wasn't anywhere near as bad as what they did to his friend Gus Courts. Gus had a little grocery store, too, and a bus business for the farmhands. They put him out of business. Oh, they shot him, too, but they put him out of business. The crazy crackers do the shooting, but respectable people put them out of business. Respectable people put their names in a list. Put mine in it too. Published it in the paper. People not to buy from, though I wasn't selling anything. Or people to shoot, depending on your preference. But if anything, economic reprisal is worse than the outright killing."

"I know what it means," Leon said.

"It's hard to have a life if they take away your living. That's what I'm doing. I'm documenting the reprisals. The law is plain, and the law is on our side. But we are trying to teach the law to crazy people. To people who don't see reality, who only see their own emotions. We're trying to make these crazy people behave themselves. We're trying to make them obey laws they can't even see. And what we need is work. We need details. Evidence. Documentation. Tons and tons of it. The law will win eventually, there's no doubt of that. For one thing, every time they ignore the law, they create more evidence against themselves. But it is long, hard, boring work. It's exhausting. And it is dangerous without being glorious."

The man paused for effect. He walked away a step, his back to them. Then he turned and spoke.

"Now how much good do you think we can do with a couple of raw kids who don't want anything but to see their names in the limelight?" He made it come out with a crackle of anger.

"I ain't a raw kid," Leon said. "And I ain't afraid. I believe you just have a complicated way of laying low. I ain't gone lay low. I give my life for the brothers."

"For who?" the man said.

"I ain't afraid of the white man, and I ain't afraid of you."

"I don't think you understand me yet," the man said. "You can't give up your life for our cause. It wouldn't mean anything. You don't have a life. All you have is an existence. You don't have a life, because you haven't built one. George Lee built a life, and he gave it. You can't give it, because you don't have it."

"Let's get out of here, T.J.," Leon said. "We ain't gone do no good with ole Uncle Tom here. Jive-ass don't even talk like a black man."

Jive-ass? the man thought. Where did he get that? "The sooner you get away from this joker, the better off you'll be," he said to T.J.

"Come on," Leon said, and pulled T.J. out the door.

The man was trembling. He took his glasses off again. Let the bastard get to you, he thought. Go back over it in your mind again. You've done it a thousand times, do it again.

You have seen the pattern, and you have seen that it is a trap. This anger, uncontrolled, is a trap. It is a trap for the manhood of the black man. Give in to it, and you will lose to the white man. He will have you where he wants you. There is only one way to be a man, and that is to break the trap. Even if it goes against the grain, against instinct. Refuse to indulge your anger, use it instead. Learn how to use it. If you are angry because those are your only choices, because you cannot live a normal life, then use that anger too. It would be different if you did not know that these things were true. Then, in ignorance and hatred, you could do simply what you felt like doing.

But you do know that these things are true. No point raging against the truth. Don't blame the truth for being true. Remember Judge Brady's filthy book: "The Negroid man, like the modern lizard, evolved not." Don't rage against the truth, when there are so many lies to be destroyed.

If the only victory you are to be allowed is the victory of breaking the trap, that victory is still sweeter than defeat. It is a man's victory. And if there is no one you can explain this to, no one who understands what you feel, remember, that is a part of the trap. That, too, is something to win a victory over.

Mrs. Maples, and then the Baptist preachers, and then supper.

They can't kill you if you have ever really had a life. That has to be true. If you have ever lived, you live. Such a waste of good people otherwise. They can't kill you. All they can do is stop you. But Lord, it is hard. It is so very hard.

T.J. FOLLOWED Leon back home, Leon stamping angrily along, silent all the way. When they got to Leon's aunt's house, Leon said, "I don't want to go in there. Let's go to Mosey's for a beer."

"Mosey won't serve me no beer," T.J. said. "My daddy won't let him."

"Mosey could clean the floor with yo daddy."

"May be. Whatever reason, he don't want to go against my daddy's will."

But T.J. followed Leon on to Mosey's. They met Roger coming out the door with a paper bag full of sandwiches, the bag soaked through with grease already. "Evening, Mr. Wing," T.J. said, and Leon looked at him sharply.

Inside, in the smoky roar of Mosey's in full swing, Leon had a cold beer and T.J. had a Coke. They sat without speaking for a while, digesting the way things had gone wrong downtown.

Finally Leon said, "Well he's a chickenshit bureaucrat, all he is."

T.J. said, "I don't know. I thought he was all right. A lot of what he said made sense to me."

"Cause he sound just like yo daddy. Yo daddy got it over you so bad, you never be a man on yo own. No more know how to make it out there in the alleyway than a long-haired goose."

"My daddy's a good man."

"Sure he is. He a fine upstanding citizen. And pussywhip you so bad you don't even know your own mind. Yeah, you act just like a pussywhip lover. Never seen nobody pussywhip by their daddy before, but you sho is." Leon decided not to carry the metaphor further and suggest any actual sexual activity between T.J. and his daddy. He was thinking of the butcher knife vibrating in the wall of his aunt's house.

"Whatever you say, Mr. *Cool*."

"The son got to kill the father, fool. Don't you know nothing? The son got to kill the father. Can't be a man till you get out from under the father."

T.J. finished his Coke in one swallow, and made as if to go. "Listen here. Who that white boy you sucking up to when we came in?"

"Sucking up to nobody, *Cool*."

"What you call it, then? Yo daddy teach you to be nice to white boys?"

"That man a hand you yo head if you mess with him. He don't look much, but that is the fastest, most dangerous white man I have ever seen."

"Shit."

"Shit yo self. Why don't you go be ugly to him, you feeling so mean, ain't nobody mean enough for you, no black man or white man anywhere mean enough for ole Mr. Leon Cool."

"Shit."

"I seen him spar."

"You what?"

"Fight, I seen him practice fight."

"Practice."

"All right. I ain't tellin you nothin. I'm going home."

"Well go on."

"I am."

"Well go on then."

"I am going on, when I get ready to. What you gone do?"

Leon did not answer, but turned back to his beer.

"Well I'm going on now," T.J. said. Again Leon did not answer. "Maybe I'll see you at school," he said. Leon drained his beer, and leaned over the counter to pull another one out of the box. Mosey lumbered out of the kitchen to collect for it.

"Well so long," T.J. said, and left.

Leon had three more beers and ran out of money. That pissed him off, running out of money. Chickenshit fool sittin up there gettin paid for tellin his own people to fuck off. He a be drinkin all the beer *he* wants, for damn sure.

When he went by the laundromat, he saw Roger inside, sweeping the empty studio area. "Now what," he said to himself, and stopped to watch. "He live in there, or he work in there? Wouldn't be working here this time a night."

He went in. Roger had stopped sweeping when Leon stopped to watch, and now stood facing him.

"I hear you pretty tough," Leon said.

"No," Roger said. "I'm a Christian. Aren't you a friend of T.J.'s? Seem like I've seen you with him."

"T.J. can't keep up with me. He said you was pretty tough." Leon was having trouble reading this little white boy. He seemed conciliatory, eager to please, but he also seemed perfectly relaxed, as if he were not at all afraid of this large, sullen black man in front of him.

What he did not know was that Roger was in that rare case of a man utterly without physical fear. Emotions could frighten him: he hated for people to be angry with him. But he had lived for so long with his body's perfect capability to take care of itself that he never worried about getting hurt. Ever since he had cleaned Dibby McDonald's clock, he had been perfectly confident of himself in a fight. That had been his first fight since he had started practicing karate. The way he had handled Dibby had felt spontaneous, but it had been the result of his training. Roger had realized then that all he had to do was practice, that he didn't have to worry about his reactions—if he practiced, the reactions would be there. He had had only a few minor fights since then, mostly when somebody got pissed over a low block in football practice, and once after a game when the right tackle on the other team pulled and clipped him and then did it again after Roger had told him not to do it again. You could wipe Roger out in a game—he wasn't very big or very good. But word got around that you had better do it clean.

"Naw, I'm really not," Roger said. "He probably just means I do a lot of jujitsu."

"They have that in L.A.," Leon said. "Go ahead and thow me down."

"Naw, it don't work that way. You would have to like attack me or something. You can try to hit me if you want to. I could like demonstrate a little of it."

"Yeah, you demonstrate," Leon said. "Demonstrate this," he said, flicking a right at Roger and lashing the opposite foot at his nuts immediately after it. But Roger was inside the right sideways to Leon and blocking down on the kick with his own right arm. Leon felt a sharp pop on the inside of his thigh, and nearly fell as his leg flew out in the wrong direction. Almost simultaneously, as he caught his balance, he felt three light thumps on his lower belly, his chin, and his chest just over the heart. After the downward block, Roger had cranked a side-fist blow to the belly, rotating to face Leon and coming out of the side-fist blow with a palm-heel drive to the chin. The blow to the chest was a left full-fist drive off of the retracted palm drive. "Here, here, and here," Roger said as he made the strikes.

"Of course, if you were really fighting, you would want to drive through the contact point on those blows," he added.

"That's pretty good," Leon said, stepping back. His leg was funny under him, unstable, as if its cords had all been loosened, and he was trying not to show it. He smiled. He had decided to play it like it was all a big joke, they were just joking around with each other. He checked the room. Nothing in it but the broom Roger had dropped when Leon stepped into his punch, and a sponge mop leaned in one corner. He carried a blackjack in his back pocket that he liked to claim (in the right company) he had beaten up a gangster for. It would have to be the blackjack, then. If the man give him a chance.

"That's pretty good," he said again. "I seen that stuff, but I thought it was all sissy stuff."

"No, it's not," Roger said.

"Well, I thought it was. But you don't hurt nobody with it. You didn't hurt me none."

"I wasn't trying to," Roger said, bending over to pick up the broom. He turned away to put the broom in the corner with the sponge mop, saying, "The whole point of it is"—

Leon pulled the blackjack and struck at the back of Roger's head. He never did know what happened. Everything jumped. Then he felt like he was falling, but something was pressing his face and his chest and one elbow hard. Things were in the wrong direction. Gravity was in front of him, pulling him into a wall, and there was nothing under his feet. Then his mind rotated things, and he realized he was on the floor.

"I think I fell down," he said, and rolled over. The white man was standing over him. His blackjack was nowhere around.

Roger was thinking, Kill the nigger, kill the goddamn nigger. Hahaha wipe the floor with yo ass nigger try to get up now I kill you son a of a bitch mess with me goddamn black bastard nigger son of a bitch. He was filled with a high sweet vicious elation.

What he was feeling was a deeply American emotion.

I never knew I hated Negroes, he thought next. Then he thought, I'm saying Negroes because I'm afraid I'm a bigot. Then he thought, I don't hate them. I don't hate Marcus. I don't hate Mr. Gandy. I don't hate T.J. or Mrs. Gandy or the little girl. I don't even hate this stupid son of a bitch on the floor here.

I don't even think they are inferior to me, he thought. They aren't niggers. They are just people I know. I'm not a bigot.

Well somebody here is, he thought. Somebody here is full of hate and frustration and ready to kill the people he lives around because of it. What's going on? There's somebody here I don't know thinks he's me, and he hates a bunch of people that don't even exist called niggers and he is ready to kill a bunch of other people that do exist because of it.

Jesus, I hope I'm not crazy, he thought. I hope I don't have a split personality. I don't feel like I do. Maybe it's the Devil. Satan waiting for a weakness and stepping forth. Bullshit, it's me.

It was the most introspection he had ever done. He did it in the space of time it took Leon to roll over and say, "I think I fell down," and look up at Roger. What Leon saw was the kill look on the white man's face, and then he saw it fade and another face rise up through it as it disappeared, a clear face, a waiting face offering nothing but not threatening either, a face that simply waited and watched.

"I have an idea," Leon said.

Everybody Has an Idea

LEON HAD HIS idea the same day somebody at Ole Miss had the idea to send James Meredith's application back because he had sent it in too late. Although it would have been interesting to know how being earlier would have done him any good. After all, the man in the green room had sent them *his* application back in 1954, and all he had gotten for his trouble was a headline in *The Jackson Daily News:* "Negro Applies to Enter Ole Miss."

And then there was Clennon King in 1958, the professor from Alcorn who applied for summer school. They gave him transfer credits to Whitfield. That was pretty funny, when you thought about it. Nigger *had* to be crazy, didn't he?

Leon had his idea three days before Burke Marshall had an idea: his idea was that the NAACP would accept Meredith's case, and that the case would be given to Constance Motley.

He had his idea a month before the special board of Roger Tutwiler's bank had the idea that the bank needed to take certain special measures. The special board was made up of those members of the board who belonged to the Citizens' Council, which was all of them but one, and he was Jewish. They wanted to set up a special fund for special legal emergencies, like say just in case the federal government decided to get involved with the Meredith situation, which surely they wouldn't, the American people would not stand for that sort of usurpation, but then again here they were deeply involved in voter registration in Hattiesburg and there had as yet been no general national outcry against the outrage. And then, too, their idea involved closer cooperation with the law enforcement agencies, and perhaps even a special militia for the bank itself, just for protection in case the social order broke down even a little more.

They turned to Roger Tutwiler to carry out their idea. Even though he wasn't on the special board, or the regular board either for that matter, he would be someday, and they all knew it. He was an up-and-coming young man. Roger Tutwiler, Tut, as they called him, agreed to carry out the idea for them, but only if they would accept his suggestion to set up a scholarship fund for black college students. "Tut," they said, "why in hell should we do that?" Tut reminded them how the liberal out-of-state press tended to distort things, and how they might distort the perfectly natural idea of a defense fund for Ole Miss. Whereas now if they had *also* set up a scholarship fund for black students ...

Roger Tutwiler thought banks were a good idea, and he wanted this one to survive. He could see what was coming in the next few years, and he knew damn well who was going to win, and he did not want his bank's investment position to suffer when he *was* on the board. He knew there was no way to talk the special board out of what it wanted to do, so he tried to minimize the damage.

Leon's idea was The Black Shadow League. He knew what was coming as well as Roger Tutwiler did, though he was more interested in money than he was in banks. The Black Shadow League would be a cadre of elite black warriors, like the Blackhawks, with him as the leader. They would get this white man to train them in his tricks, and they would also all have knives and pistols. Someday they could have jets, and work for the government as secret agents, after they whipped Mississippi and a black man got elected President. Hell, you could have a President who *was* a secret agent. Wow, what an idea. Nobody ever had that idea. Be a hell of a comic book. Somebody ought to work that one up. Go ahead and take it, it's free, Leon got plenty more ideas where that one come from. Leon's too busy to work that one up, you can have it. Cut him in on it, and you can have it.

The members of The Black Shadow League were black, and they

would wear black. They would be invisible in the shadows, like Lamont Cranston. But black. It tickled his sense of humor to think of it. Black people had always been white people's shadows. One day soon the shadows would suddenly quit just following the white people around. They would jump up and turn around and grab them by the throats and start choking them. And when the war came, this honkie duck-fucker that had thrown him on the floor would be the first one to go. Right in the middle of the forehead. Boom, with Leon's big gun. Right now, we need the man, though. Turn on the old Leon charm. Lying on the floor looking up at him. All a joke.

"You pretty good," he said, smiling. "I had a little of this in L.A., but you a lot better than I am. I figured you was, way you stopped my first try. But I have to test you, you know. Looking for the right man."

"Right man?" Roger said.

"How you like to make a little money?" Leon said.

But it was a little while before Leon put his plan into action. For one thing, he didn't really have any friends he could get to be members of The Black Shadow League. He could probably patch up with T.J., but he needed to get out and make some other friends.

In the meantime, Mr. Gandy had an idea he needed to take Snower Mae and visit Alligator to see his sister one last time. He hadn't heard from her in three months, and he had been afraid what that meant, and then his nephew had written to say that Sister had had a stroke and was paralyzed on her right side and breathing like somebody trying to keep their face above water.

They didn't have money for a wheelchair, Nephew and his wife, and Mr. Gandy did. It would bust him for a long time and he dreaded thinking about it, for it had taken him and his wife two years to save up 300 dollars. Even if he bought the wheelchair on time, he knew how the payments would eat him up. When a colored man bought on time in Mississippi, he paid 200 or 300 percent interest. But Nephew said Sister didn't need the wheelchair anyway, she was too far gone. She couldn't talk and he didn't think she knew where she was.

Mr. Gandy read the letter over and rubbed his bald head and worried. He read it late at night in his study for a week before he decided to go. He felt relief that he didn't have to get Sister a wheelchair, and then he felt guilty about feeling the relief. Nephew said he didn't need to get one, but then why did he bring it up in the first place? Sister had brought him up after Mother died, and she had always said, "I have plenty of food, and a dry roof over my head, and

God in my heart. What else do I need?" And here he was wishing not to have to make her last days easier. But really it sounded like there wasn't any point. That was T.J.'s college money. T.J., his special boy. He had been so worried about him last summer, messing around with that worthless Didier boy. And no steady girl. But he had come around, like he always did. His sweet smart boy always came through, his big-heart boy. For the last month, there had been a warm glow in those eyes when he looked at his daddy.

And sometimes Sister, after she asked, "What else do I need?," would smile at him and say, "A hug from little brother, that's what."

So they decided to go back to Alligator for a while and see Sister one last time. He had three weeks vacation time built up, and Mr. Bingham at the hotel would actually let him take it if he could get a replacement, and would even give him a week or two of personal leave if he needed it. Mrs. Gandy did cleaning for three white families, and she could leave so long as she had a replacement. They didn't want to take the kids out of school, or at least Mr. Gandy didn't, especially not in T.J.'s senior year. School was too important. So they left T.J. in charge, and asked Roger to help him keep an eye on things, and they left enough money to go to the movies once a week, and they went.

The first time they went to the movies, Eleanor Roosevelt had the idea she didn't want to go. That was no surprise, because she was sensitive, and didn't like sitting up in the Jim Crow rows with all the black people and watching the pretty white people all together and happy down below. T.J. didn't much like the Jim Crow situation either, but he had the feeling that if you stopped and tried to get it straightened out, you might wind up missing the cartoon and even the first part of the movie. He didn't feel comfortable about leaving Eleanor at home alone, and went over to ask Roger to stay with her, but Roger was nowhere around. So he told her to watch out the window for Roger, and as soon as she saw him, to go tell him T.J. needed him to stay with her.

When Roger came in, Eleanor Roosevelt was waiting in the studio. She said, "They left me by myself and I was scared."

"Where they going?" he asked.

"Movie," she said.

"Well, they should've took you," he said. "Do you want to stay here till they get back, or go over to your house?"

"I like yo place," she said.

"I don't know what we're going to have for supper," he said.

"You have a television?"

"No. You know, I was just going to have a baloney sandwich. I really don't have anything good to have for supper."

"I don't need nothing. I thought you would have a television. Yo parents have a television?"

"Yeah. Really you need something to eat." Roger was beginning to think of the awkwardness of having Eleanor Roosevelt in his place for several hours. There was nothing for her to do here, and he didn't want to make conversation, and he wouldn't be able to relax and just do whatever he wanted to. "It ain't healthy for you to go without a good supper."

"I thought they would," she said. "I reckon you just ain't got yours yet." She twirled, and Roger was aware, for the first time, that she had on her pretty white Sunday dress, the one that was really too small for her now, though her folks were putting off getting her a new one just a little bit longer, since she would outgrow it too. Her skirt spun up and showed her young legs a little, and Roger noticed that he was noticing them. He looked away.

"Do it make you need to pee when the water running?" she said.

I didn't have any idea how hard it would be to write this part down. I don't know how much of it I can tell. There's no reason for me to lie about it, because Roger never did. There's no reason to cover anything up about it, because Roger never tried to hide it or cover it up.

But I don't think I can set the scene anymore. In brief, she kept up a happy little conversation on topics just innocent enough that he didn't quite get shocked enough to say no, just forbidden enough that he didn't want her to quit. When he turned away with a hard-on, she touched it. She lowered her blouse, and let him know it would be ok to do other things. She knew about other things, Marcella Timmons had told her all about them, and she had seen Marcus and T.J. She was thirteen. Roger was crazy horny, and kept telling himself no, no, no, just another minute I have to quit this in just another minute. He came standing up between her legs just as he was saying to himself, only a minute, just the tip of it for only a minute just to see what it feels like I need it so bad. She had no clothes on at all.

Every time I think about it, I think I may have to kill him after all.

When he came, he fell to his knees, his face in his hands. At least I didn't put it in, he thought. At least I didn't do that. But even as he thought it, he felt a terrible surge of desire to get up and take her and put it in. He bit his hand, bit into the heel of his hand praying no no no and help help help and thinking at the same time, Come this far might as well this is just as bad so you might as well it would feel so no no no that's the devil talking bullshit it's me me me kime find kime bite kime bite through it, his eyes squeezed shut so praying in darkness, the taste of the blood in his mouth and the hard feel of the hunger in his penis one angry red scar like frozen lightning.

Eleanor Roosevelt wiped his white sperm off of her dark thighs with her panties, and knelt beside him and kissed him on the ear, and got up and put her white Sunday dress back on, and slung her shoes by two fingertips over her right shoulder, and said, "You can be my boyfriend now. I'm on go fix me some supper," and walked home barefoot humming.

Roger didn't see Eleanor Roosevelt for a week. He stayed away from the neighborhood as much as he could, taking long walks (and getting stopped by the police a couple of times as a suspicious character and brought back home, which made him an even more suspicious character when they saw the neighborhood he lived in). Then he gave up and stayed home and prayed that she would stay away and hoped she would come over. But she didn't seem to need any repeats, and when he finally saw her, with T.J. and Marcus, she acted perfectly normal, except that she seemed happy. T.J. had asked Roger over for an early supper before he and Marcus and Eleanor went to another movie (she was going this time). He felt he was filling in for his father, and Mr. Gandy had made it a point to have Roger over at least once a week.

Roger went because his curiosity was killing him. By this time he had converted a fair amount of his guilt into anger at Eleanor for leading him on. An interesting facet of this anger was that the same anger served as a response to another frustration, the fact that she wasn't leading him on any more. So he was very curt and snippish with her, treating her like a little girl, but she did not seem to mind. She stayed light and happy and humming, as if she were living in another world, a much nicer one.

By the time another week had passed, the whole thing had begun to seem unreal to him. It had happened, but life had gone on as before. The same thing had happened with Elrod the drunk. Big drastic changes, but they disappeared under the surface of everyday life without a ripple. That was where he wanted them to stay, submerged, invisible, unreckoned. Wavering in the current with all the other bodies.

All the other bodies under Mississippi, the bodies and dead deeds. That's a whole separate territory, like Lower Slobbovia: Under Mississippi. Some of the scariest stuff in Under Mississippi is the stuff that Aunt Wilma Riley absolutely does *not* wish to consider. The scared and the profane. Nice people think profane people are terrible. What they don't realize is that some of the profane people are just trying to make Under Mississippi a decent place to live. It's only a closet because it has skeletons in it. Get rid of the boogermen and it might turn out to be a nice little A-frame by the lake, you know. The boogermen that the nice people sent there, getting up in the weird of the night and mailing us their bad dreams.

And the *dead* shall *rise* again. Jesus, I hope not. There's a good movie on tonight.

Be that as it may. In late March, almost three weeks after the second big thing Roger didn't want to think about any more, nine people got themselves arrested at the library, and the shit hit the fan. The nine people were by coincidence all black, and by coincidence people from Tougaloo, and by coincidence people who had never been allowed to use that particular public library. Hooo-law and boy howdy! Mississippi's first organized public passive resistance! When I say the shit hit the fan, I mean one turd after another stood up and sprayed himself all over the papers, I mean without let-up for at least ten more years, on up until the time the state gave the largest plurality of any of these United States, 79 percent, to a man who surely wasn't a Communist even if he did look like a crook, talk like a crook, and finally act like a crook.

The next day there were mass meetings at Jackson State to protest the arrests. This was upsetting to the administration of Jackson State, which had managed so far to keep it from becoming such a haven for trouble-makers as Tougaloo had become.

And then on the first day of April, a crowd of blacks and whites gathered across from the Municipal Court Building to protest the arrest, Mississippi's first biracial public passive resistance. Several of the whites were just high school kids so not really responsible individuals. One of them, for example, was a girl who had painted her room black, and lit it with a candle in the shape of a skull. People like that, well, honey, you just form your own judgment, but if that's the kind of people that are in this movement I think I'll just stick with good old American prejudice.

The girl was amazed at the effect it had on other people that she had painted her room black. She couldn't get over the fact that they thought they lived in her room. They couldn't have been more upset if she had painted their faces black. She was amazed at the supposed-to's that rigidly governed everybody's lives but were invisible because you could never look at them.

And then the Freedom Riders let it be known that they were heading for Jackson in May.

It was these events that radicalized the special board of Tut's bank. The Communists were apparently ready to go to any lengths to split up Mississippi's happy community of harmonious blacks and whites, the goddamn Earl Warren court was already totally Communist, and anything could happen.

Roger Tutwiler thought of two people for the special militia for the bank, William Percy Alexander Sledge of Sunflower County, and Roger Wing of the Orient. As far as he knew, they both needed jobs. Percy had been let go from the Rebel team halfway through the season last year, and had not attended any classes since. He was in fact living in Jackson now, and Roger Tutwiler knew where to get hold of him. He did not know how to get hold of Roger Wing other than driving over to his studio, which at this point in the state of things he was just not quite willing to do, thank you. He thought he knew someone who would get hold of him, however: that friend of Katie's, June.

He got Katie to get June to give him a call. "When was the wedding?" was the first thing she said when he answered. "I've been watching the papers, but I must have missed it."

"Shoot, honey, you ought to know we would have invited you," Roger Tutwiler said. "Naw, we postponed it. Naw, things just got so busy we just had to. Naw, we not thinking about June, we don't know when just yet, probly be this fall. But you'll be the first to know, you ought to know that. Well, listen—"

"Katie told me what you wanted to talk to me about. I'll be happy to get in touch with him for you, but I'm just so curious I could die. What in the *world* is going on down there? Are you busy for lunch, I have to be downtown anyway. Delmonico's?"

They had a good lunch. June had not realized Roger Tutwiler had such a good sense of humor. His idea on the special militia for the bank was that it was a damfool idea, so he was going to hire a couple of damfools to do it. Naw, not really, but he definitely did not want any professionals. He wanted a couple of people he could control, a couple of proxies he could keep neutral and harmless and yet who would impress the special board as tough enough. He was going to have them dress as bank guards, arm patches and all, as if they were from one of the agencies around town.

As shrewd as he was financially, Roger Tutwiler was being pretty stupid about the special militia. He was right that it was a damfool idea. But if you want a couple of armed men you can count on to stay neutral and under control, you *want* professionals, not amateurs.

On Saturday, April 8, June drove over to Roger's studio. He was surprised to see her. He was also very grateful to see her. She was outside the routine of his life now, and she could freshen him and carry him off from the things he did not want to think about.

His gratitude came across as warmth, because he was too courteous to allow his desperation to show. June found the warmth heady and pleasing. Urban renewal had bogged down completely, and she had not been feeling too great about little Juney McMullen, as she sometimes thought of herself. She remembered the physical pleasures of working out, the happiness of sake. She talked Roger into giving her a lesson, which she insisted on paying him 25 dollars for. She had to wear one of his ghis, and then when the lesson was over, she had to take a sponge bath in the little restroom to cool off and clean up. Then she took him out to eat. He really was a dear. A goose, but a dear goose. It felt awfully good to both of them to have broken out of the staleness that had come over their lives. June felt that something important was about to happen in her life. She had had the feeling before, and she had never been wrong, but she hadn't had it in a while. Maybe she was never wrong because the feeling meant she was about to do something to shake herself up, but she thought of it as a sense that something outside of herself was about to sweep her up.

When they got back to the studio, she came in to get her half-slip, which she had left in the bathroom. At the door, she looked at Roger, trim and clean and earnest in his khaki slacks and penny loafers, his Ban-Lon pullover. She looked at the studio, a ridiculous home perhaps, but clean and trim, and so spartan that it felt spacious, the late afternoon spring sunlight coming in the big front window. "I really like it here," she said. "I like the way this place feels. You are so free. Just what you need, and nothing more." She sighed, and let her shoulders drop. She stepped up and pressed her mouth on his.

So it was that Roger finally did it. Knee and nipple, mouth and languor, smooth run of back to hip and belly curve, the throat, the inner elbow like a throat, the throat of the wrist to kiss and rub against a cheek, the hair just where hair should be, the raw surprise in all that smooth skin just right, just right, and easing in with nowhere any stop or no or bad but good, base of the brain all down your loosening back between your legs collecting where a cool hand held and you went in and came.

At eight that evening, Roger got out of bed to answer a knock at his door. It was Eleanor Roosevelt, with another little colored girl. "This here's Marcella Louise," she said, and faltered. June had come up, wrapped in the rumpled sheet, to lean her head on Roger's shoulder. Roger was astonished at what a child Eleanor Roosevelt was. He hadn't seen her for nearly two weeks, and he hadn't remembered her as being that young.

"Oh hi, honey," June said to Eleanor Roosevelt, whom she remembered having met last summer. "You too," she nodded to Marcella Louise Timmons.

"Nice to meet you," Roger said to Marcella Louise. "I'm busy now," he said. "Say hi to Marcus and T.J. for me," he said, and closed the door.

Mr. and Mrs. Gandy were gone until the middle of April. They had been lucky in that Sister had gone ahead and died while they were there, so they didn't have to abandon her and worry over her from a distance. Her face had relaxed in the moment before death, Mrs. Gandy said. The paralytic grimace had disappeared, and she had smiled, according to Mrs. Gandy, and her eyes had glowed. "She was seeing her Savior's face," Mrs. Gandy said. "It was just the sweetest thing." Mr. Gandy hadn't seen all of that, but then he didn't have his wife's eyes. He wasn't a Christian, or maybe he was, but if he was, he wasn't the kind of Christian that people who call themselves Christians would call a Christian. He believed that when Jesus said, "God is love," He meant it literally. He believed that if you wanted to see God, you had to look at love. It didn't work the other way, you couldn't look at something called capital Gee oh dee and see love. He believed Jesus was the Son of God, all right, and he worshipped him. But he didn't believe he was the Son of a Virgin and he sure didn't believe Jesus never fucked up. Take the blasted fig, for example, where Jesus was coming in from the desert and was so hungry He was starving and saw a fig tree and said oh boy I'm gonna get me some figs, but when He got to it it was barren and empty, and so He cursed it and it withered away. Bad temper, pure and simple. Was it the tree's fault there wasn't enough water that year, or the right kind of wasp never came around? Maybe He should have taken it up with His Daddy before he blasted the poor tree.

But the expression of such dangerous and heretical ideas would have distressed his wife, and he loved his wife, so he kept quiet, and went to church, and pretended not to be an evil and Godless junglebunny.

Eleanor Roosevelt had already begun to pull her hair out when they got back home.

The Stuff in Eleanor Roosevelt's Bottom Dresser Drawer

TOP LAYER, left-hand side: seven pair of white cotton panties, ironed and folded.

Top layer, right-hand side: one pair of nylon hose, dark brown, six pair of white cotton socks, three pair of colored wool socks.

Middle layer: two slips, a half-slip, two training bras (one black, one white), an old t-shirt, a man's old dress white shirt, a nylon scarf and a wool scarf.

Bottom layer: one Kotex box with Kotex; also one empty Kotex box refilled with extra shoe-strings (loose), book matches, two empty nail-polish bottles, one plastic lens from a pair of sunglasses, a five-pack of balloons from Walgreen's Drug Store, and a thumbnail-sized cartoon book; also six movie magazines, various titles, a rubber from Marcella Louise Timmons's boyfriend, wrapped up in paper towels in a used compact circled with rubber bands, a box of 48 wax crayons, and three bubble-gum-machine adjustable plastic rings; and finally, one twice-folded sheet of paper with a mimeographed message in fuzzy purple ink, dated October, 1957, in pencil in the upper right-hand corner:

> Do you know that some people in our country want the Negroes to live with the white people? These people want us to be unhappy. They say we must go to school together. They say we

must swim together and use the bathrooms together. We do not want to do these things. "Why do some people want us to live together?" you will ask. They want to make our country weak. If we are not happy, our strong and free country will grow weak. Did you know our country will grow weak if we mix our races? It will.

Summertime

ROGER WING WAS astounded by Roger Tutwiler's office. It had wall-to-wall carpeting (a nice blond color), and walnut veneer panelling, and a solid wood desk. It had a plant, a live plant, over in the corner by the window. That alone astounded him: bringing the outdoors in. What a radical idea. He wished everyone would do it.

Roger was realizing that Tutwiler was an important man, a wealthy man. He had never thought of him as anything but one of his pupils before. Suddenly he was the pupil and Roger Tutwiler was the master.

Little Wide Load was not impressed particularly by the office. He had seen a lot of them, and he knew that Roger Tutwiler's office was run-of-the-mill. Anyway, he figured he would have one of his own soon enough. This bank guard job was a step in that direction, maybe just a small step, but a step.

T, as Little Wide Load had taken to calling Roger Tutwiler, was explaining the job. He called him T because he wasn't about to call him Tut. Tut was an uncle's name. You had to be somewhere a long time to be called Tut. You had to be rooted like a live oak at Natchez to be called Tut. Tuts were not born, they just existed, *a priori*. He could have been Bud, or Bo, or maybe, just maybe, Mac. Not hardly Tut.

One of the things that T was explaining was that this wasn't a bank guard job, but Little Wide Load knew that it was. He could tell that T wanted them to think that they weren't just bank guards, that they had some higher function. He could see that Roger Wing ate that up, but he knew they were just bank guards.

The other thing that T was explaining was what their duties were.

Their duties were very complex, he said. There were a lot of special situations arising in the state, and they were to monitor those special situations in regard to their application to the operations of the bank or the bank's officers, without however rushing into action unless there was some direct and impelling necessity, and with of course special attention to the actual grounds and building of the bank itself. To that end, they had been provided with appropriate uniforms and licenses to carry weapons had been issued in their names and a special security room had been set aside in the basement of the bank building. He was at pains to stress the importance of not taking action unless it was absolutely necessary. They were to consult him before doing anything at all, unless of course people rushed in the door with machine guns, but otherwise they were to be trained observers only, bringing their special martial-arts training to bear on given situations, but essentially not repeat *not* acting without consulting with him, Roger Tutwiler.

"We're bank guards, Coach," Little Wide Load translated later for Roger down in the security room. "We have to walk around a lot, but we don't have to do much of anything. We carry guns, but we ain't police and if we ever take our guns out of our holsters, we're fired."

The security room had wall-to-wall carpeting too. It had a big closet with nothing in it but two uniforms apiece. It had a bathroom with towels and razors and shaving cream and toilet paper and a shower and Lava soap, though what they were going to be doing that would get their hands that dirty, Roger did not know. The security room had fluorescent lighting and two chairs and a workbench and a cot and a big coffee pot and shelves all along one wall. On the shelves were boxes of ammunition and handcuffs and tear-gas bombs and wrenches and screwdrivers and hammers and nuts and bolts and a police radio and a color television. Not just a television, but a color television.

"This is all right, Coach," said Little Wide Load, looking around. "I could live here."

That was exactly what Roger had been thinking, since the place was more luxurious by far than his studio, though a little smaller. He was impressed by his gun, a big blue-steel .38 with a walnut stock. When he was alone down in the room, he twirled the chambers and held it and sighted along it for hours. He could not get over it, the economy, the beauty. He loved the dark well of the muzzle, the fluting of the carriage. This one thing, this compact massive elegant cool device outdid all his training. It was centuries of thought. It was point your finger and kill, a straight line from brain to target, pure mathematics. Reach out and touch. He felt his sphere of influence enormously enlarged, and yet he could touch any portion of it. Pow. And Pow. Too bad it blew the sucker up when you touched it, but at least you had concrete evidence of response. It was not a weapon, but a magic wand, the monkey's happiest dream of power.

> Boom to the tiger,
> down you go,
> boom to the big bad dominant
> Daddio.

And yet he had no real desire to fire it. That would have been noisy and disappointing. He just liked the weight of it, the thought of it, the cool perfected quality of its working. He didn't like wearing the thing, either. He liked holding it in his hands, and he loved wearing his uniform, the peaked cap he thought of as a policeman's cap, the blue shirt and black pants and badge and leather, but the gun dragged in its holster. It was off-center. He had spent too many years training for balance and harmony, and now he could not be comfortable with anything else. He was too far gone. The gun pulled his right side out of line, and he was aware of it all day long.

Perhaps there was irony in the fact that the gun, which was so harmonious and balanced and self-sufficient a work of art, was the agent of such imbalance in combination with that other symmetry, a man. The man had to reorganize around the gun.

Or maybe Roger was weird. Eccentric. Though he could have sworn it was the pistol.

He worked days, 8:00 to 4:00, and Little Wide Load worked evenings, 2:00 to 10:00, so that they overlapped for two hours in the middle of the afternoon. Then he would take off the gun and go home. It was his first real job, and it wore him out, though all he did was walk around the bank and tip his hat to the men in suits and ladies in hats, or sit down in the security room on the cot and watch the game shows and soap operas. There were people around all day long, and you had to react to them, however minimally. Work was like school. It was designed to depress you by giving you a rough idea how many other people there were. Watching other people, you began to realize there was a tide in the affairs of men, and you were stuck in the salt-water with all the other starfish.

A curious thing began happening after the first week, which was orientation, and during which time Roger and Little Wide Load had both been there all day during regular hours. The top executives of the bank began dropping by in the middle of the morning, or after lunch. They would have a cup of coffee in one of the crockery mugs Roger had bought (he could not abide Dixie cups), and a cake doughnut with powdered sugar, and sit on one of the chairs and watch tv with him. They would loosen their ties and kick off their Florsheims and talk about duck hunting or the new preacher out at their church or how their girlfriends stacked up against their wives. The CEO himself would come down at 12:30 sometimes with a box of Krystals (which every waitress in every Krystal in Mississippi referred to as Kryshtals), and he and Roger would have about ten of the little wafer-sized burgers each, and then he would go to sleep on the cot. Roger would sit there watching *Young Doctor Kildare* with Emerson Smoot the Third snoozing away beside him. After a while, he was giving these guys rides home so Smoot Four could use the station wagon and Mrs. Smoot the Caddy, or they would have him babysit the house while they went down to Cypress Gardens for the water-ski championships, or sometimes they would even have him babysit the baby while they went to a ball out at the country club. It all came loosely under his job responsibility to monitor the safety of the board members, Roger assumed.

They were comfortable down in the basement with Roger, far more comfortable than they were up in their own fine offices. They almost never talked politics or business, though from time to time one of them would tell Roger to put a little money in this or that fund, and though they sometimes had a little something to say as regards the race question. The race question was not politics, in spite of the fact that politicians were necessarily involved. It was superior to politics. It was the survival of our way of life.

Roger was making 575 dollars a month, an incredible sum, from which he was able to save 250 or so. He was amazed that it was so easy to become rich. He discovered that he was no longer interested in fixing his own meals. He was too tired, even with cutting his workouts back to one a day except on weekends. He wound up going over to the Gandys' near suppertime and waiting to be invited, and then he started showing up at breakfast, which was really the best meal of the day. Mrs. Gandy made fresh buttermilk biscuits every single morning, high and fluffy, with a mildly crisp crust and a wonderfully delicate and spongy interior. Roger would melt about a half a pound of butter into a couple of these and wolf them down as appetizers. The next four or five he loaded up with strawberry preserves, but he treasured those first two, washed down with a pint of ice-cold milk. The Gandys did not drink much milk, so he had to bring it over. Then he asked Mrs. Gandy if she would mind picking some up next time she was at the grocery store. Then he realized he was making a lot of money, and was also eating a lot of food. He spoke to Mr. Gandy about it.

"When a man is no longer able to offer the hospitality of his home, he is in a sad way," Mr. Gandy said.

"Well I don't want you to feel that way about it. I'm over here all the time, and it isn't right for me not to carry my own weight. If *I* had any hospitality, I wouldn't be over here so much, probably. So you shouldn't feel like you owe *me* any hospitality. Shoot, I'm like. Like." Roger couldn't quite say "a member of the family," not because he had any personal reservations, but because he did not know whether or not Mr. Gandy had any. He knew Mr. Gandy did not always approve of him, though he always tolerated him and often seemed to like him.

"I don't think you understand," Mr. Gandy said. "The hospitality of the home is a attribute. It's just something a true home is supposed to have, like a library. I don't have but a po imitation of either one, but if you was to take away my library, you would have lessened the kind of home I can provide, and if you was to take away my hospitality, you would be doing the same thing."

Roger understood Mr. Gandy's point in a dim theoretical sort of way. Mr. Gandy had ideas of the way things ought to be, and as well as he could he drew images of those ideas in his own life, like rough drawings on the wall of a cave. Not really like the cave paintings of Neolithic tribes, for those were, in their way, finished works by trained artists. But more like something scrawled in chalk a hundred years ago by a couple of small boys.

To Roger, Mr. Gandy's visions were comprehensible, but not very realistic, and he was impatient with them. But he could make no headway with Mr. Gandy, and finally he gave up and discussed the day's news, as usual. Mr. Gandy liked to analyze all the front-page stories, and some of the others, from a historical or a Biblical perspective. He thought what was going on in the South right now with the colored people was like the Hebrews in Egypt, a startling thought to Roger, since all his life the white people had talked like *they* were the Hebrews: despised and afflicted, persecuted among all the other desert tribes, and yet possessed of a great secret, because they were the special ones, the Chosen of God. And like the real Hebrews in the Old Testament, they kept that same aggrieved aggressive whining persecuted-but-special feeling going for a long time after they had come out on top.

Roger pointed out to Mr. Gandy that the Freedom Riders at least were talking about riding back *into* the kingdom of Egypt. Mr. Gandy, to give him his due, was quite aware that his comparison was not particularly original. He thought it was especially accurate, however, and went on to develop the parallels in much greater detail than was usual. It was easy to describe Martin Luther King as a Moses, but Mr. Gandy went on from there to state that, like Moses, Reverend King had become a political leader because he was a religious leader, and that the irony of this was that the leadership was exercised in a religion the subject people had adopted from the rulers. Mr. Gandy was firmly convinced that the Hebrew tribe had had no formal monotheism, knocking around in the desert before being taken into Egypt, but had worshipped a ragtag collection of jackal- and goat-headed gods like the rest of their desert neighbors. Moses had been powerfully influenced by the theories of Ahkenaton, just as Martin Luther King had been by Christianity. Which was itself an echo of the Osiris rituals. It seemed like the fulfillment of prophecy because the pattern of Jesus's life resonated so strongly in sympathy with that suppressed vision.

Roger excused himself as soon as he could. Mrs. Gandy let him out the door. "You could just give me some extra money to get you some groceries with," she said.

"What?"

"What you was talking to Mr. Gandy about."

"Oh yeah. But what about." Roger hesitated. "Well he says. Well, I don't want him to feel bad."

"It could just be from you to me, just like for the milk. He worry too much. I don't want to worry him neither. He would know because he do the budget, but if it was just like to pick up something for you cause you wanted it, he would let it go."

Roger began paying Mrs. Gandy twenty dollars a week for groceries and eating with a clear conscience.

Eleanor Roosevelt was mostly eating in her room all this time, because she was ashamed of her hair. She had pulled most of it out, and she looked like nothing so much as a child's old pickaninny doll, abused and balding and indestructibly round-cheeked. No one saw her pulling it out, but they knew she was. Mr. Gandy had taken her to the doctor, eight dollars he could (as they say) ill afford, especially after their prolonged visit to Alligator. The doctor told him there was nothing physically wrong with the girl. He had seen this before in adolescent girls. He recommended that Mr. Gandy get her some psychological counseling. He knew there was no way Mr. Gandy would be able to afford that, but what else was there to say? *He* couldn't help her.

"But what's wrong?" Mr. Gandy asked him. "Why would she be doing this?" He was as horrified as he had been the time he had seen the cat eating her own kitten, the little truncated body going down into an appetite it had been born to trust. Natural order was violated, and violated in the body of his own daughter. But by what? Everything was nature, and how could nature violate itself? How could this happen to his sweet defenseless baby that maybe he hadn't paid enough attention to lately? She was not the prettiest girl in the world anyway. And now this disfiguring blight, striking her in her weakness. How could it be? The irrational stalked near.

"I don't know, sir," the doctor said wearily. "I cannot tell you what is going on in her mind. You will need professional help for that."

"We could get a wig," Eleanor Roosevelt said, out on the street, her head wrapped in a large scarf. It was as much a mystery to her as it was to her father. She was afflicted, under attack. Invisible hands plucked out her hair when she was not aware of it, leaving her to endure baldness and shame.

Mr. Gandy grabbed her up, though she was five feet two, and carried her like a baby back to the car, her head laid on his shoulder.

Eleanor Roosevelt ate with the family some of the time, though. Mr. Gandy would get worried about her keeping to herself so much, and he would decide that contact with others might help her come out of her shell. More accurately, a week would go by in which the family did not see her at meals, and he would once more allow himself to *hope* that contact with others would help. At these meals, she sat at the end of the table, wispy and whispering, her eyes on her plate. She had lost weight, and Roger did not feel he was even looking at the same person as the young girl who had appeared in his studio and seduced him. That had been a mistake, but it was a one-time mistake, and he did not think about it any more. That girl had disappeared somewhere. She no longer existed. And she had taken the reality of that evening with her, leaving only the skeletal trace of factual memory.

No one had said anything to Roger about Eleanor Roosevelt's illness, but Roger could see she was sick. He figured if they wanted to talk about it, they would, and meantime he was unwilling to embarrass them by prying.

So Roger spent his time that summer: his days on one side of Missouri Street, his evenings on the other. The Freedom Riders came, got whacked on the head, dog-bit, booked, beat up some more, bailed out. Bum Festrich had this to say about that:

Commies Play on Your Sympathies

What would you think about somebody who burglarized your house, and then tripped on a roller-skate on your stairs and broke his leg? You would probably think that he was not among the smartest of individuals, for one thing. But as a good Christian, and in spite of what he was trying to do to you, you would feel sorry for him, and you would telephone for the nearest medical assistance immediately.

Now suppose that this uninvited intruder goes into court and sues you for negligence, and a soft-hearted jury awards him damages that amount to more than the value of your entire house? Suppose that this jury, furthermore, is made up of members who do not even live in your state, much less your community. Never mind that there are absolutely no precedents in the statutes for such a happenstance, not even if we go all the way back to the English Common Law.

Now let us suppose that this same unauthorized and larcenous individual actually returns to your house again, again with the intention of ransacking all your precious valuables, which to you represent priceless memories, but to him represent merely the opportunity for crass material gain at the expense of another. In fact, let us suppose that he returns not merely once, but time and time again, and that every time he gets a nick or a scrape or a bump, he takes you back to court, and instead of himself receiving a sentence for his determined and repeated miscreance, he somehow plays on the sympathy of the court to the end that *you* are bound to pay *him* damages.

Ludicrous, you say, but if such a thing did occur, I would surely consider myself justified in arming myself and taking whatever measures were necessary to secure my property and my dreams against the invasions of this individual.

Ludicrous?

Oh, Mississippi, tear the veils from your eyes! For this is happening *now*. The Communist-inspired traducers are burglarizing our very Way of Life. What is more, the godless ones have a secret weapon on their side, a secret weapon more powerful than the stolen H-bomb itself, a weapon they have ever resorted to in the last analysis.

There are those among us who see the outsiders thrusting themselves into our business uninvited, who see the rude persistent stridencies of the attention-getters who have not lived here and have no desire to understand our special problems; there are those among us who see renters and drifters sashaying into a state they neither love nor understand, and interfering in the rightful pursuit of any reasonable form of government in that state, and who yet refuse to condemn these aliens as outlaws.

And why is this? It is because of the softness of our hearts, the tenderness of our sympathies. We have learned Christian charity at the knees of our mothers, and when we see a few heads clubbed here and there, a sprinkling of mostly minor blood, we cannot help but feel a welling-up of sorrow and fellow-feeling for these unfortunates—never mind that they asked for what they got, that they were disturbing the civil peace, never mind what was going on inside those same heads.

It is this that is the secret weapon I spoke of. Having no morals themselves, the Leninists count on using our own morals against us. It is the oldest trick in the book, and they are using it for all it is worth. While we hesitate, concerned and irresolute, they are acting. They are most assuredly acting.

In this we must finally and reluctantly imitate our enemies, save that we do it in the cause of justice. Let us, as did the Lord Himself, harden our hearts against the evil-doers. Let us purge every drop of the mistaken milk of human kindness from our veins, and stand firm, the rock of the Southland, on which shall falter all the ships of the iniquitous!

One evening in June Roger told T.J. and Mr. Gandy about Gloria Laverne Floyd, the nine-year-old who had gotten herself lassoed and dragged down the street by a bunch of white boys in a convertible. I say T.J. and Mr. Gandy, because although Mrs. Gandy and Marcus and Eleanor Roosevelt were all there, they were never very interested in this sort of table conversation. Roger had heard the story from Ellis "Buddy Buck" Buckaloo, the executive VP at the bank. It had actually happened several weeks ago, but Buckaloo had had a more detailed version than the one that had appeared in the papers. He had gotten his from one of the boys in the convertible.

Roger did not feel compelled to render the story in quite the way that Buddy Buck had rendered it, however. In that version, some fun-loving boys from one of the local high schools had tied one on and gone out to rope steers, but all they had found was a little black filly. Didn't do her no real harm, and she sure did bounce good, heh heh heh. Roger's version was not so picaresque.

One thing Roger was aware of, and that may have affected his storytelling, was that T.J. had gone back to see the man in the green room and was now transcribing records part-time for the NAACP. He would come home with incidents from the files sometimes, which he related in a matter-of-fact way to his father. Mr. Gandy approved of T.J.'s job, though he had his doubts about stunts like the Freedom Riders. His idea was to work hard, educate yourself, and leverage yourself eventually, arduously, into such a position that your equality could no longer be ignored or denied, no matter how the white man felt about you. T.J. secretly admired the demonstrators more than he let his father know, but he supported Mr. Gandy by saying that, yes, Roy Wilkins himself had begun to complain about the rising legal expenses the riders had incurred. Those people were getting the headlines, and the NAACP was paying the freight.

Roger told his story defensively. It was an example of injustice: the villains went free. It was his contribution to the stew. It made him an honorary nigger.

"Wa she ugly?" Eleanor Roosevelt said. She seldom spoke any more, and the others were surprised.

"What?" said Mr. Gandy. "What you say, honey?" A wild hope sprang in him. "Tell Daddy what you say, baby."

"Wa she ugly?" Eleanor Roosevelt repeated.

"She was a little girl," Roger said, not understanding.

After the Freedom Riders, most of the action that summer

occurred in air-conditioned places, the courts primarily.

A Mississippi summer is an awesome and boggling thing, a slab of steaming time, a hundred cubed: a hundred days at a hundred degrees and a hundred percent humidity. Resin bulges in big globby tears from the trunks of the pines, a sheet of paper wilts in your hand—by noon you can wipe your face with it like a handkerchief. You wake up glued to the sheets, the window fan puffing like someone out of breath huh huh huh huh blowing rags of wet exhalation over you. You think that's the sound of the subconscious mind after a few years, a window fan laboring unnoticed near you, and you get where you can't sleep without it. A lot of older Mississippians, they have air-conditioning now, but somebody should market a tape of a window fan running so they could get a little sleep.

So it's morning and you rip off the sheets like Johnson and Johnson tape and go outside in your shorts. The grass is grey with dew, every blade bent in a drop-loaded curve. The trees drip. Things are *soggy.* The sun is just over the treeline and steam rises from the ground, the entire Gulf of Mexico soaked up during the night and filtered through buckshot mud and red clay and now evaporating back into the air.

Breakfast you have a half pound of animal fat with some eggs and pork stirred into it and some biscuits for binder, so all day a thin film of grease comes over your face. Wipe it away, cold water in the basin and towel off, and five minutes later it's back.

Ten o'clock you can't believe the hammer blows of wavering heat. You've had your last rational thought of the day. It makes the headlines believable, the way everything shimmers unreal. Your mind shakes like the Shadrach air. The last scrap of fog is gone, partial pressure of water vapor is way down as the ambient heat skyrockets. The blacktop pools with liquid asphalt, barefoot children trying to skip across to the store for a Nehi (their folks make them do it to kill the hookworms burrowing into their feet). The children get stuck and squeal. Squeals turn to screams, but the sound is far away and tinny, sound doesn't carry in this heat, or maybe your ears have melted. The children char, collapse on themselves, subsumed in the asphalt. All winter their parents will drive over their trapped bones. By January the old folks' brains will have cooled off enough to wonder what happened to the kids.

I want to say that the humidity factor has never to my knowledge been taken into account in descriptions of Hell. You talking eternal fire without no humidity, a Mississippian is gonna think you mean

Heaven or Southern California. Humidity is Satan's device to keep you from getting rid of your own body heat. A good wet summer day is like taking a shotgun and making your granddaddy drink two quarts of Early Times in quick succession and then making him put on his long wool underwear and run around the house till he sweats it all out and then making him sleep in the underwear for three straight days without letting him get up to go to the bathroom so he just has to leak right there in in his long-johns, and then you make him take em off and you take em out in the yard and wet em down good with the hose with the water that is still running hot from laying there in the hose in the sun. Then you take em and wrap em around your face. Suck in a good lungful.

Eleven or so, and the green stuff jumps. Corn grows two foot an hour, Johnson grass strides over the turf saying *ha* to the lesser grains, thunder lizard of grasses. A rabbit goes down, the kudzu has him. Snarls, slobber, slurping sounds. A burp. Time to find the craziest most retarded redneck teenager in the county and send him in with a slingblade, a sacrifice to chlorophyll. You're cheating Parchman, but the rest of us may get to live another day. He's white-haired blond with freckles and pale blue eyes so flat they must have tin-foil backing. Takes off his blue work shirt. Ties a red bandana around his neck. Wades in. *Eeeeeyah.* Goodbye. At least this way you won't get bumpy with chiggers in two three days.

High noon. Radiators boil over if you even turn the key. Exhaust manifold on the tractor is cherry-red. Reflections kill. The hell with lasers. A '58 Mercury in the parking lot can punch a hole in your chest. Death star of blinding scintillation. Only a fool drives. Stumble out of the car with cinders in your sockets. A flash off the lake will print your shadow on the wall forever. Must be lunchtime. Set out front in a lean-back chair with a can of Vie-eena sausages and a plastic thermos top of warm sugary coffee, or baloney and cheese and crackers and a cream soda, or a slice of Wonder Bread covered with mayonnaise and rolled up in a tube to bite in half.

About this time something darker than sex lets go in the Mississippi brain. A basalt gland, a venous network of black bubbling fluid, way thicker than blood, stiffer even than frozen tar until the right heat hits. Is it a web of nerve and sense, a vision unseeable until raw flame cooks the apparent earth away? Is it a plasma, rather, a pumped injected flow, lava hormone?

But then they understand unreality. No human can live out there in that air and sun. Their state has become the surface of a star. Stay in your cool cubicle under the front porch roof, or in your raggedy cylinder of shade-tree shade. Suspended animation. Out there the bass hum of The Other Stuff. The flies have gone atomic, rocketing orbital quantum particles you see like dots in the dazzle, singing. The clank of giant mosquitoes off in the swamps, waiting for cover of evening to come suck your soul. Fat moccasins throbbing beside the ditch, bawoomp bawoomp bawoomp. Something has *made* your world and not particularly with you in mind. Now they are breaking it down to basic flame, and maybe it will still be Mississippi when they get through with it and maybe it won't, and maybe you'll be a greasy picture on some green lizard's wall, the way the world might be if it wasn't a lizard's world, something to laugh at torn from a magazine.

And in this unreal stupor, rolling the crumbs of gristle and suet around a tongue in a soup of tepid caffein, nigger and noggle are one and the same, did they but know it. Noggle being a No-Good Goddamn Lap-Eating (White Man). They are not but one race with the one black blood that is not blood between them. It is the same grandfather's face under the tractor cap, one dark and one pink, it is the same voice telling jokes, and the same hot world they see. The little frail deacon in his boxers and underwear should be rolling with naked big fat momma smearing her juices all over his whiskery face and Jimmy Lee Vandeventner, sixteen-year-old deb, should be snoozing with her cute nose jammed in old Chicken Itchy's sweaty grizzled armpit, his big black dick rolling rubbery on the left-hand cheek of her pearly little ass as he snorts and snores. Or down in the library black Professor Morton T. Headbone says to his little white professor friend, "Dr. Rambustious, this here deconstruction stuff is nothing but a load of crap put out by them damn effete Northeastern pinko intellectuals. It is no more than a perfectly obvious and trivial fact which anybody who has ever tried to make any sense about anything has run into, a perfectly trivial fact I say elevated and inflated to the spurious realm of philosophy," and little white bearded twinkling-eyed wise Dr. Rambustious pats his companion's monstrous waddling fanny like a football player and says, "Yassuh, brother Headbone, you sholy right about that, you sholy is, yassuh yassuh yassuh." Or the black insurance man says to the corporate controller, "I ain't gone lie to you, boy, yo rates a going up. You show a three-year experience increase averaging 41.4 percent with no increase in contracts, and when you adds in the mandated major medical at 80 percent for mental and nervous even without retention you can see we lost our ass on you last year," and the controller answers, "Well, you've always been honest with us brother Elmore, so I guess we will just accept your increase as proposed." Or Leonard the garage mechanic says to Boston B. Coon, billionaire black banker from out of town whom however redneck Leonard don't know he has any money at all, driving as he is a rusty '65 chevy and wearing overalls, Leonard says: "Well we broke your carburetor down but it turn out to be your pcv valve blowing oil into your air intake so we ain't gone charge you for the carburetor only the valve, which is $18.34 overall."

But that ain't what we have is it? That ain't what they want, the big mechanical mosquitoes out in the swamp, the clanking alien bugs that tear down our world every day and build it back as ugly as they possibly can. They want the wound, the middle wall of partition, the whole state a landing strip for bug-eyed devils from hell in flying saucers.

Because all of that heat and vision, that was really the Old South wasn't it, horrible with hope. With what could be if we could have burned till hate was burned away. One mind, one speech. A home for a way of loving, a territory for a way of seeing.

No, that ain't what we have. The bugs made us a New South. A New Improved South, with everybody cool in their own big buildings. With everybody talking about what the New South means, like everybody else in all the other new new things are always chattering away about what it means to be a part of the New New Thing. And I'm setting here thinking of the old old story. We have integrated schools in the new new thing. We have equal opportunity employment. All good things to have, sholy, and way too long in coming. But it ain't like it all ended without ever healing, is it? It ain't like the crime quit without neither punishment nor forgiveness, is it? Don't nobody hate nobody no more, do they? Americans aren't getting more and more fat and vicious and sullen, are they, feeling like something has gone wrong but they don't know what, feeling like things have gotten out of hand, empty and nasty and speeded up? It ain't like the koo-koo klux klan could start right up again, only this time all over America. It ain't like some invisible huge bug out there in the shimmering Venusian heat is whispering *Hate. Hate. Hate* into our mental ears, is it? It ain't like we hate our jobs and hate our families and wish we had a more expensive car and eat cancer and wear clothes that choke us and hate the insolent naked teenagers we go to the movies to see naked and having more fun than ever we did if you can believe the lies of the old jerks our age that made the movies.

We ain't spoiling for a fight, are we—any kind of a fight, a fight with anybody, Arabs or commies or Cong or terrorists.

What we have is not Pentecost of noon after all, but the high hot unreal time backing off a little by 2:00, and then by 4:00 maybe even only 97 degrees or so, livable flame. Drink some beer and baste in your own juice awhile.

What we have is summer cooling down like so, till our minds come back from the other side, and we find ourselves back in our old familiar personalities, except with our suit-coats stuck to our backs. We're watching the lawyers coming out of Judge Mize's courtroom, where all the way through June and July the Meredith case gets delayed. Hearing dates are set and then changed, until finally it gets itself put off on into August, too late for a settlement that would allow James Meredith to attend Ole Miss in the fall. Along the way we have had the pleasure of hearing one of the registrars allow as how he isn't really *sure* whether or not there are any blacks attending Ole Miss already, since there are people there of "varying degrees of color."

Or maybe one day in early August we're sitting down in the basement of the bank with Roger while Buddy Buck says, "What gets me is the way this Franz Boas fellow infiltrated *all* the universities without anybody noticing it. Not one single solitary soul. The communists always said they would conquer us without a shot being fired, and this is the way they do it. They're going for the minds of the children. They're poisoning all our ideas. Like Festrich says, as far back as fifty years ago that McShuey fellow had *proved* beyond a shadow of a doubt that a Negro's I.Q. was ten to fifteen points lower than a white person's. You might not like it, but there it is, it's a scientific fact, and there's no use arguing with it. So the way the communists work around that, how would you do it? Oh, it was brilliant, I give them that. You start with the so-called experts, you take a bunch of these anthropologists, and they are supposedly the ones who know. So they spread throughout the world preaching their humanist gospel, everybody is exactly equal. You dilute the minds of the young with ideas like that, and you weaken their resistance. Take control of all the media you can, like even at Ole Miss this Barton fellow that was the communist who belonged to the NAACP, and what was he? The editor of the campus paper. And the next thing you know every liberal in America just bleeds for the poor Negro. And your own children get confused, because they are good-hearted kids, and when their *professors*, that they look up to, when *these* people are telling them that stuff. Because you are a young man, Roger, and I was too, I know it can be confusing. I'm just saying consider the words of somebody who has been there. Because you want to love everybody. But when you look at it from the point of view of efficiency, which you can bet your bottom dollar that's what the communists are doing. And I know about efficiency, because I run a bank. And I can tell, what they are counting on is when everybody in America is averaged out according to the false gospel of this humanistic evolution theory equality stuff, when the white man isn't doing what he is best at and the colored man isn't doing what *he* is best at, well then you are not being efficient, my friend. And you better believe me, Buddy Rough, when that happens, they are just going to march right in here ripping off our eagles and seizing our asses."

And Roger saying mm-hmm, oh, and hmpf! and not looking at Buddy Buck because he doesn't really agree, but he doesn't want to contend. Because the only way to contend is to say, "You are a goddamned foul-mouth lying fool, and I am tired of listening to this crap." Certainly you will not reason with Buddy Buck. He is in *place*, he is in *his* place, and he has no doubts.

And finally quitting time and Roger gets on out of there. To home, where this day there is no peace, but a whirl of crowd and ambulance and police car and policemen, blinking lights and high contradictory gabble of arguing onlookers, doors open and two men in white hunched over fast-stepping a stretcher down the front stoop of the Gandys' building. It is Eleanor Roosevelt Gandy, who has washed her face with Drano. Rubbing until she cannot see, until her hands will no longer work. Yelling with pain, not screaming, but yelling without realizing it, thinking she's smiling and singing, until it doesn't hurt any more, and she *is* smiling and singing, although Mr. Gandy, breaking open the bathroom door, cannot tell that she is.

Then there is Mr. Gandy, face in his hands, saying to Roger when Roger pushes through the circling crowd, "You get out of here."

Not because he has found out about Roger and Eleanor Roosevelt, but because Roger is pink, his skin is pink, and his daughter has just been wheeled out saying, "When it grow back it a be pink. When it grow back it a be pink."

Home Missions

MR. BINGHAM, A.L. Gandy's supervisor, was a little white-haired pink-cheeked balding man, not above five feet four and with a round little belly he kept busily in motion up and down the corridors of the hotel. He smoked Camels in holders. I don't want to get him in trouble, but the truth is he defrauded an insurance company. Maybe the statute of limitations has run out. It has for everything else, so why not?

Mr. Gandy did not work a 40-hour week for the hotel. He worked a 33-hour week. This was true for many other Negroes across the state. This was explained as a fringe benefit, since it allowed these children of nature an extra hour a day to go home and follow their essentially amoral pursuits. See, you are not expected to furrow your brow quite so intensely as the white man. We know you like to have a good time. In fact, practically speaking, you cannot be expected to put in any work at all unless you are allowed a to have a good time on a regular basis.

It was of course ok to put in seven or more hours of overtime a week, which was paid up to ten cents an hour higher than regular time. In fact, you were encouraged to put in overtime. In fact, you had better do it if you wanted to keep your job. This was never stated outright, but it was not that hard to decipher the message. Mr. Bingham was not so strict about this as other supervisors, but his bosses had their expectations, too, and he had to keep them satisfied.

One of the largely unnoticed side-effects of the 33-hour work week was that you did not qualify for group health insurance, since at that time you had to work at least a 35-hour work week to be considered a full-time employee, and according to the master contracts of most of the companies chartered to operate in the state, group policy coverage was available only to full-time employees and their families. Since then the requirement has been lowered in most areas to something like 30 hours, I believe. Informally, the 33-hour arrangement served to identify and cull a high-risk sector of the population.

What Mr. Bingham did, first of all, was go to the hospital and sign the necessary papers to get Eleanor Roosevelt admitted. What he did next was go straight to the hotel. The night staff was on by now, but they were only mildly surprised to see Mr. Bingham, who was known to be a workaholic. Mr. Bingham went straight to work on A.L.

Gandy's timesheets. He was not one to suffer agonies of conscience. If you were going to do it, do it. By 6:00 in the morning, there was a clear record showing that A.L. Gandy had converted to full-time status as of the first of January, well over the required 90-day waiting period. There was also a parallel record of pay stubs showing that he had been paid as a full-time employee, and that the cost of a family contract had been deducted from his pay. Mr. Bingham had a completely separate budget for his area of the hotel's operations, maintenance, so all he had to do was square the new numbers with the monthly balances he had been showing. That's all. Get a C.P.A. to tell you how easy that would be. He managed a believable facsimile by morning. He also managed carbons of letters and forms to the insurance company canceling his own family contract as of the first of January and requesting the installation of Mr. Gandy's as of the same date. And that was about all he could do. The insurance company had not issued Mr. Gandy an I.D. card, of course, and they would have no record of any of the fictional correspondence. What one had to hope for was a settlement. Presented with the evidence Mr. Bingham had created, would they assume the simplest hypothesis, that they themselves had lost or misplaced the files? Would they prefer settlement and payment of claims to a court case? Mr. Bingham felt the odds were pretty fair, worth taking the shot. He was correct, and most of the claims on Eleanor Roosevelt were eventually paid. The Gandys were a lucky family.

The only other difficulty Mr. Bingham faced was his superiors' displeasure at his mismanagement in allowing Mr. Gandy on the full-time payroll in the first place, but he could survive that. It would be easy to demonstrate that Mr. Gandy was an unusually valuable and hard-working employee, and Mr. Bingham himself had 29 years of service with the hotel and was nearly irreplaceable.

The only guilt he felt on this particular morning was that he would not be at home to make breakfast for Mrs. Bingham. He normally brought her a small tray with juice, a soft-boiled egg with the top cut off, a sweet roll, and a pot of fresh coffee before he went to work. They would have coffee together and read the paper. Mr. Bingham ate breakfast at the hotel. Mrs. Bingham was five ten, and weighed about a hundred and fifty. Her voice would be soft and sleepy when he called later to wake her. Throaty and breaking, full of a drowsy hoarseness. "Hi, baby-boy," she would say, and yawn audibly. "I feel goooood today. Wish you were here." He sighed.

Mr. Bingham went to the restroom and shaved with the kit he kept in his desk. He washed his face and torso and changed into one of the fresh shirts he kept in the linen closet. He combed a few strands of his white hair back over the top of his head, patted his cheeks with aftershave, and went back and worked straight through to 5:00.

The Gandy family closed ranks, more or less. Life goes on. Life most cruelly goes on. What is it that does not go on? What is it that we stare at, there where someone important has disappeared? As if to stare into the other realm, to see just a glimpse of where they went, of what else there is. Older people, most especially, who have seen so much of disappearance. Mr. Gandy at 71, say, a lean old man with all his faculties. A harsh man, you might say, if you visited with him, a man who looked at you with a disinterested evaluating glance, as if you were a stranger and an interruption, although he had nothing to do with his time. A man who raked that glance over you momentarily and then went back to staring out over his nephew's yard there in Alligator, Mississippi. A man of small conversation. As if he were an Indian scout, peering intently out over the plains. In perfect stillness, but bringing all his experience to bear. A fierce and total concentration, waiting for the one clue, the one odd tiny detail that will tell him what to expect, what is going on. A focus of so many and such interrelated levels that he cannot afford to leave it in order to bandy idle chatter with you, and with the others who do not understand, to whom it would be impossible, for years yet to come, to explain.

Eleanor Roosevelt was in the hospital for a month and a half, finally coming home in mid-September. There was no question of her going back to school, in spite of the truancy laws. Technically she should have been either in some place like Whitfield or in a private sanitarium or in school. But they kept her at home, and no one ever bothered them about it.

She was permanently cheerful now, with wide pink or white-and-purple mottlings on either cheek and on her brow. Her hair had grown back in except where she had scarred herself above her forehead, and her mother kept it cropped close to her head for simplicity's sake. She had done such damage to her hands that they were extremely sensitive to pressure and to cold and heat. The cheapest and most effective way they found to protect her was with kitchen mitts, those mitten-shaped pot holders. She wore them everywhere around the house, wore them to shuffle through the pages of her movie magazines, or to help her mother fold towels. She became, in spite of her hands, very helpful. After a few years it was not even necessary to buy her new movie magazines. She was perfectly happy with her familiar stars. She had lost weight in the hospital, and now she stayed thin. She always did have a big butt, but she never got fat like her mother.

Wearing her mitts all day, she looked a lot like Mickey Mouse, except for the ears. Marcus had dreams of Mickey Mouse for fifteen years and never knew why. They were scary recurring dreams in which, sometimes, horrible things happened to Mickey Mouse and, sometimes, Mickey Mouse did horrible things, had slavering teeth and ate parts of his father or simply laughed and laughed in an unidentifiably frightening way.

Mr. Gandy did not entirely resign as head of the family, but he stayed out of things more, and when he did rule on an issue, he was harsher. He seemed angry, and yet he never spoke of his anger. He drew apart from his wife, who had begun drinking again. She had stayed away from alcohol since the first five years of their marriage. There had been bitter scenes back then, arguments every day. She had never been confident of herself. She thought she was ugly, and could not believe that Mr. Gandy really loved her. She drank every day, and got mean, and became convinced that he was running around on her.

"There ain't no other woman can *take* me away from you," he had said to her once, "but there's another woman could *chase* me away from you. And that's the woman you turn into when you drankin like this. I *chose* you, Snower Mae, and now you insulting me. Telling me I don't have no sense, lying in my face that I'm running around on you. Woman, *can't* you see you drinking the very same poison that's coming out yo mouth? Ain't nothing but hate-yoself there in that bottle, and you are drinkin it right on down. I'm on tell you once, I can't live with nobody that hates Snower Mae Gandy, not even if it is Snower Mae Gandy herself."

Snower Mae had turned to Jesus, and turned her back on the bottle. And now her husband took it hard that she had started back. Now when they needed each other most of all. She knew it drove a wedge in their feelings, but she went on and did it. Sitting there at the table blindly when she got home from work, drinking glass after glass. "Po little baby," she might say. "She hate her big lip so. Po little baby, haf to bear her ugly cross. Haf to be ugly like her momma. It's the sin on me. The sin on me has hurt the child. I known I should not ever marry, but Lord I wanted me a man. The sin on me."

Mrs. Gandy continued to work, but often now she went straight from the house in her belted-up houserobe and worn flat shoes splitting with swollen feet. Always before she had worn a clean dress every day, and white trim nurse's shoes with a good heel. Now even when she did wear a dress, it might as easily have come from the dirty clothes pile as from the line. At work, she did her chores about as well as ever, out of long habit, but she began to forget the ones she didn't want to do. She raided the liquor cabinets when she was alone in the houses, and she talked back when asked to do something extra. It would not be long before she began to lose houses.

Mr. Gandy felt betrayed. He gave up trying to ease her grief. He spent long hours in his library. He read the paper more intently than ever, and was highly critical of T.J.'s involvement with the NAACP. It wasn't that he disapproved of the work that T.J. did, but he demanded to know the details of everything, and nothing they did was as smart as it should have been. He always had something to say about the right way to do it.

T.J. grew up. Half of the time he did the meals, even after school started and he had homework and evening work at the NAACP headquarters. He gave up football, not much caring one way or the other how well Lanier would do without him. His coach was in tears, but T.J. just could not care any more.

He talked patiently with his father, though most of what he heard was criticism, and sometimes he had to go out and pound the wall till he could calm down. He came on to Marcus as though he were now the father. He absolutely would not tolerate playing hooky, he leaned on Marcus to do his homework and do it right, and he insisted that Marcus take over a large share of the housework. Marcus put on a small rebellion, but T.J. squelched it. He did not waver in his expectations, and he actually grabbed Marcus up a couple of times and turned him over his knee and spanked him.

Marcus was barely ten years old in late 1961, and he hadn't gotten his growth yet. He would not grow much until he hit fourteen, and then he would grow like a weed, pretty much the pattern of all the Gandy men. And he was thin. As a result, he felt himself very small in a land of giants. Even his sister was nearly a whole foot higher, and his mother, though a good four inches shy of six feet tall, carried nearly the weight that Mr. Gandy did. Marcus talked tough, but way in the back of his mind he saw himself as a tiny ridiculous piping figure, scuttling between the ankles of larger beings. In his dreams, that's who he was, a little rabbity boy who could be terrorized by even a weird and ear-less Mickey Mouse.

That sense of his small nature stayed with him for years, long after he was a full-grown man, six foot four like his brother and able to press his weight plus 113 pounds.

The first spanking was a big turning point for Marcus, a big shock, and not all to the good. There was nothing unfair about what T.J. had done, but suddenly Marcus had lost a hero and gained a tyrant. He was alone in the world. His sister was spacey and out of it forever, his mother lost in drink, his father fierce and unapproachable. And T.J. took no shit. Every hand turn hard.

And as for Roger: the rest of that summer and into the last of the year he kept away. It wasn't so much that Mr. Gandy had ordered him off: it was that a smell of trouble and sorrow hung over the Gandy household, and he instinctively avoided them.

He had a regular job, and his savings account kept growing. Every time it hit 800 dollars, he took 400 out and bought some silver, or put it into one of the funds that Buddy Buck recommended. He wasn't thinking of silver as an investment. He just liked having some solid cash.

He bought himself a tv.

He had a regular lover.

"I'm not exactly in love with you, you know," June said one time.

"I know."

"I don't mean I don't love you. You feel really good to me. But. I don't know. It's not very nice, I guess, but I'm not thinking of getting married."

"I'm not either."

"We're really two very different kinds of people," she said.

"I know," Roger said.

He knew what she meant. He was not sure her family knew he even existed. She had her own home, not far from her parents' house, but they had only gone out to it a couple of times. It was a brick three-story with high Colonial pillars. The floors were polished oak, and the carpets were old and oriental. There was a lot of brass, and it all looked new. There was a twelve-foot table in the dining room, which was across the hall from the kitchen.

"I want to redo this someday," she had said in the kitchen. "Something more modern." Two long counters ran along either wall. The walls were of bare unfinished brick, and on one of the walls two huge old ovens were built in, venting up through chimneys of the original brick. A colored woman who was cook and maid sat smiling and nodding on a high wooden stool. "This is all so antebellum-ish, and it isn't really an antebellum house. It was my cousin Duncan's house before he died in the war, and I think he just let his mother do it however she wanted it done. And I like the house, but it isn't my kind of kitchen. It's Duncan's mother's kitchen."

They had made love in the high old four-poster bed upstairs. Satin sheets, and more big soft pillows than all of the pillows in all of the rooms of his stepfather's house. The mattress a cloud, and made cloudier still by a wonderful old comforter. That was the height of something for Roger, the best that making love could come to. Deep in a woman, naked and swaddled in comfort, serene and cool and rocking, high upstairs in a quiet old house.

He was calm now that he was getting some regular pussy. He could take it with equanimity that theirs was not a romance for the ages. He saw that you could get what you needed without having to have a romance for the ages, without bribing fate. He was able to think ahead, to think that there might be more of this out there, other women who found him desirable, other warm beds to take and give pleasure in.

A curious thing happened. He grew two inches. He was nineteen, and he had not grown since the age of sixteen. He had assumed that five foot seven and three-eighths inches was it, although he had a feeling his real father had been much taller. It was strange not to know how tall his father had been, but his mother did not like to talk about those days. Once he had asked her and she had said, "Tallish—it doesn't matter." Another time he had asked her, and she had said, "He was a lot bigger on the outside than he was on the inside."

Now here he was, nearly five nine and a half. Wow. He figured it was the sex that had done it.

June didn't like going over to Roger's studio anymore, in spite of the fact that she liked the studio itself. She didn't feel safe in the neighborhood. In fact, after a year of peace, there had been a brick or two in the night. Roger had had to replace his window once. He had put in safety glass, and the new glass now showed a couple of radiating scars. He had thought of it as simple vandalism, despicable but normal. June made him think, for the first time, that it might be racial. She thought he ought to move out. He was making good money now, he could live in a better section of town. He considered it.

They wound up making love at the bank a lot, late at night, down on the cot in the security room. It was ok, but it was missing something. That may have been one of the reasons their love affair did not feel fated. It's hard to feel fated on a cot in a back room.

Roger Tutwiler walked in on them once. Coming back late to do some extra work, he heard a noise and went downstairs to check it out. June was on top, riding hard, her legs astraddle the sides of the narrow bed, grinding herself chock-full. She heard the door open behind her and turned her head but could not quit. She saw Roger Tutwiler recognize her, but then there was another shift in his face, a second shock, like a deeper recognition. She couldn't blush because she was red all over already, even her hips. His eyes fell to those driving hips. He didn't go away, he watched. Roger Wing's eyes were closed, and he was completely unaware. *"Oh,"* she protested, *"Oh oh no oh go—oh nooooooh."*

She collapsed on Roger Wing's chest, panting. She refused to look around to see if Roger Tutwiler was still there. He was. He looked at the hairy root of Roger Wing's dick, where it went in. Roger Wing opened his eyes and saw Roger Tutwiler. "Uh-oh," he said.

"Don't worry," said Roger Tutwiler, and closed the door, and went upstairs to work.

Leon Cool had not forgotten The Black Shadow League, but it had been put on hold. His mother had asked him to come back to L.A. for a while, so he had been out of town all summer. He missed the excitement over Eleanor Roosevelt. When he came back, she was already home from the hospital, and T.J. was acting uppity. Didn't want any smoke, didn't want to knock around, and acted like *he* was giving the orders. But by then Leon didn't need T.J. anymore anyway. Leon had money now, and he had a plan to get more.

Leon's mother had missed him. She had begun remembering him as a shy little boy following her around the house. She wondered if they couldn't get back to that place again. But her invitation had come across more like an imperial summons. Leon was tired of being ordered around. He couldn't seem to break free. Everybody ordered him around. He was tall and smart and good-looking and he had a special fire, but everybody ordered him around. Or put him off and put him down, like Mr. Big with the Niggers who Always Act like Christian People. There, see. Tole you I was smart.

Now here his momma's letter with the bus money. Bus money, shit. Be a 30-hour trip. Fun. Keep the damn money, don't go. But he knew there would be no more monthly allowance if he did that. Well go then. Besides. Might be a way to make some money out there. Sell some shit or something. Sho can't make a livin here. Yeah. He would go. Keep the money and hitchhike. No way. Cops a never let you out a the state.

He went out on the bus. And until they passed into Kansas, he rode in the back of the bus.

There was a big billboard coming into L.A. It was a gigantic billboard. It had been erected by Ford Obsolete. It said, *Save the Nation. Impeach Earl Warren.*

Leon did make some money selling some shit. But he and his mother got into a tremendous argument, and he got so mad at the world in general that he cheated his supplier. He lifted a couple of extra lids and stowed them in his jacket pockets. The fellow tracked him down, and *they* had a big argument. In Leon's mother's kitchen. With her standing there aghast. Hearing this shit, knowing she was going to cut him off. He and the supplier had been friends in the past, so the man didn't threaten him with a gun or a blade or anything, but he took a big swing at Leon's head. Back in Jackson, Leon had been practicing moves like the moves he had seen Roger Wing making. Like shadow-boxing. He was a good mimic, and he got the feel of some of the moves right, not that he really knew what he was doing. Now, instead of ducking, he stepped inside the punch and chopped his friend in the throat. It worked because it was not anything that the man had been expecting. The man went down. He bucked on the floor, his eyes rolling back.

"Don't mess with Leon," Leon said to him, standing in a clenched crouch like an angry Green Lantern or Superman. The man quit flopping around. His eyes were locked back in his skull, only the whites showing.

"Fuck you, bitch," he said to his momma. "This is the last I'm on do for you," he said, and dragged his friend's body to the window. He went through the pockets, helping himself to the roll he found, and the spare lid of grass. Then he heaved the body up, and over the sill. It caught on the wreckage of the fire escape, then slowly, slowly dragged over a snagging spear of twisted re-bar. Finally it let go, and dropped two more stories to the street, arms and legs wombledy-bombledy. Whap. Down like a *rock*.

It was the finest thing Leon had ever seen. He was exhilarated. But it had been over so quick. He hadn't realized that a fall was so quick.

You didn't get a chance to enjoy it, really. It sliced through your attention, and whap. Just as you were about to get ready to *really* watch it. But fine.

"You don't know nothing now," he said to his momma. "Po-lice won't bother you now. This the last time I'm on see yo ugly face."

He went by his friend's place. The man's girlfriend and little brother were there. They watched silently as Leon went through everything. He found it up under the couch, in the springs. About five pounds of grass already stemmed and rolled in separate little baggies. A nickel-plated .45. Leon stuffed the cache in the bottom of his duffel bag, went to the bus station, and bought a ticket for Jackson, Mississippi.

He did not sleep on the way back. He was too high, without even getting into the dope. He was one of those strange people with glittering eyes you sit next to sometimes. They talk to themselves. You get up and sit somewhere else. Leon was laughing to himself. He was saying, "Leon killed his man."

This was not true. The jolt of hitting the fire escape had somehow cleared his friend's trachea. He damaged three vertebrae and broke one arm and one leg. He wound up with a bad limp and a back brace and continual pain in his back and a long diagonal scar across his chest where the re-bar had sliced him open, but he lived. The experience changed him. He saw that it hadn't particularly been Leon, it had been his own way of life that was to blame. Sooner or later, somehow or other, something like this was bound to happen. Maybe worse. He could have been dead. He had been living scared as an outlaw anyhow. Didn't have the temperament for it. He changed his ways, without knowing exactly how to do it. He combed the town until he got a shitty job that was, for him in his crippled condition, nearly an hour's walk away. The walk turned out to be good for him, a sort of informal physical therapy, and it cleared his mind as well. He kept the job for years, made friends, and finally wound up with a better job, making almost 10,000 a year. When the Southern Baptist Convention began their big metropolitan push in the mid-'60s, he found a focus. The Baptists had always had Home Missions, but it had been a sleepy division specializing in providing help to little bitty understaffed country areas in the South. Foreign Missions had always been the glamour branch. Now they began to realize that there were American cities as foreign and dangerous as Africa or Brazil. They set up a mission in Los Angeles near Leon's friend's home, and he became a

Christian. He never saw Leon again, but he prayed for him for years. Leon, from the Arkansas line on in, rode in the back of the bus.

Killer

IN OCTOBER, a policeman found it necessary to defend himself against Eli Brumfield, who had thought he was just passing through Mississippi. Brumfield did not survive the defense.

In October, 400 students boycotted Jackson State because Jacob L. Reddix had suspended the SGA and kicked out its president. He had taken these measures because the SGA had continued to get involved in all of these unseemly protests and demonstrations that made life difficult for the Negro by arousing the ire of the white man. Jackson State had finally got radicalized. It was finally catching up with Tougaloo.

In October also, Leon Cool showed up one Saturday with two companions at Roger's studio. It was the day after Race and Reason Day, starring Carleton Putnam. Leon was ready to start The Black Shadow League. One of his companions was the man who had put the knife in Elrod's throat.

Roger went numb all over, but it was an odd, buzzing numbness, almost electrical. His skin tightened to gooseflesh, and a chill racked his spine like the wave in a whip. His pupils were pin-point, and he was whiter than typing paper. Not that Leon or his friends paid much attention to differences in the shade of a white man's skin.

All Leon knew was this honkie was tight, way tight. He had a edge on him he didn't have when Leon had tried the sap. He looked good and dangerous, and Leon was glad, because he wanted to impress the boys. He put a twenty down on the sill of the big window. "We gone pay for em one lesson at a time," he said. "That way everybody's fair."

"That ain't enough," Roger said, jerking his head to look at the bill. His mind wasn't on the twenty, and he didn't give a shit about conducting any kind of fart-ass karate clinic for Leon's Losers, but he had to keep the situation going while he figured out what to do.

"All right, my man," Leon said grandly. He pulled out another twenty and put it with the first one. "I thought you might say that. But there ain't no point paying more for something than you have to, is there? That ain't the way the rich man got rich, is it?" He smiled. He waved Roger's eyes back to the two other men. "This here's Clovis, " he said, indicating a man Roger never even saw, "and this here's Killer."

"What?" Roger jerked his eyes away again, back to Leon. He was outraged. "*What?*"

"Whoa dere, Rastus," Leon said. "They just call him that. Name of Achilles, you can see why. What's up witch you, brother?"

"What's his—what's your—what's y'all's addresses? I need your, for my files. I got—wait." Roger ran to his valuables box and pulled out copies of the insurance claims forms he had been issued the week before by the bank.

"Hey man, this say Blue Cross," Leon said.

"I know. It's for if you get hurt, like a form for we're not responsible if you get hurt, you know."

"Disclaimer."

"Yay-o. I couldn't think of the word to save my life."

"Look like a claim form to me, man."

"Well, it's all they had. I can change the information over later, but I like need your names and addresses and signatures and all."

"I ain't got no address," Killer said, taking the form Roger held out to him. He looked Roger straight in the eyes, his eyes flat, unreadable. It was that no-expression look that somehow manages to be just short of insult. He crumpled the form in one hand. Never taking his eyes off Roger, he pulled his waistband open and jammed the crumpled paper in down to his balls. He cupped his balls in the hand with the paper and rubbed the crackling paper around on them. He pulled it out and threw it at Roger's face.

Roger did a strange thing. He attacked the *paper*. He blurred into a front snap kick. The paper disappeared. It didn't tear or get knocked looping away. It just disappeared. Roger never found any of it. It was weird, like he had kicked it into hyperspace. It was no place for a miracle. This one was too small, and it didn't contribute, but there it was.

Since it was so small, they acted like it hadn't happened. "He's a cop, man," Killer said to Leon. "Let's leave." He said it with a look at Roger that meant, I'll take care of you later.

"No, wait," Leon and Roger said together. They both had reasons to want to keep it going.

"I'm not a cop," Roger said, at the same time realizing that in a way he was. "We can skip the forms for now, I guess. I'll need em later. You want a lesson?"

Leon held onto Killer, talked him into staying. Killer wasn't really worried about cops, but the way Roger had been staring at him, he figured the man was insulting him. That was all. Ain't gone let the man get in *my* face. Killer knew the cops weren't going to mess with him. He was too mean. Made his own knife. File down a saw-blade, wrap wire around and around and around two pieces of flat wood for a handle. Wrap that wire tight as a mother. Sharpen up the blade with a whetrock. Wicked blade, thin and flexible.

It was a strange lesson. All Roger wanted to do was keep them there till he could figure out what to do about Killer. Realizing he *couldn't* figure out what to do before they went, he wanted to make sure they came back. He had learned that people wanted to go right to the blows and kicks. They were not patient with stretches, warm-ups, and meditation. Normally he insisted. Today, he went immediately to the action stuff.

"Try yo knife on im," Leon giggled when Killer acted bored. Roger gave Leon a hard look.

"You don't go bringing a knife into a lesson," he said. He was sweating, and he had relaxed. The exercise had calmed him. Even in the presence of murder, the forms of his discipline had cleared his thinking and steadied his heart. "A knife is serious stuff. This is *practice*. It isn't that it isn't for real, but it's *training*. When you bring in a knife or a gun or anything, training is over. You don't practice on somebody with a knife. You don't pull back. You don't try not to hurt em."

Leon smiled. He was thinking, Keep on talking, white man. Keep on laying down the law to Leon. Yo time is coming. But he had a plan and he knew he had a plan, so he could smile.

"Something wrong with this. Something wrong with this chicken-shit white man," Killer said. "Damn hi-i-i kachoppy shit."

"I think it's interesting," Clovis said. He was a medium-height wiry Negro with a friendly face and a mustache. He should have been called Uncle Jim, because he had an uncle mustache and he was a nice guy.

"See how high I can kick?" he said, unlimbering a long-legged if unfocussed and rubbery kick that did indeed sail a good foot over his own head. "I use to be a drum major," he added.

"You a damn fool, too," Killer said.

"Pretend you have a knife, then," Leon said. He wanted Killer knocked on his ass like he had been. He wanted to solidify his control. He wanted to use Roger as a surrogate for his own dominance.

Roger was wondering how much of a game they were playing. Did they know he knew about the murder? Were they in cahoots, and were they toying with him? Or maybe they weren't *sure* he knew, and all this knife business was just a way to test him.

He decided that wasn't real. If they really thought he knew, or even just thought he *might* know, they would have sneaked up out on the street and slid a knife into him. And there was no reason for Leon to be in on it with Killer. The killing Roger had seen had been spontaneous. There had been no motive. It had been like throwing firecrackers at children when you drive by. It was something Killer had done when he was doped up, and Roger was sure he hardly ever thought about it. Maybe it wasn't the first time Killer had murdered a bum. Maybe he caught cats and cut them up.

But Leon was definitely up to *something*.

In all of this, Roger was not thinking of Elrod, except in a marginal, abstract sort of way. Elrod was dead. What there was now was the situation his death had made. Roger was caught in his responsibilities to the situation. That was not at all the same thing as sympathy for the departed, he was learning. Sympathy was quick and easy, it hurt, but it hurt good and let you go on your way. The need for right action never let up. It was another thing the whirlpool did to you. Freedom was being small, being out of it, freedom was when it didn't matter what you did. Elrod had been free. He had disappeared down the center of the vortex. Now here was this mean nigger, Killer, whipping in crazy orbit close in to the core. He was breaking apart without knowing it, he was throwing off intense radiation.

"I ain't pretending nothing," Killer said. "I'm thoo with school." Roger shivered with *déjà vu*. This had happened before, but when? The weird sense of repeated time seemed connected somehow to all the other weirdness: like a power shunt was running from the night of the murder to now, warping time and space around it. Moonlight and shadow, Captain Mississippi and the alleyway and the glittering knife, all somehow existed right now, in a pocket of this bright day.

"I want some a that shit you was promising me," Killer said to Leon.

"Shut up," Leon said angrily. "Come on, then, we'll go then if

146

that's what you want." He waved at the two twenty-dollar bills, still on the low windowsill. "There's more where that come from," he said to Roger.

After they left, Roger walked down to the grocery store. He went the long way around so he wouldn't have to go by where Elrod had died. He called the police. He had to get change from one of Leon's twenties to do it.

"There's a man out here who killed another man," he said to the man who answered the phone.

"Out where?" the man said. "Who's calling?"

"I don't know where exactly, I don't think he has an address, I think he just bums around. Out near Smith's grocery store, near Valley Street, in that neighborhood."

"When did this happen? I can have a car out there in three or four minutes. Where are you? Is the killer still in the vicinity?"

"No. I mean yes, I think he is, but it didn't just happen, it was a few months ago."

"And you're just now calling? Hey, bud, you trying to get somebody in trouble?"

"No, this is a real murder. Listen, it happened like a week before Christmas. His name was Elrod something. Out near Smith's grocery."

"What's going on, buddy? That's almost a year ago. Wait a minute." Roger heard the phone put down on a wooden desk. There was the background crackle of papers, an occasional voice cutting across the humming silence. The aural smell of another place on the line. A thing that hold and call-waiting have taken from us and replaced with Hawaiian music from the Phantom Zone. Roger would have sworn that he could hear the silence of the desk, the lives in its files. Were they tracing his call? No, that was Dragnet stuff, that wasn't real.

"Is your name Roger Wing?" the man said, back on the line. How had they gotten that? He had never talked to the police. He felt the drag of the whirlpool. Paranoia lifted his hairs.

"No," he said, "my name is Leon Gandy."

"Yes, well, Roger—"

"Leon."

"Right. I tell you what, friend, we have that death listed as an official suicide."

"Suicide? He was stabbed in the throat, man!"

"Roger, I'm just telling you what the file says the coroner said. You want to get that changed, you welcome to try. But there ain't no evidence left. The only thing there is is what you say. You willing to testify?"

"Leon."

"You willing to come in and make a statement? Because otherwise this case is closed. Listen—Elrod was colored, right?"

"Yeah. So what do you—"

"What about the guy you say wiped him? He colored, too?"

"Yeah, but what's the point?"

"Well Roger Leon Gandy-Wing, the reality is that you being white—you are white, ain't you?—your testimony might have a pretty good chance against the killer's. But what *is* the point, that's my point. They have their ways. What's the point of you messing around into it?"

"Goddammit, I'm getting sick and tired of all this goddamn *bigotry* shit!" Roger squeaked. "Elrod was a sweet old guy even if he was worthless, and the meanest son-of-a-bitch who ever lived stuck a knife in him for no good reason, that's why!"

"Watch who you call a bigot, nigger-lover," the cop said calmly. "You livin in a bad neighborhood, Leon. I would be moving out of there if I was you. It could be hurting your reputation, you know."

"Fuck my reputation," Roger said.

"Yeah. Everybody hates the cops. You could have spoke up when this happened. Take a look at yourself. Listen, I got business here. The way it is, you want to make a statement, you come on down. You know where we are."

He hung up.

Roger looked at the phone. He wanted to bang it on a rock. He called Patsy.

"Roger!" she said, and her voice was full of delight. "I'm so glad to hear your voice. We *are* still friends, then? You don't hate me?"

"No, I don't hate you. I understand why you did what you did." Roger was frustrated. He felt wrapped in a cloud, a thick slow fuzzy cloud that impeded his movements. He didn't want to say these words, he had words he needed to say, and here he was having to run through this rigamarole before he could get to what he wanted to say. He was out of practice with these words.

"Oh, I'm so *glad,*" Patsy said. "Because I think, when it is the Lord's will, it always is for the best, don't you think, even if we think maybe it is not quite what we thought it would be like. Or don't you think so?"

"That's what I wanted to talk to you about," Roger said, seizing the conversation. "The Lord's will. I have got a situation where I don't know what it is, and I need to talk to a good Christian about it."

"Have you prayed about it yet?" Patsy said.

"I haven't had time to pray about it yet."

"Roger, there's always time to pray."

"For crying out loud, girl!" This was the manliest thing Roger had ever said to Patsy, the first time he had refused to defer to her. He was changing, and whether it was the regular sex or the extra two inches or having a job or the damage he was beginning to see in the lives around him would have been hard to say. Even with everything else that was going on right now, even with his heart still pounding away because of Killer, he felt the small shift down in his soul, the tiny reordering of his possibilities, a change on a scale as invisible as the switching of a gene in his DNA, and as thoroughgoing.

And while I'm thinking of DNA, I want to tell you they didn't have no genetic code in 1961. You want to remember that, brother.

> Didn't have no genetic code
> in 1961
> Nigger had to hit the road,
> white man had a gun.
>
> Send in yo hate to this address,
> we'll run it through the machine,
> we'll digitize yo lies I guess
> until they come out clean:
>
> truth enhancement for the asking,
> tv on the wall,
> cancer's answer, multi-tasking,
> super-micro-small ...
>
> Too bad the dead they had to die
> before we learned these tricks:
> I love a techno-moral high,
> gimme my future fix—
>
> I breathe an air that never was,

149

right and wrong go quaint,
my vision for South Africa's
sustained by things that ain't.

Naw, didn't have no genetic code
in 1961
Nigger had to hit the road,
white man had a gun.

Nigger, what *are* you doing? You got to quit this digressing. You got to *finish* this book. Blowing yo story-line like that. Must be crazy.

Patsy said, "I'm sorry, Roger. I was being awful prissy, wasn't I? Like some old preacher or something."

The truth is Roger wasn't about to take this to the Lord in prayer, and that was why what Patsy had said had bugged him so much. He had a gut feeling that taking this to the Lord in prayer wouldn't do a damn bit of good. And he wanted to talk to Patsy not because she was the best Christian he knew, but because she was the best moral person she knew. It wasn't that she couldn't fool herself. But she was straight-ahead with whatever she thought was the right thing to do. She didn't count the cost to herself.

"So what's going on?" she said.

"I know about something really bad that has happened. I mean, I know who did it, and nobody else does, and I don't know what to do about it."

Roger realized that what he was saying sounded like a bad suspense story on tv. He knew it wasn't, but he didn't know how to say it so that it didn't sound that way. That was a part of the cloud that was interfering with him. If he had known how to make it real, how to remove it from that realm of glassy fiction, then perhaps he would also have known what to do about it.

"How bad is it? I mean, is it like a crime? Can you like call the police?"

Go ahead and say it was murder, he thought. He saw the moonlight, the hand, the blade coming out of the throat. No, you can't do that. You can't do that to people. You can't just *kill* somebody.

He gagged on the words. He couldn't say it. He couldn't say it to her. The moonlight was his to bear, his to carry. The moonlight itself was like a blade, a blade in him, letting out his life, leaking his energy from its proper time into a scene that had happened nearly a year ago.

"It was real bad," he said. "Real, real bad. So bad you can't, you can't imagine it. I tried the police. They don't care."

"Oh, Roger, I don't believe that."

"You don't understand, Patsy. This isn't like some Dragnet story or something. I'm not lying about it. I can't go to the police, I can but it won't do any good, that's why it's so bad of a problem of the Lord's will for me, if I could go to the police then it would be all ok, it wouldn't even be my problem at all."

"Well I don't understand why the Lord would make it where you can't go to the police."

Captain Mississippi, he thought. I can't go because of goddamn Captain Mississippi. But he couldn't say that, and he felt guilty to have the secret, and again he took it out in anger.

"Well goddammit, Patsy, I don't understand it either, but that just gets into a whole lot of other questions I don't understand about how it could even happen at all and where have I been for twenty years and why aren't there rules for this stuff if it happens all the time, and you are just going to have to take my word for it."

"Sweetie," she said. Pause. "I can't really help you, can I? You sound so different. I don't have any experience with this kind of Lord's will. I have mostly been doing little stuff, I guess. Just kind of girl stuff. Are you safe? Is anybody going to hurt you?"

At the sound of her concern, something let go in his chest, and tears came into his eyes.

"No, I don't think so," he said. "I mean, I don't think anybody's going to hurt me."

"Sweet Roger. You sound so bad, like you feel so bad. I want to just kind of cuddle your face and make it ok. But I'm not really the kind of person you need, am I?"

"No," he said, and it was a curious relief to admit it.

"Are you crying?"

"Yeah, a little."

"I really love you, you know that?"

"Yeah, I know that."

"You know what I think you need? I think you need some old, experienced person to talk to. Somebody who's very wise, and who knows about this kind of thing and would understand why you can't go to the police. Do you know anybody like that?"

"Yeah," Roger said, surprised to realize that he did. "Yeah, I do. I *do*."

"Well, then."

"Wow," he said. "Boy, you helped. You really helped me."

"Really?"

"Really. I mean, you can't give me the answer, but what you said. Wow. It really does help. I feel a lot better."

"Oh, that's so nice. I guess when we ask the Lord, He doesn't give us His help the way we are expecting it, maybe. But if we just stay close to Him, and trust Him, He will provide."

"Yeah," Roger said.

They talked a lot longer, small things. His job, her classes. She was happy he had a girlfriend. "I'm so glad you called," she said, finally. "Don't be a stranger next time. Just because we aren't in love any more ..."

"Yeah. We can still be good friends. We can still love each other."

"Just not that way."

"Yeah, just not that way."

They were each suffused with a sense of the infinite possibilities of love, a sense of healing and plenty not unlike the vision that Mr. Blake had had a couple of years ago.

"Well, goodbye."

"Yeah, goodbye. Listen, I do love you."

"I love you, too."

"Goodbye."

"Goodbye."

"I love you. I'll see you," he said, but she had hung up.

Roger told his story to Mr. Gandy. They were sitting in the tiny library. Mrs. Gandy brought in coffee, just as though there would be brandy and cigars to follow.

"No, I don't know this Achilles. Nobody I know around here named that. He might be some drifter. How you know he kill Elrod?" Mr. Gandy was still stern and distant, as Roger had known he would be. But Roger had realized that it didn't matter how stern and distant Mr. Gandy was. Mr. Gandy had something he needed. Mr. Gandy was exactly the man to talk to, and Mr. Gandy's discomfort and Roger's own nervousness were not important compared to the importance of getting the right information. This was a revelation to Roger, even if he *had* realized it all on his own, this attitude toward getting a problem worked out. It was very much an adult attitude, and he was proud of himself for being able to have it.

"I don't want to say how I know," Roger said. "But I do know. I absolutely and for sure do know."

"And you want to set it right. See justice done. That what you wanting, that what's worrying you?"

"I don't know about justice. I don't want it to be where one man can just walk up and stick another man and he dies, and that's it. Everybody forgets it. He just walks away, and even he don't think about it anymore. That's it, that's all. Even if it is a bum. If I didn't know he done it, it would be all right with me, I'm sorry to say. I wouldn't worry about it. But I do know he done it. And it makes it like time don't count. Like nothing is written down, like the stuff that holds the universe together is coming apart, like anything can be anything else and it don't matter what happens. But I don't know about justice. Is that justice?"

"Yes," Mr. Gandy said, looking at him hard, "that's justice. And you don't believe this Killer-man is going to hell. You ain't willing to wait for God to punish him?"

"I don't know about that either. I don't *feel* like he's going to hell. I'm a Christian, but it don't seem like heaven and hell has much to do with it. He just walked away, like nothing happened. When I think of God punishing him, and that being the answer, it's like a cartoon in a comic book. I can see it in my mind, but it's like a story I'm reading. The real thing is him walking away like that. If God is going to step from behind a curtain and say, 'Surprise, Elrod's alive after all and is going to heaven, and Killer has to go to hell because he has been bad,' I don't know, that's like a game. You say, what's the point? It's too hard of a test to have that kind of a answer. And what would be even worse, what if Elrod had to go to hell, too, like for being a drunk or something. Down there with Killer all that time. I really am a Christian, but I'm starting to wonder if you don't have to decide whether you believe in justice or in heaven."

"And you ain't gone kill him," Mr. Gandy said.

"What?"

"I say, you aren't gone go out and kill him, are you? Take justice onto yourself?"

"Kill Killer?"

"That's what I say."

For the fourth time that day, Roger's head turned completely around. He had never even thought of himself that way, as someone who was physically capable of killing a man. For all of his years of training, he had not thought of it. He had beaten Leon up when Leon pulled a sap on him, but he had not thought of it. He supposed he had known it in an abstract way. But here he was, with his hands. He could do it. He could fix Killer good. He could murder the son-of-a-bitch. Jesus, that would feel good! For a moment he felt a wind of freedom and exhilaration blow by.

But then he realized that wasn't justice, either. That was just action and reaction, just cancelling-out. Killing Killer wouldn't have any more meaning than the murder of Elrod had. It would be like scratching a great big itch. Roger wanted more, wanted there to be a pattern, an order to things, something to depend on. He felt a responsibility to do something, but not something unilateral and solitary. The proper order of things was screwed up, suspended temporarily. He wanted to do something to restore that order, allow it to resume its natural course.

"No," he said at last. "No, I ain't gone kill him."

"Hm," Mr. Gandy said. He thought a while. He looked up at his books, as if he wanted to go look up the answer in one of them. Roger wondered if you could do that, if maybe something just like this wasn't written down in one of them somewhere, and what they had figured out to do about it.

"Those are all the choices you have," Mr. Gandy said finally. "For one reason or another, you don't feel like it will do any good to push it with the police. No, I agree with you. You got your reasons, but they ain't interested in what you're thinking of as justice, not these police, not right now. So anyway, that's social justice.

"And you don't believe there's going to be any religious justice. And what other source of justice is there? There's personal conscience, but Killer don't have any. And there's individual or vigilante redress, but that ain't acceptable to you.

"Son, you just going to have to let Elrod go. You done used up all your options."

Roger shook his head. He couldn't.

"I'm on say it ain't Elrod is worrying you any more, it's you. You know that, don't you?"

"Yeah, I know that. But it don't make anything any easier. It don't make it go away."

"You see a lot of grief after a while. Longer you live, the more you see happen you can't do anything about. Some of it you ought to be able to do something about, and you just ain't man enough, and some of it nobody could do nothing about. I tell you what whittles you

154

down, and that's not knowing which kind of trouble is which. The stuff on the borderline gets to you, it surely does. Grief is like a flood river that turns a hill to an island, and you standing on the island looking across at everybody else knowing you bed not try. And then it starts whittling down the island."

"But what am I going to do the next time Killer shows up for a lesson?" Roger said.

Mr. Gandy shook his head. He didn't want to talk any more. His eyes were shining, as though with tears. He saucered some of his cold coffee, blew on it.

Later, when he took Roger to the door, he said, "People like Killer find their own fate. I don't know if that will be any consolation to you, but he *will* have a bad life and a bad end. Nothing will have no meaning to him. What people like him do to people like us is like a accident. It's like a rock falling on you. It ain't good, but it ain't a contradiction either. You can't take it to heart. It ain't like a human has vanquished yo spirit. I don't know if all of that helps you. It's true, but it ain't justice, exactly."

When Mr. Gandy went to bed, Mrs. Gandy woke up a little. "Wha'd he want, honey-love?" she mumbled. A wall broke in Mr. Gandy's heart. It was the first she'd said to him out of sleep since Eleanor Roosevelt.

"He just want to talk," he said. "Nothing much. Just want somebody to talk to."

"Well I'm glad you getting back together," she said. He put his hand on her huge hip. "Mm," she said, and scooched up against him. It was the beginning of the healing of their marriage.

Roger didn't have to decide what to do about Killer next time he showed up. He never showed up again. Leon said he didn't know where he had gone, maybe he left town. He heard he did. Leon had replaced him with a wino, a grey-stubbled little man with wide hypnotized eyes who went through all the moves in slow motion. He was like a little grey shadow of Clovis and Leon and Roger, something thrown by moonlight and not really all the way real. *Wooo,* he would say, floating through a strike with slow, exaggerated steps, or doing an extra shuffling pirouette after a roundhouse back-kick, both arms out for balance. *Wooo. Wooo.* Maybe it was his version of the focus-cry.

Leon went through the sessions with a ragged ferocity. If sheer intensity could have made him good, he would have been a master in a matter of weeks.

Roger was planning to cancel out when T.J. showed up for one of the lessons. He was looking for something physical for release, now that he did without football. Roger decided to go along for a few more sessions. T.J. was slow, but smooth and patient, and Roger enjoyed working with him. T.J. began coming over in the evenings during the week as well, to share a short, relaxing workout.

Roger had been about to move, too, but now the rock attacks had stopped, perhaps because people could see him through the big window, working out with blacks. And 160 dollars a month more from Leon was really very nice, as much of a piss-ant as Leon was. It was easier to accept the money now that it wasn't paying for Killer. Where Leon was getting it, Roger had no idea.

June broke up with him in mid-November. "This is really starting to make me feel guilty," she said, holding her diaphragm up pinched to a boat-shape, "putting this thing in. It's all so cold. All we want to do is do it. We're just out for ourselves, and what we can get. It isn't like we can't resist it any more."

What she said was true. They had been watching more and more tv downstairs at her place, in front of the windows in a lighted room. She was sweet about it, but she didn't like his haircut and seemed embarrassed by his uniform. She wanted him to buy a good suit and some shirts and ties. She was starting to bug him about all manner of small things, like he had a cavity that needed filling and he sopped gravy with his bread. It was a novel sensation, being bugged by a lover. He had never before had the luxury. He had always been so desperate he didn't dare to let himself feel any irritation at all.

Their relationship had really not ever been the same since Roger Tutwiler had seen them down in the security room at the bank. Roger supposed that the shock of being discovered had made her feel ashamed and unclean, and that it had also taken away her sense of security in the security room.

Leon showed up at the bank one day. There he was, down in the basement. It was a shock. He wasn't dressed with his usual weird elegance. He was wearing some sort of green coverall with writing over the pocket, like an auto mechanic or janitor or something. He sat around awhile, watched tv, did a snatch or two of the monologues he thought of as small talk. Never gave a clue to what he wanted.

From then on, he dropped by at least a couple of times a week, never for very long, always in the green coveralls. When Buddy Buck or another officer was down there, he would fiddle with something on the shelves at the back of the room, and they never paid him any mind. He made Roger nervous, but there was no reason to tell him to leave. At least he didn't act uppity when Roger's bosses were around.

A pair of boots showed up in the closet, tall black leather boots. It was odd. Then a belt with a holster, no gun. Then a gauntlet, a white cavalry-style gauntlet for the right hand. Roger assumed they were Little Wide Load's, but he still couldn't figure out what they were doing there. Maybe they were appearing from the same void the wadded paper had vanished to.

When Roger had sought out Mr. Gandy's opinion it had broken the ice, and he was back in the bosom of the Gandy family, which helped him over the loss of his lover. He had lost two lovers, now. Wow. He was getting to be quite a man of the world. He guessed you could count Patsy, even though they had never quite done it. Until somebody told him different, *he* was going to count her.

The Gandys were doing better. Eleanor Roosevelt really did seem happier than she had ever been, in spite of her limitations. Mr. and Mrs. Gandy were loving again, though she continued to drink quite a bit. T.J. was coming along so fine. Roger was fun to have over for supper. "What was that?" he had said one time, wiping his mouth after a plate-full of rice with some sort of brown hamburger stew. "That was *good*."

"Oh that was skillet-full-of-doo-doo," Mrs. Gandy said, and then got embarrassed. "Oh, *my*."

"That's Marcus name for it," Mr. Gandy said, grinning like a fiend. "We all got to calling it that."

"What it look like," Marcus said, having another helping of it.

"Skillet-full-of-doo-doo?" Roger said. "Skillet-full-of-doo-doo?" He began laughing. Then Mrs. Gandy started to giggle. Then they were all laughing until they cried, saying "skillet-full-of-doo-doo" to each other and breaking apart with laughter, even Eleanor Roosevelt giggling and giggling. Marcus, dignified and solitary, ignored them all and went on eating.

Yes, things were looking up. Maybe the worst was over.

On December 12, Judge Sidney Mize ruled for Ole Miss on the injunction to allow Meredith to enroll immediately.

He was immediately overturned by the Fifth Circuit Court of Appeals, ruling in review. The Fifth Circuit Court said that segregation was "a plain fact known to everyone." It also noted that Jackson State was now an accredited school, which meant that Meredith could no longer be kept out of Ole Miss on the basis of invalid transfer credits.

And then one day not long before Christmas, T.J. came home from the grocery to announce that Reverend Smith had qualified to run for Congress. He was running against John Bell Williams.

Mr. Gandy, who had been critical of the NAACP for so long, was delighted. The Reverend was making good. He was going to be a candidate. He would actually appear on tv.

"Reverend Smith," he said, grinning and slapping his thigh. "Reverend Smith for Congress. Ain't that a killer," he said.

Americans

REVEREND SMITH never had a prayer. But it was something to see a black man on tv, a black man with dignity and reason in his voice. Roger brought his tv over, and though it had only a rabbit-ears antenna, the picture was very good. Channel 3 was inside the city limits. The Reverend had originally been scheduled for six appearances on Channel 12, but then they had chickened out, afraid that he and the Reverend would both get lynched by the peace-loving white people of Mississippi. That was funny, since WLBT and WJTV themselves often functioned as incendiary devices to the superatmosphere of methane floating up from the thought processes of the people of the state. It was funny to see the station manager afraid of what he had made. But funny or not, the Reverend had to go to the FCC to get air time, and what he wound up with was a couple of gigs on WLBT.

Roger left the tv at the Gandys', and now after supper they all had tv in the evenings. Mr. Gandy absolutely would not let him pay for his meals, not with them using his tv that way. Besides, Mr. Gandy had been promoted. Any black man who had earned full-time status had to have a lot on the ball, they figured, and with Mr. Bingham's concurrence, he had become second-in-command. Maybe soon Mrs. Gandy wouldn't have to work anymore. She could sit home and watch tv and drink her vodka like a white woman. Her drinking no longer threatened him. He saw she had been irretrievably hurt, long before he had met her, long before things had gone wrong for Eleanor Roosevelt. Let her soften the edges of the pain with vodka, then. She stayed blurrier, but happier and more gentle.

Roger stopped the karate lessons for Leon and his Black Shadow League. It was the first relationship he had ever ended. Always before he had waited until something happened or someone else dropped the hammer. Doing it gave him a tremendous surge of adrenalin. He felt immensely superior to Leon.

Leon said, "That's what I was gone tell you. I done learn all I need to know from you."

Another gauntlet showed up in the bank closet in February, and then a sword, a whole sword.

On the third of February, Sidney Mize pulled a judgment from the same place that the boots and gauntlets and sword had been coming from. Having ruled for Ole Miss on the injunction, he now ruled for them on the case itself. He declared that yes, segregation had once been a fact in Mississippi, but all that had ended with the Supreme Court ruling of 1954. Everybody got a good chuckle out of that. Supreme Court thought it was the law of the land, didn't it? So sholy, since they said segregation was unacceptable, Mississippi must have given it up right away. Oh, a good old involved Southern joke. The punchline? You don't get it?

So the Nine Old Men and the Interfering Do-Gooders (the IDG, also known as the Interfering Yankee Do-Gooders, or the IYDG) come back and say, Yeah, but you didn't *obey* us then.

And we grin, and without us saying it, you know we thinkin: So we gone obey you *now?*

And then there was a curious, dreamy lull, on through March and into the spring and the early summer. I don't mean nothing happened, but there were no murders and fewer head-crackings. There was a lot of rhetoric in the air, but most of the moves being made were legal moves. Interposition, the brainchild of Ross Barnett. Mississippi, like Jesus, interposed her precious blood. It was as if they believed interposition might really work, as if they might get away with it in the courts, and so could afford to not kill anybody. It was as if they believed their own bullshit. And they did. That is what you have to understand. Every mother's son of them could come up with some totally cynical theory or strategy that contradicted every other belief they professed, such as that Negroes were not as far up the evolutionary ladder as whites (when they could turn right around in Sunday School the next day and denounce evolution as a pack of godless communist lies), and crack bad jokes with other good old boys about how they were going to really put it to the Yankees with *this* trick—and then, when the pressure was on, they would *believe* themselves. They would turn around and there would be this enormous slick and steaming turd that they had just laid, lying there hot and fresh and shiny and big as a hump-back whale, and yum yum they would say, and slurp it right up, sliding it down small end first to swallow it whole and slippery. Oh I do love that good old Mississippi home-cooking.

It was a tingly interval, a time of gathering awareness. The Whippissippians had always lived inside each other's heads, that was the only way to make sure nobody was thinking wrong thoughts. I say Whippissippians, by which I mean White Mississippians, of course. There needs to be a distinction because the colored are Mississippians, too. But say "Mississippian" to yourself: Do you see a white man or a black man? You see a blond man in a white linen suit, that's what you see. That's the whole point. That's why I'm writing this book. Whippissippians and Blappissippians. Mississippians. Americans. America is Mississippi now. You don't think it is. You wrong. Start paying attention.

No it ain't why I'm writing this book. I don't know why. Won't know till I finish. Might suspect, but won't know.

So anyway. All over Mississippi little rabbit-eared boxes were pulling the story of Mississippi out of the air, and feeding it into the minds of Mississippians. They gathered around the boxes as if they gathered around a fire, but now there was no storyteller beside the fire, the fire had become the storyteller, and the fire had become no longer a fire. More electrons per second shifted position than there are words in this book, more than there are letters in this book, more than there are letters in all of the books of stories we have written, and as the electrons went, great waves went through space, meters and meters long, and something woke in the little boxes and something woke in our minds. The huge waves went through our bodies, went through Marcus and Mr. Gandy and T.J. and Snower Mae and Eleanor Roosevelt and Roger and Leon and Killer and June and Patsy and Little Wide Load and Johnny Vaught and Ross Barnett and Roger Tutwiler and Medgar Evers and Elrod's bones, went through Judge Sidney Mize and Sissy and Mr. Bingham, through James Silver and

John Doar and Evans Harrington, through Joe Patterson, Reverend Smith, Mosey Froghead, went up to Memphis and went through Elvis Presley and down to Gulfport and went through Johnny Wink, went all the way to Texas and went through Edwin T. Walker and maybe Chicago and went through Lerone Bennett, the huge waves went like the angels of the Holy Ghost, went through us and went on. And maybe if we made the tiniest imprint on those waves, cut the faintest shadow in that expanding front, maybe then there we are, 25 light years out in space, dancing the dance we thought was ended.

Maybe. But back in Mississippi, the waves went by, neutral as angels, and from the waves we fed the energies of whatever we already had in us. Hate added to hate, somehow, courage to courage, and hopelessness to despair. And everyone in the state felt everyone else out there in the darkness on the other side of the fire. It was a different sort of story. We were in this story. Were in it and therefore nearly helpless to see its next turn, much less change the direction of that turn, and yet we were trying, each of us, with all our will, to turn it our way, whatever that way was.

T.J. began to be frustrated. How could this silly stuff go on and on? How could the white men lie on the news day after day? Didn't the news have to be true?

He had been reading case reports for months now, of course, but that was different. That was cold print. Now, every evening, he saw living men, editorial reporters actually live, that moment, radiant with violent slander, like revivalist preachers on fire for Jesus.

He was a teenager. He was not patient.

He was still working out with Roger two or three evenings a week. "Sometimes I think ole Leon is right," he said one evening. "Black man gonna have to fight the white man in the streets."

"Leon wadn't never right about nothing," Roger said, grunting into a hamstring stretch.

"Leon ain't all bad. He's just confused."

"He's all bad," Roger said.

"No he ain't. He was sho right about me, you got to give him that. Ever since I stand up and speak for myself, everything been going my way. It all work out if you only respect yourself. Leon trouble is, he wants more than he is."

"Everybody wants more than he is," Roger said.

T.J. thought it over while he completed the same stretch as Roger, hands grasping his ankle, elbows up like wings, head resting on kneecap. "I don't," he said when he sat back up. "I'm happy just being T.J. Gandy."

"Yeah," said Roger, "but you already have everything. You're big and brown and handsome, you can have any girl you want, you're smart, you're going to have a good education—"

"I got good parents," T.J. agreed, "I'm coming into a time where the black man won't be held down so bad. Yeah." He did not argue the point about having any girl he wanted, although he was just now maybe about to get close to this one special girl at school.

"So you see," Roger said.

"I still like Leon. We had a fight now, but he was my friend when I didn't have no other friend."

"Be your own friend," Roger said.

T.J. was beginning to get irritated. "I didn't *say* we was friends now," he said. "All I *say*—"

"Ok, ok," Roger said.

This was the last day of May. Roger had not even seen Leon for nearly four months, though he understood that T.J. had been seen at Mosey Froghead's a couple of times, drinking a Coke while Leon sat beside him and drank a beer.

But he saw Leon the very next day, at work, as if his conversation with T.J. had summoned him.

The bank was robbed. An old black man shuffled in wearing cracked shoes and dirty work clothes so furred and imbedded with grime they had all turned the same sea-grey color. He wore a punched-out hat pulled down over his eyes, and one shoulder showed through his coat. He mumbled and shuffled right up to the counter. The ladies in line shrank back. Just as the teller was fixing to say, "Now, uncle, you'll have to go on back outside. No loafing in this here air conditioning," just then, the old man pulled a nickel-plated .45 from his baggy pants pocket and handed over a note.

"Don't nobody move," the old man whispered when he had the money. He backed up to the door to the rear exit, waving his pistol in both hands. He disappeared through the door just as the sirens began.

Roger had been down in the bathroom when the red warning light over the sink went off. He stared at it a minute, and then caught on. He charged up the front stairs, only to find that the bandit had already gotten away.

"Your fly is unzipped," said the teller who had been robbed. People were pouring into the lobby out of their various offices. A squad car pulled up out front.

"Oh shit," Roger said. He realized he had come up without his gun. He had let the thief escape, and now the police would see him without his gun. "Oh shit," he said again. "I'll be right back," he said and took off downstairs after the gun.

He charged straight into the room and into the closet where he kept the gun. Behind him, Leon said, "Howdy, Rastus. What's going on?"

Roger looked back over his shoulder. Leon sat on the cot, jaunty and neat in his green uniform. A lot of things ticked into new arrangements in Roger's head, all in the one moment. He turned with his gun in his hands.

"Just how much of a fool do you take me for?" he said, holding the .38 on Leon.

"Pretty much of one," Leon said, pulling his .45 from under his thigh and firing point-blank three times. "Yo fly is unzipped," he said, waiting for Roger to fall. When he realized he had missed, he pointed to fire again, but Roger had already flung his pistol into Leon's face. It bounced off his skull, knocking him flat on the bed. Leon grabbed his bleeding scalp, rolling over into a fetal curl. "Broke my head, you broke my head, broke my head head head," he was crying in a high baby voice, and he was crying tears, too, Roger could hear the rips in his voice. Blood was everywhere.

"Don't shoot im!" Roger said to the cops jumping into the room.

"Your fly is unzipped," said one of the big ones.

Roger was a hero. For a couple of days he actually led the news, until the fifth of June, when the Fifth Circuit Court reversed Sidney Mize. He was a modest hero, refused interviews and stayed off camera as much as he could. For one thing, he couldn't see where he had done anything heroic. It had just been some stuff that had happened, was all. It wasn't like he had saved a life with karate or anything. All he had saved was some money, and in fact, far from saving a life, he had really sent one to jail, even if it was one he hated.

For another thing, he was afraid to be noticed. He was afraid the cops would find out he was the same Roger Wing that was mixed up in the Elrod case. He had a bad shock as they were leading Leon out, a towel wrapped around his head to keep him from bleeding on their uniforms. Leon had quit crying. He was happy and haughty now.

"Leon planned it this way," he said. "It all a be just the way he plan." He was talking to the policemen, who were grinning as they hand-cuffed him. "The Black Shadow League gone spring Leon. The blood

will flow. Leon a martyr to the cause. The Black Shadow know karate.
Chop yo head off. Great White Ghost teach karate to the Black
Shadow. Yo own reject you. Leon kill his man. The blood will flow."

Leon's voice dwindled into the hall. Roger heard him shouting
something like *ha! ha!*, as if he were striking blows, and then as Leon
shouted again, he realized that was not right. "Hawk-aaa!" Leon was
calling out: "Hawk-aaaaaa!" His voice was cut off by a grunt of pain.

The cop remaining in the room seemed to have been unaffected by
anything Leon had said. Roger was shivering. He felt giddily weak.
His teeth were chattering. He felt guilty as hell, and felt like it showed.
It did, but Roger had just been shot at and had taken out his attacker,
so to the cop Roger seemed quite normally agitated.

They worked it out that Leon, thinking himself terribly clever, had
come down the back way to the security room instead of hitting the
street, stripping out of his old man's clothes and ditching them for the
green uniform. It was the old purloined-letter trick, though Leon had
never read Poe. Leon had thought it was the essence of genius.

Sure enough, they found the old dirty clothes in the garbage can in
the corner.

Until Roger got home, it had not occurred to him to wonder how
his neighbors would react. He had bounced a pistol off of a Negro's
head, he realized. Not only a Negro, but a Negro from this very
neighborhood.

But Mr. Gandy was proud of him at supper. "Now come on, don't
you be sulky," Mr. Gandy said to T.J. "You know a man like Leon just
make it harder for everybody else."

T.J. wasn't sulky. He just didn't know how to react so kept his face
from showing anything at all. He had a sort of loyalty to Leon that
now he would have been glad to let go of completely—but that would
have felt treacherous. He wouldn't defend Leon, he decided, as long as
no one picked on him too bad. Maybe he would visit him in the jail.
After a while.

"Now maybe they'll see," Mr. Gandy said. "We don't approve of no
criminal no more than nobody else. We have one, we catch him and
give him to the police."

"Roger is white," T.J. said, carefully watching his plate.

Mr. Gandy and Marcus both looked at Roger. For Marcus, the tv
had been an education. All of his life, he had mostly lived with black
faces. He had not needed a world any bigger than the world of those
black faces. On tv all of the faces were white—except for Reverend

Smith, and a few angry faces, demonstrators and crooks. This evening Roger had been on the news before supper. But his had been a familiar face. Now Marcus saw it was White. A strange world was beginning, a world beyond the one he knew. You could be in both worlds at once, he saw. You could be in the old, close, familiar one, and you could also be in the new big strange one. And if you could, then you had to be. If there was a world you could see but couldn't be in, then you weren't all the way real. It was scary not to be real. But in the new world, the one he was going to have to be in, most of the faces were white, and they said bad things about the black faces.

Although right now, right at this very moment, the most important thing to Marcus was the chance to see *Mickey Mouse Club* and *Superman* after school and *Twilight Zone* after supper.

"Yeah, but he's *from* here," Mr. Gandy said.

After supper Mr. Gandy took them all down to Mosey's to have Coca-Colas and fried pies and celebrate. Almost all. T.J. decided to stay home. Roger was afraid to go, but when they got there, it was like a party. It was Friday, and everybody was talking and laughing. They crowded around congratulating him, patting him on the back, talking it over.

"Thown a *gun* at that sucker!"

"I'd a kilt him. Kilt him!"

"He wadn't expecting no thowin, see. Roger done it to surprise im. Catch im off-guard. He jump around dodgin them bullets, you couldn't eem see him. I drawn his fire. Then he fetch him upside the head with the gun fore he known it. Leon say, Sho wadn't expecting no thowin. I heard him." This was Mosey, explaining above the roar.

What Roger had not realized was that all of these people were Americans. But they were, and Americans love to catch bank robbers, almost as much as they love to imagine getting away with robbing a bank. And they knew Roger, and he had caught a bank robber. It wasn't even that they didn't like Leon (they didn't). It was just that they were Americans.

Roger had the good sense to go ahead and enjoy being a hero even though he knew he really wasn't one. Who was he to spoil the party for everybody else?

But he was relieved to hear what Reverend Smith had to say about it in church that Sunday.

Roger had started attending church again—well, not really again, since he had never gone to much of anything but YFC before. He had tried several churches in Jackson. First Baptist was too big, and the people too well-dressed. Too, he had filled out a visitor's card, and they had come after him like insurance salesmen. Thirty-two different people had shaken his hand after the services. Then they had sent him a bunch of questionnaire cards about how they could help him with his spiritual life, and he had also received a pledge card and envelope. The church bulletin started coming in the mail. The assistant pastor came by twice to invite him back.

He tried First Methodist, but the day he went they turned away a group of blacks.

Finally he just wound up going to church with the Gandys. He hadn't given up on Jesus. Jesus made sense to him. He figured he needed to learn a lot more, as confusing as life was right now. He had no doubt that there *was* a sensible moral way to live, he just had to go out and learn it, as he had learned jujitsu. He was just having trouble finding a church that knew anything about Jesus, that was all.

This Sunday, Reverend Smith said that the truly fine thing that had happened to "our visiting friend" was that he had held a gun in his hand and had not fired it, even when he himself was being fired on. He said it was a truly Christian act, not because it was passive, which it was not—Roger had subdued the robber—but because it was a refusal of anger. Anger, he said, was a loaded gun. Everybody had one in his hands. And there were times when nobody would blame you for firing yours. "And that is just what our friend did not do," he said. "He found another way, the way that is the way of Jesus."

Being called "our friend" and being the subject of the sermon made Roger feel like he wasn't really there, like he was an invisible ghost, outside of his own life and just sitting in on it. He was glad to hear that something fine had happened in the scene at the bank, but he himself knew that he not done anything fine. He had not *decided* anything. It had all been too quick. He had just done what he had done.

And he was not entirely satisfied with what the Reverend had said. Not quite. He had not killed Killer, and he had not shot Leon. He was glad he had not, in both cases. But that was what he had in both cases, and all he had: he had Not. Not was not enough. You couldn't sustain your soul on Not. Somewhere in Jesus there had to be something that wasn't Not.

Roger made it into Bum Festrich's column that day, too. Festrich, in fact, concurred with the Reverend that Roger's act had been a Christian act:

This Friday a young white man gave the lie to all the blind venom that the hate-mongering Yankee press has spilled on our heads of late. It is safe to say that with all the multitudinous and carefully selected photographs that have been appearing in national picture magazines, showing this or that Negro with a bloody head or held at bay by a well-trained dog, there can hardly be a soul outside the borders of this state who can envision a white officer of the law as anything but a slavering demon, ready on the instant to beat and murder the poor helpless black man.

Two days ago, Roger Wing flung the lie in the teeth of a press that has been not so much unprincipled, as after the principal. Brutality, real or imagined, does sell copies, and reporter's salaries do go up. The truth has never been profitable.

But the truth is that a young white uniformed Mississippian, under fire at point-blank range from a drug-crazed black man, rather than return the fire, risked his own life in a dramatic struggle to disarm and subdue the criminal without causing him physical harm. We have it from informed sources that the miscreant in question has long been suspected as a major figure in a ring of drug-smuggling revolutionaries, and is known to be totally ruthless. Startling evidence, which we cannot elaborate on at this time, is about to emerge, evidence which will at last and conclusively demonstrate the active involvement of organized crime in the financing of the so-called Civil Rights Movement, which might better be called the Criminal Rights Movement. The Communists know that it is essential to disrupt our society, and they are covertly joining forces with elements of organized crime and the labor unions. It is well known that the Russians regard Mississippi as a test case for this sort of insurrection. The robbery which Mr. Wing thwarted was but a small first step in the funding of this siege.

Let them try: If in spite of all that the liberal and appeasing press can do to slander them, young men such as Mr. Wing still dare to exist in our state, young men of courage who yet exemplify the compassion that the Negro-baiting Yankee denies it is possible for a white man to possess, let them do their worst. Mississippi shall survive. She shall not merely survive, but prevail. And to young Mr. Wing, I say, "I salute you, my captain. Mississippi has need of your like."

Roger found this column very disturbing. He wrote Bum Festrich a letter. It took him a lot of tries to get the letter to sound like it said anything like what his feelings really were. He was amazed that it was so hard. I mean, there your feelings are, right there inside of you. You would think it would be easy to say them. He wrote:

Dear Mr. Festrich,

I hope that the reporters are not lying about Mississippi as much as you say they are. That would be too bad, and I don't know why they would, except for money like you say. But I hope not. But I do not think that I am a good example to use for them. Because I was not compassionate, I flung the gun at Leon because I was mad at him. Maybe if I was good with a gun I would have shot him, but I am not. To squeeze a little trigger with one little finger is not good enough for me, my whole body wants to do something. I was not scared because he was shooting at me because I am brave but because I was too mad. I have met Leon before and he has a way of aggravating you. And what I really felt was there he was messing up my whole day again by robbing the bank and then when he shot the loud noises *really* made me mad. So I flung it at him and it hit him and he bled pretty good, so they could also probably get a pretty good brutality picture of me and him too as far as that goes. I don't mean to disagree with you, but I have a hard time imagining Leon as an important criminal or anything. Maybe they are thinking of someone else. Not that he is not smart, he is. But in a real dumb-headed way. Where he gets on your nerves all the time and acts bigger than he really is and messes up everything he tries. Please print this to set the record straight. I enjoyed your column and sincerely yours,

Roger Wing

Roger was not really satisfied with this version either. He had lied in the last sentence, but he figured you were supposed to. And there was a problem in the sentence about not being scared. He couldn't figure out what it was, but it didn't sound quite right. Finally, he gave up and sent it. He watched the column for weeks, but his letter never showed up.

All this time, he was expecting the police to question him about his involvement with Leon, not to mention his involvement with the murder of Elrod. He was very much afraid they would think he was a part of whatever insidious criminal ring it was that they were after. He was even more afraid that they would think the Gandys were somehow involved, and that that would make trouble for them. They did question him, right after the robbery, and told him that he would probably be called as a witness when it came to trial, but that was it. Apparently the police only made certain connections, and you could never tell which ones they would be. Or maybe they just didn't care.

In the meantime, he had gone home to Clinton. His mother was infinitely proud of him, and wanted him there to show off to people, and the bank had given him a couple of weeks off as a reward, and he felt safer there. Perhaps when the police came he could, without really lying, make out like he had *really* been living in Clinton and only using the laundromat as an office and sometimes sleeping over. It was sort of true, because he *could* have been doing that and *had* done it for a little while at the beginning. He hadn't really meant to stay that long. He was definitely going to sell the place and move, now. He would miss the Gandys, but.

But within two weeks, he was no longer in the news. In fact, he had been out of the news so long, his worries wore off.

He had bought himself a car while he was in Clinton. He bought his stepfather's 1960 VW, a little cream-colored bug that rode like a tin sled, had no options at all, and got 36 miles to the gallon. He bought it for 1,000 even, which was maybe a little high, considering depreciation, but as his stepfather pointed out, Roger knew the car and knew how well it had been taken care of. His stepfather threw in a full tank of gas, and that decided him.

Mobility was amazing. He was light-headed with it. He could go anywhere he wanted to. He could drive right out of Mississippi, go find a girl somewhere.

He drove back to the studio Sunday two weeks after the Festrich column, to get ready for work the next day.

At that point, there were about 7,500 blacks in Forrest County, 25 of whom were eligible to vote. They had a very difficult voter registration test there in Hattiesburg. A month after Roger went back to work, the Justice Department filed an injunction regarding that test. It went to Judge Cox, who neither granted the injunction nor denied it, and then it went to the infamous Fifth Circuit Court on appeal, and they granted it. Hard on the heels of that, Judge Cameron from Meridian, who had not so far reviewed it, issued a stay in the

Meredith case.

So there was plenty to kick around in the papers and on the tv.

One Friday night nine weeks after Roger had gone back to work a banging at the front door of the studio woke him up. The moon was nearly full, and the studio was full of that strange light which is like a telephone call where the person on the other end of the line doesn't say anything when you say hello, but you know it is somebody close to you, though you cannot say who. Perhaps your dead father.

A big shape was at the door, black and shifting. It banged again.

The world was very odd tonight, he realized. It was as if he had waked up outside himself, in some adventure tale whose ending no one could foresee.

The black shape banged again. Roger got up and padded to the door.

It was William Percy Alexander Sledge, and he smelled of alcohol and carried a bottle in his hand. "We're fired, Coach," he said.

"Say what?"

"From the bank. We're fired. Fired, fired, fired." The way he said it, it sounded like *fart, fart, fart.* Apparently he thought so, too, because immediately he cut a tremendous blatting honker. "Speak, O Toothless One," he said.

"Percy, what the hell are you talking about?"

"We're fired from the bank. You and me. You made too much attention. Banks don't like attention. Like it nice and quiet. You supposed to find out Monday. Told me this evening. Couldn't get ahold of you."

Roger was beginning to wonder if all this was true. "But I saved them," he said. "They gave me extra vacation and a bonus."

"Well now you're fired. They waited till the papers won't be interested no more, see."

Percy was essentially right. What had actually happened was Roger Tutwiler had been promoted. He had never liked the idea of the special militia, and his worst fears had come true with the robbery. Never mind that Roger Wing was a hero, and never mind that Roger Tutwiler was supposed to be hard-headed and practical. He differed from many of his friends in that he saw integration as inevitable. It was the coming economic reality, just as segregation had been the previous one, and he wanted his bank to survive in the new age. But for all of that, he was as convinced as any other Mississippian that the liberal Yankee press would distort the whole incident of the robbery, and that he, Roger Tutwiler, would be remembered as having hired a cop who split a Negro's skull. As soon as he made the board, he fixed it where he would be remembered as the banker who *fired* the cop who split a Negro's skull.

Roger and Little Wide Load got very nice severance checks, but they were out, O-U-T spells out goes you, you old dirty dishrag you.

"Well shit," Roger said.

Little cut another fart. "Speak O Toothless One," he said again.

"God, that's bad," Roger said. "That's really bad." He walked away. "That's the worst thing you have ever done in your life."

"No it ain't," said Little Wide Load.

"What do you do when you're fired?" Roger said. "I never been fired before."

"You get drunk and do something dangerous."

"That's what *you* do when you *aren't* fired," Roger said.

"Yeah, but it works better when you been fired. Come on, I'm on show you something."

"What the shit," Roger said. It was the moonlight that was doing it, but he was having the feeling this was the same night that Elrod died. This was summer and full moon, and that had been winter and a half moon, but he was up and around at a weird time in a weird light with scary emotions running around in the shadows. A sick depression revolved in his gut. As if this were punishment for the evil he had seen that other night, as if this light and the punishment could go on forever. He had been found wanting and was cast out into outer darkness, defenseless and branded.

"I know what you feeling, Coach," Little said. "I been fired twice."

"I thought this was yo first regular job."

"I was fired from the Rebels. That was worse. I been a damned soul ever since then, you know. But I still love Mississippi. It's like I'm in a pit looking up, and the faces hanging over the edge are the ones that thrown me in, and I can't help it, I love ever one of them. You don't have no idea what it's like not to be on the Rebels."

"Yeah," Roger said.

"So come on, Coach. Get drunk and get mad." Little put his arm around Roger and held the bottle to Roger's mouth. The mouth of the bottle cut his lip a little, knocked his teeth. A big dollop went half down his throat and half on his chest. It burned in his throat, cooled his chest. It hit his stomach like the rising of the sun. The sick spinning feeling stopped.

"Yeah," he said.

Little dragged him out to his pick-up truck in his underwear. "Hey, I got to put some clothes on," Roger protested.

"Who wants to wait?" Little said. "You won't need em where we going." He picked Roger up bodily and set him in the old blue pick-up. He went around and got in the other side.

"Where we going?" Roger said.

"For me to know and you to find out," Little said.

"Any more of that whiskey?"

"Here."

Roger took another big slug. He was beginning to get mad. It was a lot better than feeling sick at his stomach. Little's man-handling of him had helped free the anger, though the anger was not at Little. It wasn't really at the bank, either. How could you be mad at a bank? It was just anger.

They crooked and screeched through the backside of downtown Jackson, across the tracks and out towards the east. Roger had some more bourbon, spilling half of it in a turn. He tasted salt from the cut on his lip. It seemed like they were driving awfully fast.

Little Wide Load hung a right on Highway 49. "The *worst* thing I ever did," he said, "the absolute *worst* thing."

"Was," Roger said. He was beginning to feel the bourbon. They were swimming along in the midnight moon.

"This little white girl was under the cover going down on me, and."

"And?"

"And I cut a big old fart."

"Ah, no," Roger said. "Ah, no, you *didn't*." He was appalled. Think of the *waste*. "Tell me you didn't do that."

"She was a real sweet little girl, too. She come up out from under those covers cussing me to blue blazes, and she cussed me while she put her dress and shoes back on and she cussed me on out the door and for all I know she's setting up there in her big house in Oxford cussing me still."

"Aw shit," Roger said sadly. He had slid down in his seat and was hanging his nose out the window watching the road roll by. "She's probably bald-headed by now," he added after a while. "Probably killed all her hair."

Little Wide Load liked that.

They rode on in silence for another 45 minutes. Then, when Roger had just about fallen asleep, Little Wide Load said, "Here we go," and swung them off on a little dirt road into the woods.

"What are you up to? What are we doing?"

"I'm on show you something that'll make you forget all about being fired."

"I already forgot. Ever since you farted on the girl."

"I'm on show you something everybody ought to see before they leave Mississippi."

"I ain't leaving Mississippi." The truck was bouncing around pretty good by now, sliding through the turns.

"Sure you are. You bound to. It's *on* you that you will. The marks of it shows all over you. You can't stay. Some people have to, some people can't. I'm a one that has to. You a one that can't."

"Maybe I need some more of that bourbon."

"Maybe you do."

Roger uncapped it and took a pull. "I been meaning to ask you," he said. "There's this Confederate uniform been showing up in the closet at work, a piece at a time."

"Shhh," Little Wide Load said. "It's a surprise." Suddenly he slewed the truck off the road onto a logging path. Branches scraped and squeaked along the cab. He brought the truck to a stop.

Roger had to force his door open against the springy branches, then duck under to get free. He still got scraped across his back. Sweat jumped out on his face and back and armpits now that the air was no longer moving over him, a good bourbon sweat, his body desperately adjusting against the too-much heat and toxin pouring in. He stood in the tree-ragged moon, waiting. Little Wide Load was bigger and had more trouble getting out. Finally he stood in front of Roger, blowing like a buffalo.

They were on a hill in the middle of the woods. You could see where the slope went off into the trees. It was not so much as if the trees made shadows of the moon as it was that there was a silent ongoing white-hot white-cool explosion overhead that blew a constant shrapnel into the mind, light-speed scraps of black and white. For a moment Roger had felt a tremendous silence, the ceasing of engine-roar and wind. But now the racket of crickets came up, reverberating in the gullies, and over that the loud pure chirping of the treefrogs. The night was busy and ingenious, louder and bigger than any human night. And now the mosquitoes sounded their tiny whines, dopplering loud and faint. They were on the scent.

"Now what?" Roger said.

"Follow me," Little Wide Load said. "We'll run it on in the rest of the way. Do you good. Get rid of the booze." He took off lumbering down a logging trail Roger had not even seen.

Roger was not crazy about running. His only experience with it since he was a child had been as punishment, running laps after a bad football practice. But if he stood still much longer, the mosquitoes were not going to leave much more than a rag, a bone, and a hank of hair. He took off, too, following Wide Load, little drunk hot white boy running through the unknown woods in his underwear pants. He felt how crazy it was from an outside viewpoint, but then, he was being crazy on purpose, wasn't he? And then after a few minutes they had run long enough that all he thought about was the rhythm, the activity.

He pulled up to Little Wide Load's elbow. There wasn't room to run beside him. They were running easily, loping, not too fast. You had to watch the ground, tricky with shadow, and watch the branches. You ran through flickering bars of shadow and light, irregular stroboscope. It split your mind, one side tranced and crazy and flowing, another part watching the monitors, keeping the engine humming, the body running upright. It was as if Roger could see himself running from a distance away, as if there were a third mind beyond them all, heretofore undiscovered and not quite what he had always thought of as himself.

They were running along a little ridge, apparently, the slope falling away on either side. Little was breathing heavily, but with a slow and steady rhythm. Roger had gotten loose and smooth and light, flooding with easy cleansing sweat. He was enjoying it, not thinking of doing anything else, rocking along as if this rhythm was what life was for, when Little came to a stop and Roger bumped into him. All of his minds came crashing back in.

"Shh," Little Wide Load said. "Sneak up."

Roger was bristling with scratches from the branches and undergrowth. His heart was beating hard. He heard music. Some kind of strange sad music under the noises of the night. Or was it sweet happy music? But it was there.

Little Wide Load led them to a vantage over a river bottom. They looked out from behind a big white oak and a bayberry thicket.

There was a fire down by the river, tables, people milling around, a huge makeshift pennant from tree to tree, the noise of gabbling voices. On a sort of stage beside the fire, a man was playing a guitar, a hooded man. It wasn't a stage, it was a gallows. He saw the rope.

The fire-shadows fought the moon-shadows, losing again and again. Down in their wrestle, the stirring people were sorting themselves out along the tables. They all had white hoods and white robes. The guitar player's song was beginning to catch among the other voices. It was the blues. That was why he had not known whether the music was happy or sad.

The sweet slow notes floated up, the notes that rose as they fell, the back-meat music, the music that took its own time to say it all out, that sometimes said nothing at all and let the fading resonance do all the talking. The joining voices raised prickles along the backs of Roger's arms, all through his scalp and neck.

> *I rode up to Sweet Jesus...*
> *Sweet Jesus said to me...*
> *Jump on your horse, Sweet Johnny...*
> *Kill every nigger you see...*
> *Kill every nigger you see...*

When the song was over, another man got up on the scaffold and led them in prayer. Then they fell to eating, the noisy talk rising again. There were big steel baking trays with dark meat in them, and heaps of sliced bread, there was a keg on each table, silvery in the lowering moon. What time was it? It had to be 2:00 or 3:00 in the morning. Three hours to daylight. Roger did not want the ceremony to end, this mysterious dinner in the middle of the woods, in the middle of the night. Morning seemed a peculiar notion now, bright, simple, and false, full of meaningless business, a specially repulsive brand of existence, and the last thing on earth that should ever be thought of as reality. He didn't want day to come.

The Klansmen were eating messily, happily, lifting the fronts of their hoods with one hand to gnaw on dark bones held in the other, those whose hoods had not been cut away over the mouth. It had to be barbecue. The robes were showing splatters and splotches, dark spills from overburdened sandwiches.

"What does the banner say?" he whispered. "I can't make it out."

"The First Annual Theron C. Lynd Memorial Barbecue and Cross-Burning," Little Wide Load whispered back.

"It does not," Roger said.

"They didn't spell it all right," Little Wide Load said.

"It does not," Roger said.

"Shhh."

They lay there another half-hour while the eating rose to a peak of fury and died slowly down. The mosquitoes, meantime, were having their own unrelenting feast. Roger burrowed under the leaves, rolling and grinding the moist earth into his skin for protection. It helped. He kept a hand waving about his ears.

After a while, the man who had led the prayer rose to the scaffold again. He said a few things that Roger could not decipher but that brought bursts of laughter and hand-clapping. He waved theatrically off to one side, as if introducing the next performer. Two white-robed men walked out of the trees with a Negro between them, and up the steps to the scaffold.

Roger stood up. "That's it," he said. "I'm not putting up with any more of this. I'm going to go kill me some people."

Little Wide Load yanked Roger down beside him in the dirt, keeping a grip on his arm. They were face to face in the darkness. "Quiet," he whispered. "It's all an act. They ain't gone hang him. If they hang him they won't get no more of his business."

"I can't take that chance. You on their side. You might be lying."

"That's trash down there," Little Wide Load said. "I ain't them." Roger had never heard his voice so deadly.

"I don't never lie to the coach," Little Wide Load said to himself.

Roger was looking back down. They had the Negro kneeling now. They fitted the noose around his neck. Roger started, but Little Wide Load had his arm in a hand as in the jaws of an alligator. "Watch," he said. Roger was whimpering like a lonesome chained dog.

The moderator, below, raised the skirts of his robe, undid the front of his pants. The Negro raised his face to accept the thing that had spilled out.

It was Killer.

Later Roger would be certain he had been wrong. There was no way it could have been Killer. From that distance he could not have possibly seen enough to know. It had been someone else, someone whose face was like the face of the murderer.

Tonight he knew it was Killer. There was no way to doubt it.

Killer gave suck. First to the moderator, then to the two who had brought him in, and then in turn to those who had formed a line at the foot of the scaffold. Tears stood in Roger's eyes. This was worse than the hanging would have been, worse than the murder. This was the worst of all.

His arm was numb. "I think you're breaking my arm," he said to Little Wide Load, whose grip had tightened almost enough to burst blood vessels and the sheathing of muscles. Little let go.

It went on too long. Jokes, and catcalls, and unintelligible sentences that had the same cadences as any other sentences said while standing in any other line anywhere in the world.

When it ended, the moon was in the lower trees. Some were cleaning the tables off as the last few men in line got theirs. Others brought down the pennant. At last, Killer stood up, and took the rope from his neck. The moderator gave him something. Killer examined it, looked back up and spoke angrily to the moderator, who took it back and looked it over, shrugged apologetically, and gave it back to Killer. He reached in his pocket and gave him another something. Killer jerked it away and went down the steps and disappeared into the trees. The moderator raised his hands and called out. The wandering men turned to face him. They began the national anthem, *a capella*. Little Wide Load stood up and put his hand over his heart. The moderator had a good voice.

"Percy, you got to be crazy," Roger said, burying his face in the leaves.

"I love my country," Little Wide Load answered when the last of the song had died. "It ain't America that's fucking with the South, it's just the goddamn Yankees. If we would have won, we would have been America. Can you find your own way home? The keys are in the truck."

Roger rolled over to look at him. "What are you talking about?"

"All this has just been lead-up. The real fun is just about to start. I'm fixing to go down there and mix around a while. You welcome to come."

"No," Roger said. "No, you go on ahead without me."

"I didn't think you would want to," Little Wide Load said. He dropped into a three-point stance facing down the hill. "Say 'Down set hike,'" he said.

"Down," said Roger. "Set. *Hike!*"

Little Wide Load charged down the hill, whipping around trees and yelling. He was fast. He was scary fast. He was yelling the Rebel yell. The Klansmen were looking up. Little Wide Load burst into the clearing and slammed into a knot of them, sending them all tumbling and flying.

Roger did not remember the trip back to the truck. He forced his way in and cranked it. He drank half of the rest of the bourbon. He did no thinking, he just unwound the trip they had made coming in. The sky was lightening as he came out onto Highway 49. The sun was just up as he pulled up in front of his studio.

He stood, woozy and wavering, in front of his door. He did not want to go in, stumble on in to his cave. He would lose himself when he did. This life would be over. A new one might begin, but this one would be gone, all of its history and truth and who he was. There was only a little of it left, but that little was precious.

Morning sounds, morning light. The bread truck going by down to the grocery. Black ladies off to their jobs in the white houses, hair up in nets, smoking their morning cigarettes as they walked away. Birds on the wire, bluejays after a mocker already. Not much, but all there was. Down at the end of the street Mosey and a helper were busy at the back of an old panel van, unloading stacks of baking trays filled with forks and bones.

Mr. Gerald Sheffield was walking by, on his way to Mosey's, perhaps, for coffee. He stopped and regarded Roger. Roger stood there, too tired to care who saw him, covered with dirt and leaves and muddy sweat, swollen with bites and striped with the thin and bloody lashings of branches, broken leaves in his disarrayed hair, drunken and naked except for the dirty rags of his sodden underwear, feeling already the fever coming on.

"I had nights like that," Mr. Sheffield said.

Niggers in the Woodpile

FOR TWO WEEKS Roger flirted with disease. He didn't feel actually *sick*, you know, but I don't know what it is, I just don't seem to have any *strength*, I just kind of drag around. And when I stand up I get dizzy and weak. It's like I just want to sleep all the time. My throat's a little raw, but I don't think I have any fever, do you? Do I feel like I have any fever to you?

And Snower Mae would put her big rough hand where his jawline met his throat. Naw, hon, she would say, you ain't got no fever. just walkin sick is all.

That's what I think too. I mean, my skin is real touchy. Feels real dry and sensitive, feels like paper. Feels fever-*ish*, but I don't think I have any fever.

Me neither, chile, Snower Mae Gandy would answer. She was home because she had lost her Thursday and Friday houses.

But I think I'm really sick, I don't think I'm pretending or anything.

You walkin sick.

I could just be feeling this way because I lost my job. I need to get right up and go out and get another one. But when I think of it, I just don't seem to have the energy. I can't even imagine doing it.

Why ont you lee yoself alone. You loss yo girlfriend and you loss yo job, and that ain't helpin nobody feel better, but you are for-real sick. You mights well git used to it. Lots of people don't never feel so good. You ain't got nothing you sposed to be doin, why ont you just lay back and be sick a while?

I don't really miss June so much, you know. I mean, I knew it wasn't going to last forever. It's real funny how life works, because it's Patsy I miss, and that's been over with for a long time. I don't guess I'll ever get over her, really. Maybe that's because it just ended without it ever taking its natural course. I don't have no way of knowing whether we could ever of been really happy together or not.

I guess I'm sposed to feel guilty bout losin them houses, settin here drankin in the day-time. But I don't. Mr. Gandy, he don't try to make me feel guilty. But he worry over me, and I don't like that eem as much. I rather have em try to make me feel guilty. Let em try. You know why I don't feel guilty?

Well I don't feel guilty about losing *my* job. Well, sometimes I start to, and then I realize it wasn't really *my* fault, although maybe I could have done a better job at it. But what is strange, is I *dream* about Patsy all the time.

You lucky, you don't belong to nobody. You don't belong to no job, you don't belong to no family, you don't belong to no woman. You can be yoself. Just you. Just who you is, and not what can be got out of you. This world ain't for people. We in it, but it ain't for us. It's just goin some blind old where all on its own, and it a grab us up and use us to get there, but other than that it don't eem know we here. Everything that happen in the world happen on people gettin old. Use us

...is old to keep it runnin. Like a stick thown on the fire, ...rivel in on itself. Keep that old fire goin. Don't nobody ...e stick feel. All my life I been workin. Belongin and ...at's all I got out of my life, just bein used up to keep ...oing. Keep my blessed famly fed. Polish the crystal for Mrs. Abc. leen. Bring them chilren into the world so it won't run low on wood. I never eem known who my own daughter was till she broke her own self. I's too busy keepin her butt clean and her belly full. Always mo that haf to be done than there is time to do it. I bout half bleeve she broke herself on purpose. Now she don't have to fit into nothin. Don't have to be chopped up and cut up and used for something else. Mr. Gandy think I'm drankin cause I'm depress. I ain't depress. This here vodka is my retirement. I just set here and be me. Just cut it loose and whatever I see in my mind, that there is me. Whatever crosses my feelin, that's who I am. I don't eem want to watch no television. It ain't for me. It just another thing want to use me. Make me turn loose of a dollar, go to a store, vote for the man, thank the thought that get what somebody else want done done. It ack like it for me, but it ain't for me. They don't eem know who I am. Ain't nothin in this world got a use for who you really is. You can't eem walk out the door without something pick you up and try to use you. Well I ain't walkin out the door. I ain't eem moom from this here table till I haf to. Mr. Gandy don't understand why I bleeve in Heaven. He pretend he do, but I know he don't. Cause it don't make no sense for there to be something there ain't no use to. Don't make no sense to have a world full of people and they not for anything but to thow on the fire and burn em up. Heaven don't have to be no golden streets. I probably just be sweepin em. All it have to do is be a regular place, but have a good use for people. Have something you can fit into and still have yo own self. That all it haf to do, and it a be Heaven.

You have any more of that vodka in the bottle? Maybe I ought to go out and get another bottle, I drunk so much of it.

You can see if Mosey's got some laid back if you want. If you gone do it, though, you bed do it before Mr. Gandy get back. I don't want no more worryin.

You don't mind me hanging around like this, do you? I don't mean to talk your head off. There's just not really anybody else I can talk to about how I feel about Patsy. It feels good just to sit around and talk like this.

You ain't botherin me. I ain't gone let you bother me. Nobody bother me. I'm just who I am. That's all I'm doin. You can help Eleanor Roosevelt make supper, though, if it's worryin you.

At supper of this particular day, T.J. and Mr. Gandy had a quarrel. "You ain't gone go to the jail no mo to see Leon," Mr. Gandy said.

"Come on, Poppa, it ain't hurt nothin. He don't have no friends."

"I said no."

"Come on, Poppa."

"I don't trust that man. I don't like the effect he have on you. No."

"He ain't gone do nothin to me. I'm a grown man, I a make up my own mind."

"Nearly grown. You ain't grown. You still under my roof. You do what I say."

"It ain't fair. You leave us when Eleanor Roosevelt hurt herself, you leave everything to me. I have to be a man, cause you don't want to be one no more. Now you want to take over again, take it all back. You want me to be yo baby boy again."

"No matter how I felt, I was still yo father. And I still am. And you ain't gone sit at this table and talk back to yo father."

"Maybe I ain't gone sit at this table then."

"Suit yoself," Mr. Gandy said, and continued eating. No one else looked up. T.J. pushed back his chair and stomped out the door.

It was just a small quarrel. Mr. Gandy knew that. It would heal soon. Maybe the next time, or the time after that, he would let T.J win. It was almost time. Not quite. Not quite yet. There was a time when the son was ready to win. T.J. was almost there. His boy almost grown and gone. But not quite. The father need to win one or two more, the boy ain't quite ready. This a small quarrel. Be over soon. They be lovin again soon.

Two days later, Sunday morning, Roger was over at the Gandys' again. Nobody was going to church. Mrs. Gandy just wanted to stay home in her bathrobe and drink. Mr. Gandy was tired and wanted to just relax and read the paper and not have to dress up and talk to people. T.J. was still mad and was not around—in fact, he had not come home last night, which was one of the reasons his father was feeling so tired. He had spent the night at his girlfriend's, on the couch, her parents being sympathetic because they thought Mr. Gandy thought he was too good for them. They were watchful that nothing happened, but she had sneaked out to the couch in the early morning hours anyway, and now T.J. was even more sure he was a grown man.

As for Eleanor Roosevelt, every day was the same for her. She was happy going to church and not going to church. Marcus was delighted to be able to hole up in their bedroom with the few comic books he had scrounged. He could spend the whole day on them, absorbing them frame by frame. He had two Mars ones: an old John Carter of Mars, and a John Jonz, Manhunter from Mars. He had a Submariner and an Action Comics with a Bizarro story and a Krypto the Wonder Dog story. Yum yum, Bizarro love Mississippi. Me get me another helping. Mississippi taste just like Bizarro-World.

The stories in the comic books were illuminated lives. They might have been panels of stained glass. They radiated glory. The superheroes in their auras strode. One might imagine a writer praying to learn a similar prose, a style that might inform the ordinary and dear with something of the same light, a sense of color that might explain why such small things should seem so valuable. Hoping to hell not to fall to mere cartoon. Cartoon, maybe. God help us, please not mere.

First Baptist had begun televising its morning services, and that gave everybody an excuse: they could tune in to the tv services, and that would make it a little more ok to miss church. In fact, you could just turn the thing on and let them sing and chatter, and go about your regular business.

Roger was mopping up the eggs he had made himself, feeling greasy and sick at his stomach and lightheaded, but hungry nevertheless, or maybe just restless, frustrated and dissatisfied and needing to complete himself, fill up the void with something, when Mr. Gandy called from the study: "Ain't that yo friend?"

Roger went into the study. They were having a Youth Preacher. The Youth Preacher was Jimmy McMorris. He looked elegant in his suit and tie. Roger knew the suit was blue, and the tie was red, like that fellow's tie in New Orleans. He was looking up with a joke on his face.

"...a lot about preaching, but you still have a whole lot to learn about being married," he said, smiling, and a wave of pleasant laughter could be heard.

"Yes you do," Mr. Gandy said.

Married?

"But seriously, I just want to thank the Lord for bringing me my wonderful wife. Truly marriage is a blessed estate. And I know I will fall short of His wonderful plan from time to time, for I am human.

But in Jesus we have our Help, and He has given us another help as well, second only to the love of Jesus in the joy it brings in the good times and the peace and patience it gives to see us through the hard times. Thank the Lord for our wives, brethren!"

There was a rumble of *Amen*, and Jimmy partially turned to show his new bride, seated behind him in the pulpit. It was Patsy.

Roger was very cold. He was too cold to shiver. A long wave of chill ran over him, like a January breaker on a Gulfport beach, draining back bubbling over the dead jellyfish, their tendrils washing back toward the sea.

And then the first wave of heat, a strange, lifeless heat, a heat that flared like floating alcohol but left him cold in his bones, rocking under the grey dead water. He sat with a thump on the floor. Mr. Gandy looked at him curiously.

"But seriously," Jimmy said. "As a man thinketh in his heart, so is he. And brethren, we need to examine our hearts today. Brethren, we in the state of Mississippi need to take a hard look into our hearts. You know as well as I that these are troubled times for us here in the state of Mississippi. Troubled and trying times. But I say unto you, brethren, the trouble in Mississippi today doesn't have anything to do with the color of our skins. It has to do with black and white, brethren, but not with the black and the white of our skins. It has to do with the blackness and the whiteness of our hearts.

"Now I'm not the one who can lay it all out for you. I don't pretend to know what everyone should do. I am only an humble servant of the Lord."

Roger had been staring at Patsy, who kept her face steadfastly downward. "Can you help me to the bathroom?" he said to Mr. Gandy.

"What?"

"...hate in the hearts of brethren white man, and hate in the hearts of brethren Negro," Jimmy Mac was saying. "Today I am challenging our darker Christian brothers. Can you honestly say there is no hate in your heart for your white brother? We read in the papers every day how terrible it is to hate the Negro, and under God's law of love, this is true. But it is equally true..."

"I'm gone throw up," Roger said.

Mr. Gandy jumped into action, but they didn't quite make it to the bathroom in time. Roger hung with his head over the edge of the tiny little tub while Mr. Gandy cursed and mopped and ran water and mopped some more. He threw up twice more, the last time heaving on an empty stomach. Mr. Gandy got him cleaned up, and when he was sure the convulsions were over, wrapped him in his own old house-coat, leaving Roger's clothes for Snower Mae to clean up. Roger was flushed and hot and giddy. He couldn't make a sensible answer when Mr. Gandy asked him how he was feeling. Supporting him with one powerful arm around his shoulders, Mr. Gandy walked Roger down the stairs and across the street to his studio. He tucked him in, turned on one of the lights, looked around, sighed, and left. "I a check on you later," he said at the door to the studio. "Hope you feelin better soon."

When he got back to the apartment, Jimmy Mac was closing in on the end of his sermon. "God's *mercy* is indeed infinite, brethren, but so is His *judgment.* And woe unto the soul of the Negro man who has allowed murder and hatred to pollute his heart and disrupt the proper political process of a free society. Woe unto the dark heart of that man who, in a moment of personal anger and frustration, has thrown away all that the white man and the Negro have achieved together. Woe unto that evil heart that comes as a false Messiah, for the Lord has warned that in the final days there will be many of these. And as the Lord God Almighty has done with *Sodom* and *Gomorrah,* He will do with such as these. Make no mistake, a day of flame and fire is coming, a consuming storm of *Judgment* is on the way—"

Mr. Gandy switched the tv off. "Sho is a lot of different kinds of white people," he said to the God he had quit believing in but not quit talking to. "Made too many of the wrong kind, though."

Mississippi Vortex Fever

I AM A FALLING man, dwindling against the swirl: like the revolving black-and-white spiral they use for background in movies or on *The Twilight Zone,* to show a man falling backwards in time or into another dimension or down into hell.

Like a jackass looking up and braying at the great American eagle.

Praying for the great American eagle...

So much for you, Joe Patterson, Joe Patterson, so much for you, Joe Patterson my Joe...

How long you thank he been like this?

Maybe a week or two or year or two or life, living in superheated steam, falling to fractured dreams, awake standing peeing thank God the bed isn't wet but this isn't my isn't my

Went home sick Sunday. That a be four day.

Day and

(Night and day...)

broken from order, random succession of light and dark, or dark and dark or light and light and dark dark dark light dark, one or the other each time I am here: the room is dark, or there is light from not my window...

(Deep in the heart of me...)

Damn. I mean to check on im and didn't do it. Just let it go. Got to workin, didn't want to bother.

Where is my skin? Who has my skin? It burns, it burns. Make Marcus give me back my skin, Mr. Gandy. Tell him don't make a cape out of it. Don't throw it on the fire.

You thank we need to take him to the hospital?

They can't fix what he got. I seen im get sick. They a kill im. Stick im with medicine and forget im and kill im.

What he got, Daddy?

People used to get sick like that in the country. Before there was hospitals. They died more, but they learn from it.

What a happen to us if he die here? A white man die here?

He ain't dyin. Put im in Eleanor room. Marcus bed. They a sleep in the study with you.

What if we catch it?

You ain't catchin it.

We will not surrender to the evil and illegal forces of tyrannosaurus Rexall. Submit to an awful dictator of federal bubblegum. Never!

Turn off that tv.

Come on, Poppa. This is important.

You know it's crap. Ain't no point listenin to crap you know is crap. Just poison yo mine, make you hurt-yoself mad. Hurt yoself cause you can't hurt them. Ain't gone help.

Not drink from the cup of genius-eyed. Right as a slobbering state.

Maybe I ain't heard enough crap. Maybe I been livin in yo dream too long. Work hard and make good. Maybe I'm just now catchin up on crap.

Y'all bed quit talkin trash in front of the chilren you want to eat supper here tonight.

You sick, Captain Mississippi? Po baby. You be all right, Captain Mississippi. We a fight crime. Shhh. I ain't spose to be in here. Shhh. What? Night. Late night. I ont know. You want some nanna puddin? I a get it. On get me some. You awake? Shhh, ass right, you go on back a sleep, I a take care of you. Soove yo fever brow. Shhh.

PLACE ASSURED IN HISTORY FOR FEARLESS ROSS BARNETT.

You all goin to church to-mar. I don't like the way things sounin aroun here. Everybody fightin, in a bad mood all the time. Ain't gone be no more tv church. White people church anyway. Time for some Christian education roun here. Ain't gone be no discussion, T.J. Gandy. You goin. And you are too, Mr. Gandy. Bout time you set a zample roun here. Eleanor Roosevelt take care that boy. She know how to do that.

This yo mustache. See, you real pretty. Just like Clark Gable. Don't wiggle yo head like that, it a make the gum fall out. No, now you gettin it in yo hair. Well neh mine yo ears then. Just lay back on yo pillow. You Clark Gable and you sick, see. I come in, I'm Merlin Monroe. Merlin, honey, how you *doin.* Oh, *Clahk,* dahlin, I'm so sorry you *sick.* I hear you dyin. Yessim, Merlin, I am. I'm on my last deathbed, honey. Oh, Clahk, I'm just so sorry. You spose to kiss my hand. Naw, you take it in yo hand and you kissin on it. Don't hole it that way, that hurt. Don't let yo hand fall off like that. You a bad boy, Clahk. Behave yoself.

He ain't gettin no better. We bed call his Momma.

You know her number? You know her last name? He ain't got the same last name. You could probly fine it out. Go head, you want to. But she ain't his famly. We his famly. I seen what made him sick.

...please Momma I need something some aspirin please *Oh God Momma my head my head* it's gotta quit oh please call the doctor please do something *I can't stand it* please something to put me to *sleep. Oh. Ohhh. Ohhh God* please don't make me die please somebody you know how to stop it don't you don't somebody know how to *help me ah ah ah ah...*

I hate to go to work with him no better than that. And he wa hollrin all night. Didn't get no sleep.

You bed go on. I a stay.

I on want you to lose that Monday house too.

I ain't losin it. You bed go on. I a stay.

He wa hurtin. Went in, he had tears on his face. He wa beggin and cryin. Soft and then loud. He been in the woods, I be thinkin tick-bite fever. But ain't no ticks roun here.

You bed quit wurrin. You bed go on in. I a stay.

Sometime I think I'm just provin somethin on T.J. Feel so mean toward the boy. He don't gree with nothin I do no more.

You tired. You ain't sleep. You ain't thinkin right. Go on in, come home and rest. Go on now, you gone be late.

Darkness moved on the face of the waters. Howdy, Noah. Ain't it dark out here in yo submarine, can't see a thing. Nigger Noah in his black submarine. Ride on the waves with me. At night on the waves with me. Just rocking along on the sea, out on the black dark sea. Peaceful here witch you. I'm invisible, Noah, but Noah know I'm here. Soul come walkin the water a thousand mile, a thousand mile to be witch you. We lean on the cockpit, arms in the breeze, smoking our pipe, Noah and me, out in our submarine. Out on the long slow waves, out in the dark invisible sea.

> *Hush up, Roger Wing.*
> *Listen to Snower sing.*
> *You a silly thing,*
> *hush-up wing.*

> *Rock in the rocky chair,*
> *nobody else be there,*
> *fever burn yo hair,*
> *hush-up wing.*

> *Hush up, Roger Wing,*
> *silly silly thing,*
> *listen to Snower sing,*
> *hush-up wing.*

ON YOUR GUARD—COMMIES USING NEGROES AS A TOOL.

...transferred! He ain't crazy!

I'm fraid he is, son.

*They just doin it for meanness. To dig the black man. You eem **try** to fight em, you ain't eem taken serious. You ain't eem a criminal. You just a fool, just a crazy man.*

Paranoid schizophrenic with delusions of grandeur. T.J., that sound right to me. I think they doin him a kindness. The mood they in right now, I spected em to hang im.

Can't take no more a this, Poppa. The black man got to be a man. The black man can't allow himself to be put down in the dirt no more.

You talkin bout the black man, or you talkin bout black man T.J.?

It's the same thing! It's the same thing now!

Ain't done it, T.J. Son, you ain't Leon. Don't suck into his trouble. You thinkin he the other half of you, the brave and crazy half. Got something you need. It ain't true. You everything he ain't. You got his power, you got his charm. But you got you. You got a self to hold it all together, and he don't. You a fine man, T.J. I'm proud of you.

*Now you gone make me a man. You made me a boy and kept me a boy, now you want to make me a man. See, that's my boy. Ain't he a fine man. Got it from his daddy. He a man cause his daddy let him be one. Uh-uh. This one **mine**, Poppa. I a do it.*

If that's how you feel, ain't a lot I can say, is it? Any thing I say, you a just use it to prove yoself on me.

Little Brother has evidently booga concluded that the South must be forced booga to abandon booga its booga and booga in deference booga to Asiatic booga and African booga not far removed from cannibal booga...

Oh Jongle Jim, don't you hear them drum? Natives is restless, trouble on the tom-tom, trouble on the tom-tom booga tonight.

...today issued contempt of court citations against Chancellor Williams, Dean Lewis, and Registrar Ellis. Mississippi Attorney General Joe Patterson, commenting on the citations, said...

2-4-1-3, we hate Kennedy.

...gibbering under the gibbous moon. And wham, here I am, without a name. Moon in the window of the room, ugliest moon, lopside moon. I'm in my tomb. I'm out of time. The walls are long. The light is thin. Whose house? Am I alone? The click and settle of the night. Why have they brought me here? Have they discovered my crimes?

...today agreed to cooperate with federal authorities after what has been described as "a severe tongue-lashing" on the contempt-of-court charges filed in this court four days ago by the Justice Department. A spokesman from the governor's office had this to say...

...turned away at 4:34 p.m. in spite of a restraining order from the Fifth Circuit Court of Appeals issued directly against Governor

Barnett. Meredith was accompanied by Justice Department official John Doar, and by Jim McShane of the United States Marshals. I repeat, this has just happened less than an hour and a half ago. We hope to have film in time for the late news. This just in. The Fifth Circuit Court has issued a show-cause order to Ross Barnett to appear on the 28th to show cause why he should not be held for contempt. At this moment, we are attempting to get word from the governor's office regarding the latest....

Come see us at the mansion.

You hurt real bad, Captain Mississippi. They use black kryptonite on you, you real bad sick. Sa new kine a kryptonite, shine black light. Rob yo bank and shine a zero-gun on you. What they call it, a zero-gun. Shine black light on you. Black light a go right thoo yo chest. Oompf. Oh shit, Bluejay, they got me. Black light got my heart. Don't die, Captain Mississippi, they just got the edge a yo heart. You safe now, this our secret place. We on a asteroid in our bat-cave. Look out, they comin in the windows. Bang. Pow. Pssh. I got em. Here come some more. Shhh. I play quiet. Pwwwwww-h...Oof. Unh. Pee-yowwnh.

Anti-Christ Supreme Court. Your flags, your tents, your skillets. Barnett yes, Castro no.

...escorted by the State Highway Patrol. However, the escort was halted two blocks from the entrance. Angry spokesmen for the Justice Department claimed a violation of the earlier agreement, and stated...

You think he any better?

Sleepin more. He be out of it in a couple of days. Ain't jumpin up and yellin no more.

Momma say may be meningitis.

Tick-bite. Meningitis he be dead by now. Don't know where he got it, but that's what 'tis. Car wa here every day, but he been in the trees somehow or other.

Deep in the woods. Quiet and empty like a hall. Noah's submarine sticking out the side of a hill, stove in and rusted. Million years old. Full of leafs. I don't want to see Noah's dead bones, help me. Help me. No, the woods are old, not the submarine. Not any submarine. Somebody's front porch. Never was any scary whatever-it-was. Walking down the driveway in the woods. Quiet. Leaves. Knee-high. Sound now. Walk shufflecrash walk. Down in the bottom, dried-up bottom, dried-out knees and cow-oak leaves, a cross. Old rags on the cross. A scarecrow. A ghi. Man in the ghi, a mummy, rotting leafmold monster. Head lifts up. Clean face. Looks at me. William Percy Alexander Sledge. Crying. Tears run down. Blood tears. Mouth opens. Teeth. Monster teeth. Laughing. No. Help me, please help me.

Leonard? Yeah. Yeah. Yeah, I know. Well—shut up and listen a minute. That's what I'm trying to tell you, boy. Can you line those boys up, or they all talk? No, I ain't kidding. Bring em on if you got em. More the merrier. Just whatever you go hunting with. Whatever they got. Just the marshal and border guards. They ain't gone do nothing. Hell, half those boys are *from* the South. Yeah. Yeah. Kick their asses all the way to Cuba, by God. Listen, I gotta go. Naw, I got calls to make. You ain't the only fish in the sea. Just bring em on. You having doubts, one thing you might remember, when this is all over, think of all the contacts you made. More bankers than deer camp. Yeah, I guess. Room 121, Alumni Hall, but listen, we gone be needing this line, don't call if you don't absolutely need to. I'm going now. Bye now. Come see us if you get a chance. Bye. Lord that boy is hard to hang up on. Who's next? Who got the list?

Lieutenant Governor Paul Booga's name was added to the honor booga of defenders of the states' rights of Boogassippi when the Fifth Circuit Court of Appeals ordered him to show booga...

...mysterious man in full Confederate uniform. The crowd in the rotunda literally roared in delight. Witnesses in the crowd swore that the stranger strode across the rotunda and disappeared into thin air. Could it be possible that in this time of trial our state has had a visitation from the Twilight Zone? Has some noble officer from that distant conflict risen from the shades to give us new heart, to tell us that the ancient struggle for justice is truly not yet over, that the South shall rise again? Be that as it may, visitors to the Capitol had a real thrill today, and the mood here in the capital city is like the mood before a great crusade. The night after tomorrow, the reborn Rebels of Johnny Vaught take on Kentucky, and the feeling here is that nothing can stop us now. Meanwhile, in session today, the legislature was urged to chisel out the conciliatory statements of Robert E. Lee and L.Q.C. Lamar from the stones of the rotunda. For that story, we take you to...

...just a couple blocks from here Gen'l, if you don't mind. We just so honored to have you and all, I know this ole boy'll be able to line us up some tickets, hate to ride you around like this, thought sure ole Mounger'd know where we could get you some tickets, but don't worry, we'll get you to that game, don't want you to miss the game, no sirree. Take a *right* right here...

You got to get out of here. Poppa come home I don't know what a happen but it won't be none of it good.

He be proud to shake my hand after tonight. It's all wrote down in here. All part of my plan. I known they put me in the crazy-house. Course I known it. That give me time, see. Give me time to work it all out.

This is all pictures.

No, it's writing on some of em, see, they talking. Be in them bloons.

You got to leave. I mean it. I can talk to you later, but he just out at the grocery, he a be back any minute.

Ain't no later for Leon. Ain't nothin but now. Leon *is* now. Ain't no later for nobody. All gone happen. Leon change the world. You ain't a Black Shadow now, goodbye.

I read this later. You gotta go.

Read the Master Plan. See what you missin. You coulda been the Vice President.

Go *on*.

(Hurricane coming, Noah. Waves a tearing up.) Only for you. I'm out on the sea in my submarine. Hurricane coming to tear you away, but I be here. (Please, Noah, don't lee me alone.) I ain't leem. Hurricane ain't comin for me.

Hurricane comin for you. I never see you again.

What the Governor Said

ROGER WOKE UP to a sense of urgency. There was something he needed to do. He was not surprised to find himself in the Gandys' apartment, but the place felt empty.

Something was wrong, something was bad wrong. The light said it was almost suppertime. The whole Gandy family should be here, noisy, crowding in on the kitchen.

Roger tried to get up. He was naked. His body shocked him, white and gaunt and bony. He sat up ok, but something wasn't working right. He brought a hand to his face and hit himself in the jaw. No coordination. The accidental blow sent a shock of adrenalin through him, but he was so weak the adrenalin only gave him the shakes. He rolled his legs over the side of the cot, tried to stand up, and fell in a pile of bones. "Shit," he said, but his throat was clogged with mucus, and the curse ended in a coughing fit. "Help," he said, but it was like calling for help in a paralytic dream. He couldn't get any volume. So ok, so I'll just lay here a minute, he thought. There was a sound, a faint beat of big noise far away, like surf heard from a distance.

In a moment he felt warmer. His stimulated heart had pumped a couple of circuits of juiced-up blood around his body, and down-shifted to a steadier gear. He pulled himself to his knees holding the edge of the cot. He stood shakily erect. He thought he would faint again, but he didn't. His knees were wobbling badly, as if they were perfect ball-bearings with no lock-joint. Maybe if he took a step. It helped. Moving made balance easier. He had always known that, hadn't he? Just never occurred to him he would have to use it this way.

There was a pile of clothes on the other cot. His ghi was on top of it. Christ, he smelled bad. He went for the ghi. It wasn't a pile of clothes, it was Eleanor Roosevelt under the wadded covers and his ghi. It scared him so bad he lost his balance and fell over the steel rail at the foot of the cot. He cracked a rib and an arm on the right side, and the pain made him cry. He was bruised bad.

"What's going on?" he said through the catch in his voice. "Oh Jesus oh shit," he said. "Oh Jesus that hurts. Where the hell *is* everybody?"

"They at the game. Lee me here all alone."

"What game? What do you mean?"

"Momma baby-sittin, take Marcus with her. Baby-sittin white folk for game."

"What game, dammit?"

"Leon shoot the gubner. T.J. go to catch him. Poppa go to catch T.J."

"Say *what?*"

"Lee me here all alone. I scared you dead. Turn to a ghost, grab me witch yo claws."

"Come on, Eleanor, what are you talking about? What game, Eleanor?"

"Over yonder," she said, waving at the window, and burrowed back under the covers.

Roger got up, staying bent to ease the pain in his side, and went to the window. There were lights on, northeast across the city, a backlit sky. The Coliseum. That was where the sound was coming from. Ok, Leon was loose, apparently, if anything Eleanor Roosevelt was saying made sense. And he had shot the governor, or was going to shoot the governor. If it was an Ole Miss game, the governor would be at the game. Ok, so Leon had shot the governor at the game, and damfool T.J. was trying to catch him. Or was going to and T.J. was trying to stop him. Was going to: the sound from the stadium felt normal, big but normal, not all torn up from something crazy. Was going to *try* to shoot the governor. No way that fuck-up would actually succeed.

And damfool Mr. Gandy had gone running out after damfool T.J. Roger hung his head from sheer weakness and exasperation.

So what am I supposed to do? Go running out after them, right? No good. Can't do no good. Can't make it anyway, can't physically make it.

And the police. Wherever Leon goes, the police will follow. Trouble, trouble. I don't want trouble. I hate trouble. All I wanted was Jesus and Patsy Wingo's ass. What am I doing here? God, I hate Leon. God, do I hate Leon Cool.

He began to dress. They had laid out nothing but his ghi, as if that were the only clothing they thought of him normally wearing. He had worn it to supper too many times, he guessed.

This is a job for Captain Mississippi, he thought, slipping the jacket on. "Shit on you, Captain Mississippi," he said aloud, answering himself.

"Patsy," he said, "I mean, Eleanor." He raised the girl to sitting position and gave her a quick hug. "Don't be afraid, baby. Everybody loves Eleanor. Everybody will be back real soon. I ain't dead, see. Everything's ok. Everything's real. I tell you what, I want you to watch Garry Moore while I'm gone. Turn on all the lights and make yourself some supper and watch that tv. I tell you what, I'm on give that tv to you. It ain't anybody else's, it's only yours. You can watch it all the time, and you can see whatever you want to. How about that, huh? Now get up. Get up. Come on. Good. Go turn on the tv. I got the lights. Turn it up loud." And that's all the time I got for her, he thought. It'll have to do. He was entering mind-like-water. There was a pattern here. He didn't know what it was, but time was in a pattern, and he must respond. So let the pattern enter you and tell you what it is. Don't think it. Let the pattern tell you how to respond to the pattern.

He smooched the scar on her cheek and left her to the tv.

He looked like a freak at the circus and smelled like a wino asleep in a week's worth of garbage, he knew. No time to do anything about it, the pattern said.

Downstairs, the VW refused to crank. No doubt the battery was dead. Motivation trap. The pattern was trying to clobber him. Good chance to quit, right here.

He was seeing images of Bethany church, himself a frustrated boy-child in panic tears gripping the useless wheel of the Studebaker on a back road. Not that way. Been there before.

Next level. Out of car. Not relevant, distorts the pattern around it. Ah. Air. Streets. The glow in the sky.

No way, no way, you can't do that. You've been sick for God knows how long, you're down to nothing, you can hardly move. You'll die.

Second-level motivation trap. You don't have to tell yourself what you can't do. World will tell you what you can't do. Go till you can't. Easy.

And I'm moving, anyway. Legs already running while I argued it out with my mind. Let go. Stay with mind-like-water, let the top mind fuss, forget it. Dark streets, cutting up north to Pearl. Lights, party at Mosey's. Now. East on Pearl, against the traffic, toward the stadium lights. Running on memory. Burn the memory of your run in the woods. Inside that feeling, get in the feeling, lope along. Don't think, don't check the gauges, running the hill-top now, running the ridge, remember the flow, the lights go by, you on the way, you on the way, you on the way, you on the way, you on the way...

He broke out of his trance at the fairground gates, abandoned and open now. Acres of cars. The roar from the crowd was tremendous. It filled all of space. It was the background noise of creation. It had a rhythm. Boog-ah-*boss*. Boog-ah-*boss*. There should have been cops, patrolling with long flashlights, but he didn't see any. By now maybe some motorist had reported seeing a beatnik in his pajamas running down Pearl. His heart was triggering three times a second or better. He was probably close to some kind of a blow-out, and he was burning energy he didn't have, but he couldn't tell that anything was going to go right this minute. On to the Coliseum gate. People there, staring as he jogged up.

He stopped at the gate. A lean and weathered old man with crew-cut iron-grey hair regarded him levelly. "Look at you," he said, and spat tobacco juice.

"What's the score?" Roger said.

"Seven zero Ole Miss," the old man said. "Halfback's tearing em a new one."

"I got to go in," Roger said. "My brother's in there."

The old man didn't respond.

"I didn't have time to change. I got to get my brother out before it's too late."

"What the hell," the old man said. "Halftime anyway."

There should have been people under the bleachers looking for hot dogs and bathrooms, but there were hardly any. The noise had invaded his chest: his heart was beating twice on every syllable of the chant. He broke out of the stairwell into the bleachers at nearly field-level and he could tell what they were saying.

More people than he had ever seen, row on row and tier on tier of fans in ranked descent, a square funnel of souls.

They were chanting in unison, *"We want Ross."*

No way to see T.J. and his daddy in all this crowd, no way. What are you talking about, Roger? Easiest people in the world to find, raisins in the raisin-bread. Also Leon will be creating some kind of a stir.

But the people were standing and chanting, *"We want Ross, we want Ross,"* and he couldn't see over their arms. "Hey, it's Jesus," said a drunken student in a maroon sweater, pointing at Roger. "Hidy, Jesus."

"Shut up, motherfucker," Roger said.

A.L. Gandy was across the field, in the bleacher entranceway, trying to be as unobtrusive as possible. He had gotten in because he was clearly an old Negro workingman and therefore harmless, probably there to sweep up after the game. From where he was, he could see only the other side of the stadium, and not all of that. He was going to have to step out into the crowd to look up at this side, and already a couple of creatures in maroon sweaters were leaning over the rail and dropping long syrupy ropes of spit down on him.

Then he saw Roger across the way. And above him, climbing upward, Leon in a white peanut-vendor's uniform. He waved and yelled, but of course he could not make Roger notice, he was totally drowned out in the chant for Ross. He ran back out the entranceway and around under the temporary stands in the endzone toward the other side, an old man out of shape who used to be a strong young man. The chant above him stopped, and he heard voices crackling over a microphone. He rounded the corner, and saw T.J. running up the stadium entranceway, an old white man chasing after him and yelling.

Somebody bumped into Roger and pushed him out of the way, and he tripped and fell. A black man, a big one. Rounding the corner into the stands. T.J. Here came the old gatekeeper yelling and pointing after T.J. "...kill the governor," he was saying. He was panting hard. He bent over and put his hands on his knees. "Oh God, somebody help the po governor," he said.

Mr. Gandy was helping Roger up. Where had *he* come from? "Where did he go?" Mr. Gandy said. He was intense, and right in Roger's face. "Where did my boy go?"

For answer, Roger took him around the corner of the entrance. There was a struggle some twenty rows up. Mr. Gandy saw his boy, white hands holding him. Mr. Gandy's legs went out from under him. It was the ultimate betrayal. Life itself betrayed him then. He never forgave it. Collapsed on the cement, he looked up and saw it all. No sign of Leon. His boy thrown down in a tangle. The fourteen-year-old boy in the row above whose eyes lit up when he saw a safe fight, who launched himself like a diver, his mother grabbing for him. The feet. The boot coming down on T.J.'s beautiful head. And he himself unable to move, unable to help, cheated of all his strength and force and love.

"I love Mississippi," Ross Barnett said.

Roger was bending over Mr. Gandy but about to start up for the fight. The crowd was louder than ever.

The drunken student thought Roger was fixing to beat Mr. Gandy up. "Stomp him, Jesus. Stomp the nigger," he said.

"Don't go up there," Mr. Gandy said. "T.J. dead. I seen his skull cave in. Even if he live, he dead."

"I love her people," Ross Barnett said.

The cement shook with the answer.

"Go get Marcus," Mr. Gandy said to Roger, who was bending over him. "They at her Tuesday house. Get him out of here."

"...car," Roger said, partly drowned out.

"Mine by the other gate. Key in it. I can't help Marcus no more. Too much gone. Take him away. Go."

Roger hesitated. Mr. Gandy shut his eyes. He was alone in a roaring universe. Came the governor's voice again out of the whirlwind.

"I love our customs," Ross Barnett said.

Mr. Gandy opened his eyes. Roger was gone.

"Yessir, Governor," Mr. Gandy said. "So do I."

Bluejay Speaks

DON'T NOBODY know how to tell no story. I been in yo workshop, taken yo theory of fiction, form of fiction. Only help if you tellin a story already been told some way or other. Ain't no help with a story that ain't been told.

All you can do if you tellin one of them is try to ride it out. Do anything you have to to get the story down. All you got to tell it with is who you are. Sounds in yo head run from Shakespeare to shit, the voice in which you cast your narrative must run the self-same scale, or fail to live. Maybe you think I didn't have no business going into the heads of white people, makin up what they thinkin. I admit I cheated. I used a trick. I pretended their emotions felt like mine. I pretended that they wanted pretty much the same things out of life as I did.

It ain't like you have no choice, you know. A story is a pain in the gut till you get it told. It's a life you can't live your own life because of. You don't *have* a life till you get the story over and done with. And when it is done, you don't matter anymore. You're nobody. Nobody who ever was. You're outside for the first time. You been made fresh that very minute. Blinking. Sun. Air. People talking. What?

Maybe that's *why* I told this story. To be somebody new. To split my skin and be fresh. A fresh person in the future. Not to have to be anybody from the past. The past I couldn't breathe in any more, the past that didn't have any room for me. To be able to say, I have eaten the past, and now I can begin.

No, that's not why.

This was supposed to be *my* story. Turned out to be everybody else's. I started too far back and got lost. I still don't have no story, except for my poems book, *Space Nigger and the Plasma Poems,* and you never yet heard of it, did you? And this ain't even the kind of story I wanted to *tell,* dammit. This ain't the kind of writer I wanted to *be.* I wanted to be a comic-book writer, a science-fiction writer. I wanted to write about strange and wonderful alternate realities, about glorious heroes made in my own secret image. I learn too much. Learn too much of the wrong damn useless stuff. Start seeing the rust on Captain America's shield, the semen stains on Flash's tights. Now I ain't no good for science fiction, but I ain't happy with lyrachur either. Got tricked into realism, but you can tell it ain't my home. I swear to God the next book I write will either be my own story, or it will be vampires on Mars.

But you don't care, do you? This is all just my worries. It ain't none of yours. You just want to know what happened to everybody. As far as you're concerned, I'm just breaking in, just interrupting things, Mr. Humphrey B. Unheimlich himself, in too much person.

You're right. I know you're right. It's just hard, that's all. Parts of this, I don't want it to be over. Tears in my eyes as I write, big sentimental error. It *is* almost over. There's not that much more to tell. Goodbye time. They're leaving me. Again.

There was a riot in Oxford that Sunday, the day after the game. You remember. Treachery and shit, General Walker openly inciting, telling the good Reverend Duncan Gray he was ashamed of him, Duncan Gray, who was, along with Chaplain Wofford Smith, one of the heroes of peace in all that ugliness. Yarborough ordering the Mississippi highway patrol away. The filthy-mouthed Christian coeds, the Frenchman shot in the back, the mean-eyed country lizards that weren't students and weren't from Oxford and weren't even from Mississippi.

And later three civil rights workers got themselves killed and Medgar Evers got himself shot to death and de la Beckwith got a courtroom handshake from the governor. You remember.

But in Roger Wing's mind, and so in mine, the riot, as terrible as it was for those who were there, and all the rest of the turmoil of the civil rights movement shading into Viet Nam, these things all have always seemed a kind of aftermath to the football game. There was an insanity at its most concentrated and perfect pitch there in that stadium that night. It was a sort of tornado that sucked up the wreckage of a million souls and took it north and dumped it all over Oxford.

What happened with Roger was he stumbled out to the stadium gate and found a couple of cops with their feet up on the little black Studebaker, which was canted across an aisle, blocking a half a dozen cars. One of the cops was writing out a ticket. Roger took it and thanked them and got in and drove off leaving them yelling about wrecker fees for the wrecker they'd called. He was sure they would be pursuing with guns drawn, but he couldn't worry. All he could do was keep moving. He and Mr. Gandy were both certain of one thing, and that was that Marcus was in danger. Probably he wasn't, except the unavoidable danger of a destroyed family, but something bad was moving down the line, and Marcus was the last one who could maybe be saved from it.

Roger drove to the Tuesday house and told Mrs. Gandy he had to get Marcus and take him home, she was to get the Tuesday people to bring her home. "Ain't gone like that," she said. "Trouble. Why he doing this? And when jou get up from bein sick? You ain't safe to drive."

Mr. Gandy had to take T.J. to the doctor, Roger explained. He cut himself. He was all right, everything was ok, don't worry, really it was, but Mr. Gandy had to take him right then and he had used Roger's car and Roger had to have this one to ah, he had to go to Clinton tonight, because *his* mother was real bad sick.

Snower Mae didn't like it a bit, but she let him take Marcus finally. "Sho hope he didn't get blood on yo car. Why he want to take *it?*" Roger didn't try to answer. He had nothing left to answer with.

Marcus did not want to go. He had had a bubble bath with the two little white boys and played in the great big tub with all their ducks and boats, including a big red and white motorboat that you put baking soda in the bottom and it went like fire, and he had seen color tv all night long and had had a *lot* of roast beef sandwiches and cold milk and chocolate cake. "You smell bad," he protested. "Pee-you."

And then when he had finally gotten Marcus bundled into the car and was on his way, Roger realized he was all used up. He was about to black out, hanging onto the wheel to stay upright, forgetting to press the pedal, the car slowing down to a dead crawl until he remembered and made it jump and squeal, never shifting out of first gear. He would never make it, and didn't even know where they were going.

The Tuesday people lived in a pretty high-class neighborhood. June's house was not too far away. That was the last idea he had strength for.

He drove up into June's yard through the front hedge. "Yay!" Marcus said, jumping up and down in the back seat. Roger opened the car door and fell out. Got up and somehow made it to the front door of her house. Leaned against the doorbell and prayed like hell it worked, because he didn't know if he had the strength to knock.

When she came to the door, he said, "The police are after us. Nowhere else to go." Then he did black out.

He didn't wake up until Sunday afternoon. He had been bathed and shaved, and he was wearing silk pajamas. June wasn't there. Roger Tutwiler was, sitting in a wingback chair at the foot of the bed in June's room. "Where's Marcus?" Roger said.

"Downstairs watching tv. He's all right. He'll watch anything, won't he?"

"He ain't seen much color tv. Did you tell the police?"

"What would I tell em? Wadn't nothing in the papers."

"Nothing?"

"All about the game and General Walker's in town and troops at Ole Miss. What did you do?"

"Nothing. I got to leave. Are you going to stop me?"

Roger Tutwiler shrugged. "Might try to make you eat a little something before you go. That boy eats enough for two, but you look like you forgot what food is."

June came in. "Oh good, you're awake. I was worried about you. Hi, hon." She bent down and kissed Roger Tutwiler lightly on the forehead, then stood with her hand resting along his shoulder. She smiled at Roger Wing. Her smile was crossed with a frown of concern, as if to say, You're really all right? You're sure?

Roger noticed their rings, finally. Well, good for them, but that was a long way from any of his concerns now.

June said, "What's going on? You said some funny stuff last night. Why is that little Negro boy with you?"

Roger said, "I haven't done anything wrong. But I got to get him out of here."

"Why?"

"His family's in trouble."

"With the police?"

"I think so."

"You *think* so? Are they after you, too?"

"Maybe. I got to go."

They made him eat. Roger Tutwiler took him aside and told him to bathe and shave again because it would make him look more respectable, so he did. June packed a huge picnic for them, in a big lidded basket that looked exactly like picnic baskets in advertisements, even down to the red-and-white-checkered cloth. Roger Tutwiler gave him a suit to wear and another one to take along.

"They're summer suits," he said. "I would have been buying new ones next year anyhow. Something for you and the boy in the pocket of that one. No, don't look now, look when you're on the way. I think you need to be Roger Taylor on this trip. You're going to be real noticeable with that boy. Come to think of it, though. Tell him not to talk when there's people around. Those eyes of his, he might get by."

They didn't have any boy's clothing, but June had washed and bleached and ironed to a fare-thee-well, and what Marcus did have, which was cut-offs, tennies, and a short-sleeve shirt, were as crisp as they could possibly be.

They had put the car in the garage. They wouldn't let him take it. They made him take Roger Tutwiler's Buick. Roger Tutwiler wrote him out a bill of sale for the Buick. He was taking the Studebaker in trade. "You can't do that," Roger Wing said. "I can't let you do that. Anyway, the Studebaker ain't mine."

Roger Tutwiler explained. He said that Roger Wing could either take the Buick or Roger Tutwiler could go to the police, which he might as well, because taking the Studebaker was like wearing a sign. Anyway, it was a pretty fair trade because the Studebaker was a classic, they weren't making them anymore, it would appreciate, and he had always wanted one.

As for it being somebody else's car, Roger Tutwiler would find that person and straighten it out with them. "Write his name down," he said.

"Mr. Gandy can have my car, if he's still—The battery's dead, but it works fine. Or you can have it instead of the Studebaker. Or—"

When Roger Tutwiler finally got it straight about all the cars, who owned what and where they were, he took Roger and put him in the driver's seat of the Buick and handed him the keys. Marcus was overjoyed at riding in the Buick. He was absolutely certain his life had taken a powerful upward swing. He had watched color tv two nights in a row, slept in a great big soft bed, and now he was going on an adventure in the biggest, shiniest car he had ever seen. The truth is, he had not thought about his family since they had driven into June's yard the night before.

Roger Wing could not figure out why Roger Tutwiler was doing all of this. Looking back, one can see that perhaps he did it because he was able to do it. He wasn't out more than $1,500 dollars or so really, even at the time, and that was a significant amount to him, but not a huge amount. It feels good to have enough to be surprisingly generous. Anyway, he was right about the Studebaker. In the long run, he made money on the deal.

And perhaps he was impressing June—they were, apparently, living in her house, so maybe he felt the need to impress her. Maybe also he was smart enough to be sealing off a part of her past so that it would never bother them, sealing it off with good emotions, putting himself in the position of benefactor to that past.

Could be he was feeling a touch of banker's rebellion. Not a one but doesn't feel he is secretly wilder than the image, good at the game but a crazy old boy at heart.

Wildest theory of all: Maybe Roger Tutwiler was, at heart, a kind man.

"Bye-bye," June waved as they pulled out of the driveway. "Y'all take care of yourselves, now."

The thing in the coat pocket was a gold money clip with the initials "R.T." on it, and 300 dollars in it.

Roger and Marcus made it to Vicksburg and across the river ok, and hung a right on 65 at Tallulah, maybe an hour's drive, but then Roger started getting tired. He was depleted. He simply had no strength. And it was getting dark. He pushed on to Lake Providence, and found a motel. Out in the parking lot, a cool wind had come up. The long, narrow lake glittered darkly across the road, strange in its cedar and cypress. Out beyond the motel on his side of the road were miles and miles of flat cottonfields. He felt alien, displaced, as if he were already in another country.

Marcus had stuffed himself from the picnic basket the whole way up and was sleepy. The room was sterile, the lamplight too yellow, and maybe that made him lonesome. This wasn't adventure anymore. This was too dreary. "Where my Momma and Poppa?" he said. "Where we goin?"

Roger turned on the tv to soothe him, but the only two channels he could get (and one was very fuzzy) were full of special coverage of some kind of trouble at Ole Miss. Marcus fell asleep immediately anyway, and Roger sat and stared at the tube a while, nearly stuporous. Then he got up and turned it off, and it was quiet in the room. That was when he knew he was heading in the right direction, when he had gotten it small enough and far enough away to switch off. The whole state of Mississippi. Click. Goodbye.

After that, he never would watch the news, though he eventually let us subscribe to the *Gazette*. We got it by mail, late. More distance.

And yet he drilled me relentlessly in the names and events of his own past. I had to memorize Vardaman and Lamar, Smith and Till and Melton, Duckworth and William Simmons and Brown and Love and Daniels and Ney, Causey and Prather and Rainey and Jackson and all the villains and victims, the dead and the undead. He hated history, and I loved it, but he considered it a duty to know Mississippi history. He thought everybody should be made to study it. Since he couldn't do anything about everybody else, he made it damn sure mandatory for me.

I asked him why he hated Mississippi so. "Look at Arkansas," I said. "You think you come so far away from it all. Arkansas ain't so different."

"You wrong about that," he said.

"Anyway, I don't hate it," he said. "I love it. It was my home. They taken it from me. They stole it out from under me, and I can't ever forgive em. And I didn't stop em, and I can't ever forgive myself for that."

We made it to Little Rock the next day before he wore out, but we hadn't gone far enough for him. Alma the next day, hard by Fort Smith. We stayed the night in a big motel with its parking lot full of trucks. I'm pretty sure it's the one Tony and Susan Alamo took over later on. And up in the mountains north of Alma the following morning, he said, "This is beginning to look about right." The morning light was on the trees. It struck through fog to a green river below. I was higher than I had ever been before. Nothing has ever felt higher since.

We wound up outside of Fayetteville, Arkansas. Stayed in a little cabin motel by the airport south of town, with jockeys and winos and divorced secretaries and part-time prostitutes, until he found an old farmhouse out on the east side of town. He sold the Buick and must have cashed some of his securities in, I guess through Roger Tutwiler. Surely he found it scary to cash them in, risking that much exposure, because I remember we lived like hunted people for nearly a year, never went in to town, never went to a movie or a restaurant, bought all our groceries at a little country store, and bought them only once a month. But I loved it. He did buy us a tv, and he let me watch it all I wanted to, I think as a replacement for my family. And I was free to play all day long, and the woods were another planet to me. I roamed all back along the cedar-darkened creek into the hills, I found abandoned farmhouses and read their old letters and magazines, banged on their rusted-out porcelain washtubs.

He told me my daddy had said to take me on a trip, and for me to stay with him a while. He was my uncle now, Uncle Roger, he said. I may feel guilty about it now, but Marcus, little Marcus—he was a survivor. He knew something was wrong, but hekept his head down and his mouth shut.

He sealed off those first ten years of his life. Put them in a big cedar chest under an old fur coat. Didn't *forget,* just didn't ever go open up the chest. He turned into a white man by accident, more or less. Was already going to church with Roger, simply because in that first year there was nothing else to do socially, not because Roger made him go. Uncle Roger was always a libertarian, he never forced his customs on you. Except for the comic books, and later the science fiction magazines. Fantasy of any kind he thought was terribly dangerous, and those bright stories were absolutely forbidden. Tv was an exception for some reason. I think maybe because he was basically pre-tv. He thought it was real.

I sneaked the comic books and science fiction magazines and read them anyway, of course. A source of later struggles.

Marcus was a great mimic, and he talked white as soon as he figured out his world was white. I remember the first few times in church, ducking my head and staying quiet when the grown-ups told Roger how cute I was. They thought I was shy. I knew it was important not to sound like my momma and poppa anymore.

Because of the church attendance, I suppose, they found out I wasn't in school, and the truancy people came out for a visit. Uncle Roger was very apologetic. He had been under so much stress he had let it all slide, he explained. His brother and sister-in-law had died in a terrible accident in Georgia, and he was the only one left to take care of the boy, and he just didn't know where to turn …

There were no papers, of course, but Roger came on very earnest and country, and after several meetings they worked it all out somehow. From then on, I was legitimate. They gave me some tests to find out what grade I was supposed to be in. I will never forget the expressions on their faces when they came out to tell Uncle Roger I had tested out at twelfth grade ninth month in reading, and at eleven seven over-all. It was the first time I had ever known I was smart. But they weren't willing to place me above my age level. The theory then was it was bad for your socialization. Like when you get out in life, you're only going to need to be able to relate to people who are the same age you are, you know. Country spends sixty years creating a year-by-year partition of peer groups, and then we're all surprised when there turns out to be a generation gap.

And like my socialization was just really really normal as it was.

Anyway, I went to the seventh grade white. We never talked about that at the time, Roger and I, never not once. We both just let it happen, and so another layer on top of the secrets in the old cedar chest, and lock the attic door when you go back down. Which is probably why, when it all blew up, the explosion was so damn bad.

I was a star halfback my junior and senior year. You seen my picture in the paper, boy Christian and scholar-athlete. Oh shit I was one big smart white motherfucker, the coaches loved me, the English teachers loved me, the preachers loved me, I was a shining example, and a credit to my race.

But I didn't go to college. It was 1969, and I was in rebellion. Martin Luther King was dead, Bob Kennedy was dead, and I was in trouble with the law. Smoking that stuff, the system was rotten, I was gone join the army, hell with this shit, I ain't no fucking white man you motherfucking pig bring me up to live a goddamn lie tight-ass motherfucker ain't got one gram of imagination you what's wrong with this fucking country—

I was righteous, I was angry, I was guilty, I was just beginning to realize what I had done to my past, myself, and I was trying to work up my nerve to come out of the closet: *I Was a White Nigger for the FBI*, you know. I thought it was the only honest thing to do.

The truth is that now I sincerely wish I had gone straight to college. I coulda had a scholarship with the Raazorbacks. I coulda been their great white hope, and then tried to make as a pro. Or been a Rhodes Scholar. Or a business major. Or something. Some kind of success, instead of knocking around in this sorry world for a dozen years as some kind of mediocre bad-ass, screwed-up convert to Niggerdom, which I no longer had any real talent for. Been away too long.

At least it got me in workshop when I finally decided I was a writer. It was my calling card. You got your ex-Marines, your ex-pro-wrestlers, your one-legged women and street-smart Italian kids and ex-Baptist-ministers and ex-pool-hustlers and so on, you see, and you also have your Standard Black Writer, although that's a bit passe nowadays, compared to the other categories. Passe or not, it got me an income. A tiny income, yes, but better than I was doing hustling pool.

The joke was on them, I guess. They thought they were getting a real nigger, but no. They were getting an ex-nigger. An ex-nigger the second time around.

Yeah, I shoulda just stayed white. But not me, no. I had to do The Right Thing. I was big and angry and confused back then, back when I got out of high school. Confused, hell. I was fucked up, morning till night, and scared shitless and had that old cedar chest wide open, couldn't close it, nightmare outfits all around me and I didn't know which one to wear. Roger and I had a lot of fights, but the one we had after I graduated and told him I was going to go black and join the army and piss on him and his society, that one didn't turn out like I expected.

"Fine," he said. "You grown now. I paid back what I owe. I'm square with your family and square with my own mind. I'm through, and I'm free. You're free, and I'm free. I'm leaving you the house, and you can sell it, live in it, or burn it. But I am about to live my own life for a change. My own, and nobody else's. I'll be leaving tomorrow."

And that was it. Next day he went. Wadn't nobody left but me. Oh, he wrote me. And I've been out to California to see him a few times. He runs a little karate studio out there in Marysville. Looks boring to me, but he smiles all the time. He didn't cut me off, he just went his own way. He's too good to cut you off, not if he loves you. I see that now.

I see I'm back to telling my story again, the one I thought I was going to tell in the first place and never got around to, the one there really ain't room for in this book anymore, the one I need to tell but don't know if I can tell now. The one I don't know if I'm avoiding or if it just don't seem as important as everybody else's.

Because I go back to my poppa sometimes, and sit on the porch with him and watch him stare out over those fields. Try to see what he's seeing. Don't know if he know me. Talk to me a little, but like a man he know, not like a son.

Not long after we got to Fayetteville, we got a letter from him. Roger had written him through Roger Tutwiler to tell him the Volkswagen was his and Marcus was safe, and to give him our address. "T.J. dead," my poppa's letter began (no salutation):

> Which is a mercy. They squeeze his head all out of shape. Walked him out of there like he was a drunk, taken me and dumped me on top of him. I got to hold him and feel him breathe

a little more, for which I thank the Lord. Ain't never seen no more of Leon. Lord forgive him what he done to my boy. Thank you for yo car but they done already taken it. Somebody got it. Mr. Tutwiler arrange one for me to pay on. Snower Mae hate me now. I couldn't take care a no one. Always seem like to me I was trying hard as I could, but I know now I must not of been. She ain't home a lot. All my children gone. Lord deal harshly with me, but he know best. Take care yoself.

Roger, I think, always meant to answer the letter, but he let it slide, in the way that we let people slide when we think they are hopelessly ill or hopelessly depressed. And then, suddenly, they weren't there. They had left Jackson, and no one knew where they had gone. It was years later, and I was on my own, before I remembered Alligator, Mississippi, and went there to see if I could trace them.

Driving up to that little shack in the cotton field, knowing by then only that my poppa's nephew was living there, and there he was, on the front porch, my poppa himself, lean old man staring out into space. Only a glance at me, and back to his staring.

Reading his letter now, I know how bad he was doing after T.J.'s death. Nephew showed me some of his love letters to Momma, and they were eloquent things. Wrote like a white man. "Wouldn't think a nigger could write like that, would you?" Nephew said, proudly.

So he was doing bad when he wrote it, had to be, to be writing so much like a nigger. And talking God so much.

Nephew said Momma run off with Eleanor Roosevelt, didn't know where. So they all gone. All gone, for good. Even Poppa, even though I found him. Poppa come home to find my momma, and then he just stayed, Nephew said. Quit eating a while, walked the roads all day long. Went to church once and got saved again and then didn't go back no more. Set on the porch ever since. Staring out over the fields. And don't see me.

So now I know why I wrote this book. Can't say that it helps, but at least I know. Wadn't to get revenge on Mississippi. Wadn't to swallow the past and make myself new. Wadn't to celebrate the human spirit.

Was to say, See me, Poppa. Why didn't you even mention me in yo letter? You always love T.J. so much, why didn't you notice me? See me, Poppa. Neither Jew nor Greek, neither white nor black, don't know am I a mean motherfucker or a bleeding-heart poet, see me. I'm a genius, Poppa. I'm bigger and smarter and prettier than T.J. ever was, Poppa, you loss him but you still have me.

See me, Poppa. Yo son: Marcus Aurelius Gandy: Bluejay.